There was so... Michaels brought the glass to her lips, closed her big, gorgeous eyes slowly, took a deep swig of iced tea, and then allowed the glass to come away from her mouth, ...ing it wet—so sexy that he didn't know what to do ...himself. He had to remember to breathe.

"...en you'll stay?" Jacques said, almost murmuring ...uestion.

"...love to, especially if we can just laugh and get ...w each other . . . since we'll be working side by ...the long haul."

...uer words had ever been spoken so sweetly. ...ce his condition hadn't changed, he didn't ...rward to hand her the menu.

"...you know what you want?"

...a fraction of a second she just stared at him, ...mediately grappled within her head to pull it ...her. Hell yeah, she knew what she wanted, but it ...rong, wrong, wrong, and way out of order.

Take Me There

LESLIE ESDAILE

Kensington Publishing Corp.

http://www.kensingtonbooks.com

This one is dedicated to my daughter, Helena.
Baby, yeah, you gotta work hard, but also have fun with life!
May all the gifts of Heaven pour down on you and leave
you breathless and laughing in joy.

Special Thanks and Acknowledgments

To Manie Barron who always helps me find balance between my first love, (the genre of romance), and my other projects; to Karen Thomas for always allowing me free reign with my wild and whacky characters —thanks for the ongoing support! To Latoya Smith, thank you for laughing hard with me on the telephone and answering my edit questions . . . without thinking I had totally lost my mind. I appreciate that (wink!) BIG HUG to the whole Kensington Publishing family for the years of love.

Chapter 1

Philadelphia, Pennsylvania, March

Karin Michaels sat in her gray accounting office cubicle staring at the wall. A stack of client receipts and tax forms on her desk threatened to drown her, but gave the illusion to floor supervisors that she was busily chipping away at the pile. During the winter months, not having a window didn't bother her, since everything in Philly was usually the same uniform color of austere gray, just like her conservative suit and four-by-six office mini-cell. Even the towering Center City buildings loomed gaunt and color deprived, appearing sternly uninviting as small clusters of smokers braved the whipping winds to huddle against the stark architecture to keep warm while on break.

Tax season. She hated it. But what was a brand-new CPA to do? It was a stable profession. She had always been good at math. It paid the bills. Her mother had approved the choice. She'd graduated with honors. She was at a reputable firm, although it was doubtful she'd ever make partner, since she'd never been good at office politics or subterfuge. But she was gainfully employed, she reminded herself as she listened to the incessant click-whir of desktop calculators running accounting tapes.

Her mind wandered as her hands tallied the first folder of disorganized receipts in a box of two dozen more that had been dumped on her desk by a small church. She carefully separated out her client's expenses, her thoughts drifting in between each keystroke on the computer. Excel spreadsheets were driving her insane. She'd been given all the dog accounts, small, pesky, nuisance clients. But the feeling of entrapment was only a temporary by-product caused by this time of year.

Nine-fifteen, and the big boss wasn't in yet. Good. Karin massaged the tension away from her neck. The floor supervisors would soon head out to the field for standing appointments with major accounts. Maybe, if they were all lucky, her section boss had had an important client meeting like the other partners did, and wouldn't come in until late afternoon. She instantly retracted the foolish wish. If he came barreling into the office late, bringing his hyperactivity, a hundred questions, and requests for reports with him, he'd want everyone in the office to hang around and stay till seven or eight P.M. In that regard, her boss and her driven boyfriend, Lloyd, were very similar—when they were having a bad day, everyone had a bad day; when they were stressed, they stressed everyone around them. The irony that she was sleeping with and working for men with the same personality and temperament made her stand to go get a cup of coffee.

At least without the bosses around, junior-level employees could take a stroll down the hall to the coffee room or vending machines without fear of being pulled into an office to be given more work—just because they'd been spotted supposedly wasting time, thus money. The girls, as she called them, could escape into the ladies' room, but she felt sorry for the guys who couldn't even take a private pee half the time without a male boss following them into the men's room to continue the use-every-moment-to-the-fullest berating.

"Hey, lady," Brenda said with a sigh.

"Hi." Karin offered her coworker a feeble smile and glanced at the leaning stack of paper coffee cups. Brenda was good people, shared info, and had ten years of veteran knowledge at the firm under her belt, but looked so tired and worn out by it all at thirty-five that it was frightening. Karin tried to think of something upbeat to say as she stared at the broken edges of Brenda's over-processed hair and rumpled blue polyester suit. "The sun might come out later today." The weather comment was lame, but that was all she could casually come up with at the moment.

"Doubtful," Brenda said dryly, adjusting the tight waistband on her skirt, which had been creased by a layer of flab.

"Yeah, probably not," Karin admitted, becoming desperate for an escape as she watched the depressing sight of a woman who'd literally given up. No makeup, no jewelry, and a permanent scowl on her light almond, washed-out face gave Brenda the appearance of being unfriendly when that was the furthest thing from the truth. Once you got to know her, Brenda was cool people. Boredom was the thing probably strangling the life out of her, so Karin tried again. "I heard there's a March Madness sale going on down at—"

"A waste of money. None of the department stores carry my size, anyway. *I'm* not a cute five-foot-five like *you* with a teeny waist, so I don't bother window-shopping."

Karin looked over her shoulder at her backside. "Yeah, girl, I know what you mean about how the stores don't carry stuff made for us." Grappling for camaraderie, she pressed on. "Sitting at that desk is spreading my butt, too. I always did have a big behind and thick thighs, and the stuff that's off the rack never seems to completely work. So, whatcha gonna do. But there's a makeup sale at—"

"Breaks me out. I'm allergic to everything," Brenda shot back, pouring two cups of weak coffee and handing one to Karin. "Earrings and anything near my skin that's metal makes my eczema flare up."

"Yeah, I hear ya. . . . I've got that oily T-zone thing—"

"I wouldn't care about that, if *I* had *your* perfect chocolate skin. You don't need make-up; I do, but I can't wear it."

So much for benign topics. Karin had no comeback. She let the strained conversation drop. This was as bad as talking to her mother, another depressed woman with negative responses for every possibility.

The two coworkers stood side by side saying nothing while dumping powdered creamer into their Styrofoam cups and then adding unhealthy quantities of sugar to make the brew bearable.

"Heard the boss has the flu," Brenda said offhandedly. "I don't wish ill on the man, and I hope he gets better . . . but like a week from now."

Both women chuckled and shook their heads, knowing that they might be able to finally get out of the office for lunch today, rather than ordering in and eating at their desks—a rare treat.

Karin sighed and tasted the overdoctored coffee.

Brenda's perpetual blues had taken a morning toll, and Karin could feel herself spiraling into the bad vibes with her coworker. "Shame it's so cold and not pretty outside yet, though. There's still ice on the ground in patches—too treacherous to really go walking."

"Take what you can get, kiddo. That's my motto." Brenda half-smiled and then dropped her voice to a conspiratorial whisper. "That sucker has a constitution of iron and doesn't get sick often. So, Miss Lady, my suggestion is that you bobsled out of here if you have to, because you know he'll be in rare form when he gets back."

"You don't have to tell me twice," Karin said, perking up and moving toward the door. She glanced at the clock. Nine-thirty. Two and a half hours and she was out.

She walked down the hall on a mission. Two and a half hours could seem like two and a half years, in a place like this, on a day like this. Every face she passed had the same expression of drudgery on it. People were pleasant enough, civil, but there was no life force shining in them.

However, hoping to see more at her place of employ was a crazy, idealistic thought. Work wasn't supposed to be fun—that's why it was called *work*, her mother had said, and as Lloyd had repeatedly explained, as though she were a child. But if he were free today, she could jump in a cab and get twelve blocks further downtown to perhaps meet him in the hospital cafeteria for an impromptu lunch date.

Karin slid into her chair and hit speed-dial on her phone, waiting for Lloyd to pick up. Today she'd ignore the normally brusque tone that he used when he caught her voice on his cell phone. He was probably doing routine morning rounds; she knew he worked hard as a resident and had labored to excel in medical school to get as far as he had. But if he would just make time for a brief escape-from-it-all lunch . . . She said a little prayer that his voice mail wouldn't kick in, and almost squealed when she got him live.

"Hi, whatcha doing?" She giggled and leaned back in her chair, doodling on her blotter.

"Karin, I'm on rounds. What is it?"

"You free for lunch?"

"No."

"Oh. All right." She forced the disappointment out of her voice and made it lilt with renewed anticipation. "Maybe dinner, then? Because it's been weeks since we've really had a chance to get together, and the boss is out sick, so I'll be able to—"

"Karin, don't be childish and try to guilt-trip me. I know how long it's been. How many times do I have to tell you not to call me at the hospital unless it's an emergency? I'm taking care of people here, and afterward this is my standing night to go work out and play tennis with a few of my colleagues. You know I don't break my commitments. Besides, even if your boss is out sick, this is your busy tax season, and you should be using the time wisely to get ahead so you're available when I'm off. I put a lot into what I do, as should you. I have to go. Bye."

The call disconnected, and she replaced the receiver very slowly, feeling small. There was always something in his voice that did that to her, made her feel like she didn't fit in, wasn't quite acceptable, or was in the way. Okay, so maybe he was just having a bad day like she was, and had lashed out. But it still hurt.

On paper, she reasoned, they made the perfect urban professional couple. He would soon be a doctor; she was a CPA. He was tall and good-looking, she was . . .

well . . . She was short, and had a behind that was too big and thick, unruly hair that he didn't like natural so she'd pressed it to death until it lay limp and had to be tucked into a bun or pulled into a French braid—which he also made negative comments about.

But her mom said he was stable, just like her job. Her current girlfriends said he was a primo catch, even if he did speak to everyone as though he were above them. They all said to go for it, to live the American dream . . . because most of her girls were single or had hooked up with thugs. He said he'd marry her, one day, once the foundation to his career was properly laid, and then she could give up hers to be the mother of his children in suburbia, if she could only become a tad more dignified, organized, and less needy. But they looked really good on paper. Really, they did.

She willed tears away from her eyes and glanced at the pile of work before her. Everything could be made to look good on paper, even raggedy church receipts. All she had to do was rein in that wild dreamer within her, stay within the prescribed white lines painted by society. All she had to do was keep her rampant libido on Lloyd's schedule, and stop wanting crazy things like midafternoon trysts, or hot romantic dates, or anything out of the ordinary.

Everyone had told her that she had to adapt, just like she was adapting to the job. He liked esoteric foreign films; she liked action-adventure flicks and comedies. He liked classical jazz; she liked to get her party on with everything from the moldy oldies to hip-hop. She liked to read a good thriller; he read serious, nonfiction literature. He liked things neat, orderly, in a Swedish-modern type of way; her apartment was an eclectic mix of ethnic finds from around the world—

something viscerally unacceptable to him. Her friends were down to earth and belly-laughed over wine coolers; his friends did chardonnay and intellectual, highbrow conversation. She got together with people to simply enjoy them; any time he spent with anyone represented a networking opportunity for advancement. She liked to have fun; he liked to politic. But they looked really good on paper. She wanted to cry.

A presence hovering behind her gave her a start. Karin peered up at the boss's secretary and blinked back the tears that had begun to form.

"Mr. Kincaid is on the line for you. He's really sick, and angry as a wet hen," Betty said in a quiet, urgent tone. "That's why I came around to warn you before you picked up the phone. Brace yourself, hon."

"What did I do?" Karin whispered, nearly toppling her lukewarm coffee.

"It's not you; it's his frustration at the situation," the older matron said quickly. "He's mad at himself for getting sick, all the supervisors are out in the field, none of the other senior partners are in—they're out with major clients, and he has a big one flying in from L.A. for a meeting that *cannot* be cancelled. He's been coordinating this for months to cultivate this guy and attract him to our firm from his current firm in New York. Since you're new, you were the only certified public accountant in the house not out in the field this morning, only because you haven't gotten your full assignments yet. The others in here don't have their CPA . . . and this client is edgy, an artist, and not sure if he wants to bring his business here, and you know Sam Kincaid is having a cow about the possible loss of a VIP client, all because of the flu. But the client is sorta on the esoteric side, and eats all natural and

whatnot, so he might be offended if the boss met with
him knowing he was sick."

Betty wrung her hands and had delivered the news
like the eyewitness to a drive-by.

"Aw, Lawd, Karin, pick up the telephone, I'll show
you where the client's folder is; you have to entertain
him, roll out the red carpet, and at least get him to
consider our firm until Sam gets back into the office—
or . . . Sam can be, well, it wouldn't be good for your
career path here if you don't represent the firm well
on this one. I'm so sorry to drop this on you first thing
in the morning. I know it's pressure, but . . . he's on
line one."

Karin gave her boss's secretary a nonverbal thank-
you with a nod and a shaky smile, and then snatched
up the receiver, remembering to breathe as she offered Sam Kincaid the most professional voice she
could.

"Mr. Kincaid, Karin Michaels here. I understand
there's a situation?"

"A goddamned travesty of fate is what it is, Karin,"
her boss bellowed through a coughing jag. "This guy,
Dubois, is loaded, and has to be handled with kid
gloves," he added with a wheeze.

Dubois? The name rang a bell, but not a complete
one as her mind scrambled to place the VIP who was
making Sam Kincaid birth a kitten.

Karin drew a shaky breath. "I understand, sir, I'm
on it and will—"

"No, you don't understand!" her boss shouted so
loudly that Karin briefly brought the phone away
from her ear. "His paperwork is a rat's nest! I know
the other firm had to be robbing him blind, because
this guy has so much incoming and so many people
on his entourage payroll that he doesn't know what

he makes annually! Not to mention, he's been paying people in his family by cash, buying gifts, doing all sorts of things without as much as a legit paper trail, and the feds are going to eat him for lunch—and he only came to us because another artist buddy of his in our portfolio told him we do solid damage-repair tax representation—you got it? This is a coup, but a messy one, and I am not comfortable with a brand-new, twenty-five-year-old employee handling this travesty, but to put him with a more seasoned worker who isn't certified would also send the wrong message. This guy is a real prima donna."

Several key words her boss had spit out in an agitated flurry made her grip the receiver more tightly. Entourage. Artist. Prima donna. No way. . . . He could *not* be talking about the infamous J.B. of Def Island Sounds. Karin grappled for a backup plan. If this was who she thought it was, her boss was probably right; she wasn't ready to handle a huge celebrity account like that alone.

"I could go in there with Brenda or—"

"Are you nuts? She doesn't have the polish of Madison Avenue to give the image we are trying to project at this firm."

Karin counted to ten. She understood what her boss meant, but didn't like it at all. Brenda knew her stuff and was a hard worker. If he'd said that about Brenda, she could only imagine what he thought about her.

"I'll handle it," Karin said, her voice suddenly sharp with annoyance, but respectful. "I'll explain that the other partners are—"

"No, no, no, no, no! Then he'll think our firm is slim on senior-level resources. Never mind, I'll just have to cancel the—"

"No," she said, cutting him off and standing. Her

golden opportunity to shine and do something significant was in her grasp and she was not letting her boss take it away just because he didn't think she could cope. "I *said* I would handle it, sir."

Perhaps it was his fever, the fatigue from the flu, the tone of defiance in her voice, or all of the above, but he paused, coughed, and relented. "All right. Just don't screw this up. I want a full report e-mailed to me in the morning, and I want a con-call with you and Betty to go over next steps immediately after the meeting, understood?"

Karin glimpsed Betty, who'd remained frozen by the entrance of her cubicle. "Done."

Her boss hung up the telephone without as much as a good-bye.

"What do you need, hon?" Betty asked in a strained squeak.

"Everything you've got on this guy in Kincaid's files, the name of his limited liability partnership or enterprise, what names he does business under so I can look it over and do an Internet search to see if he has anything in the news to give me insight into his personality . . . and, maybe, a prayer."

Betty smiled at her and nodded. "*That*, I can do."

With less than half an hour to prepare, every muscle within Karin's back drew her up tight and straight. Heavy volumes of tax-code books sat near her on the long, polished mahogany desk in the conference room. Every course she'd taken in entertainment-industry tax law was now mental vapor as she scavenged her mind to recall it. This was not a drill. Heaven help her. It was who she'd suspected, and as she pored over the client's file, she felt more like a groupie than a legitimate CPA.

But with everything she'd worked hard to achieve hanging in the balance, she shunted aside her appreciation of the client's talent and focused hard on his problem. Her boss hadn't lied. From an initial, cursory assessment, even she could see that the man's business paperwork was as raggedy as a bowl of yock. Karin shook her head. If J.B. didn't get a handle on his rampant spending and shield his expenditures better according to current tax codes, he'd learn how big artists went from millionaires to bankrupt in a brief ten years. The brother had obviously been on a ridiculous, undisciplined spree.

A pinpoint tension headache was forming behind her eyeballs, and the fact that she was sitting all alone in a huge conference room at the big-money, walnut table, alone, was practically giving her hives. She ransacked the files, glancing at the clock, watching time evaporate. *She* was going to be meeting with *Jacques Bernard Dubois*? International recording artist of reggae-rap extraordinaire? Kincaid might as well have lined up P. Diddy or Russell Simmons for the afternoon, too, because she was done! *Ohmigod.* Jacques Dubois?

Ten o'clock was supposed to be showtime. At quarter after, she began praying that the client had cancelled. At least, this way, it wouldn't be on her if the guy pulled out before she'd even met him. The debacle would be on Sam Kincaid's shoulders, not hers.

By ten-thirty and the third cup of java, she was so hyper that her hands were shaking from the caffeine rush and the pressure. Artists were notoriously late. Planes got delayed. He was coming in on a red-eye flight. *Please cancel, please cancel, Lord, let the man cancel!*

The beep on the console nearly sent coffee across the table as she jumped up too quickly, but caught the wobbling cup, hit the speakerphone button, and breathed a response to the receptionist: "I'm on my way."

This was complete bull. He stood in the reception area with his hands behind his back, in a wide-legged, ready-for-a-fight stance, looking out the huge picture windows at the cold, foggy sky. He could feel the muscle in his jaw twitching. Why should the government have its hands in his hard-earned money, or care if he gave his mother and friends anything? He'd paid the feds right off the top, now they wanted more? What gave them the right, especially when he wasn't from here?

The weather was awful; greedy bastards in New York were robbing him blind, skimming, he knew it, could feel it; and all he wanted to do was deal with his music. Damned media had rushed him over at the airport and then at the Ritz Carlton, and Rockko almost had to body-slam one photog to get him outta his face so he could come here and handle his business. Now some other old codgers were gonna try to take him for a ride while he was financially vulnerable. Not today. There was no need to bring his attorney along, another thief.

The only problem was, if he didn't get this mess with the IRS straight stateside, they'd seize all sorts of crap from him, including lucrative U.S. royalties provided by his American-resident label. He was a hostage. A political prisoner, the way he saw it. How many millions in fines would it take to get this straight? This was jacking with his mind, renting space in his head, and pushing his music out of his creative flow. He was an artist! Only because his best buddy had recommended this joint would he even hear their lies.

"Mr. Dubois," a lovely female voice behind him said. He didn't immediately turn, didn't feel like responding to another star-struck secretary asking him if he wanted coffee, and if he'd mind giving them an autograph for their kid—he did mind, today. Besides, he only drank herbal tea, and didn't deal with Styrofoam. He sighed.

"I'm Karin Michaels."

He let out another weary breath and finally turned around, then paused. For a moment, he didn't move. He had to keep his mind on his money and his money on his mind, but Gawd in Heaven, this was a gorgeous distraction. He smiled and extended his hand.

"Jacques Dubois, but call me J.B. Pleased to meet you."

She accepted his hand, shook it professionally and let it fall away. Pure satin was what her skin felt like, dark, smooth, satiny brown. Her gaze was level, unafraid, and showed no flicker of celebrity impression in the least. He liked that. It was new. He wondered, then, if so many stars had come through this establishment that the boss's secretary had grown immune? Good. Maybe this was a place he could do business after all, like his homeboy had told him.

"Sir, may I offer you a cup of coffee?" she said.

He frowned and was about to respond that it had been the fifth offer this morning from a host of staff members in their firm, but then she put one long, graceful, unpolished finger to her lips, shook her head, and assessed him with a slight motioning of her head, no.

"Herbal tea, from a real cup, then. My apologies. Mr. Kincaid keeps that in his office for his select clients.

Ginger, mint, raspberry, lemon . . . I believe those are the choices, sir."

Floored, he smiled. "That could work. Ginger, no sugar—unless you have raw, or unrefined honey. And I don't drink tap water."

She swallowed away a smile. Fine and famous or not, this guy was definitely a prima donna of the high-maintenance variety. No wonder Kincaid was bugging.

"I believe we have raw sugar and spring water." Karin glanced at the receptionist, who immediately picked up the telephone to communicate the request to Betty, who would play runner. Karin continued to offer the man a professional smile to keep from screaming, and bade him follow her into the conference room with as much polish of diction as she could muster.

"Mr. Dubois, while your tea is being prepared, please join me in the conference room, and if you'd like, I can hang your coat in our lobby, or we can bring it with us."

All he did was raise one eyebrow and take off his full-length leather to throw gallantly over his arm as an answer.

She could not look at this man's body. The coat hid what the fly silk shirt did not—pure cinderblock. Oh, Lawd, she had to remain in complete control, remain professional, and comprehend the fact that a six-foot-two, fine as mellow wine, hot, chocolate perfection superstar was walking behind her . . . shoulder-length dredlocks to die for, doing camel-hued leather *everything* to death; she had to breathe, she had to breathe, and was not about to lose her job by spinning on this man in the hall, pointing and screaming, "You're Jacques Dubois!" Nope. Her momma ain't raised no fool, and she had some dignity left. . . . A little bit.

"Please make yourself comfortable," she said as they

entered the conference room and she shut the door behind them. The room felt like it had grown as big as a football field, yet also didn't seem to contain enough air in it for her to breathe.

She immediately walked over to the conference room table, keeping her spine straight and professional as she sat, and then began rummaging through a spread of folders as he carefully chose a seat across from her. This was the moment of truth. She had to tell the potential client that the big boss wouldn't be coming and she was his consolation prize. She wondered what kind of hissy fit he might throw as a result, and took a deep breath to deliver the bad news.

Summoning courage, Karin finally looked up. "Mr. Kincaid is deathly ill with the flu and did not want to bring it within a hundred yards of you, knowing that your voice and your ability to tour are pivotal to your career. Therefore, he's asked me to begin the conversation with you to glean as much critical information as possible so that he may begin to fully assess your situation." She paused, held his gaze, and fought with the butterflies Jacques Dubois's intense stare released in her stomach. When he stood, she swallowed hard. "He wishes to express his deepest regrets," she added firmly. "I assure you—"

"He put me with *his secretary*, to reveal my most intimate financial business . . . and this is how this firm operates, no offense, sis, but—"

"Full offense taken, sir," Karin said, lifting her chin as she stood to match his stance, and not sure what part of her mind had snapped under the pressure. "I am a CPA, not the man's secretary, and from what I have seen of your files in preparing for this meeting, you need to have a seat to keep the feds at bay."

He cocked his head to the side and gave her an incredulous look. "What?"

Karin paused to halt what she really wanted to say to him. Deadlocked, they both eyed each other. From somewhere within the deep recesses of her being, the Philly girl in her had slipped out. It had made her head bob just a little with each word, had put the merest hint of swivel in her neck and a cutting, attitudinal edge in her voice when she'd spoken. Although she wanted to die on the spot, and she knew she now probably needed to update her résumé to look for another job, still, she didn't like the man's tone. Anyway, if she was soon to be unemployed, she might as well go out with a bang.

"This isn't working," he finally said, his tone brittle with annoyance and then glanced at the door to signal his readiness to leave.

It was reflex, but she cocked her head to the side, put one hand on her hip, and simply stared at the man for a moment. Rich or not, there was a way to talk to people. What if she had been a secretary—so what? She was a person, respect was due, and she'd had enough of being talked down to. No one deserved that. All this posturing about titles was crap. He was a musician; she was a CPA. This was her stage, and his business was messed up.

"Mr. Dubois, have a seat," she finally said, her tone more of a command than a request. She rolled her eyes and flopped down in the cushy, high-back chair she'd abandoned. "I'll give you some free advice this morning, since you obviously need it."

He neared the table, clearly outraged, and shot her a hot glare. "I don't need your free—"

"Look, save the games and drama for somebody who's got time to listen to it. We're busy in here during tax season, too, and put in long hours. That's how the boss got sick—from working ridiculous hours for his clients, so what? He didn't want to give you the flu, so he sent me, his best. You might go to another firm, whateva, but the truth is this—I'm a sister, I've got your back, and am probably the only one you're gonna meet who will give it to you straight. You've worked hard, no doubt, to get where you are. But trust me, so have I. I've got extended family I help, a momma with needs; I know what happened here when you hit it big."

She glared at him; he almost smiled. Her words and her style of delivery gave him pause, but she didn't seem to notice as she took a breath to rail on, she'd fussed at him—actually fussed—and had lost her icy, professional edge. He liked that much better and nearly laughed at the discovery, but didn't dare. She seemed to have the potential to cuss a brother out. So he waited and watched as her tirade built to a crescendo. It was like witnessing lyrics being written.

"And just for your information, Mr. Dubois," she continued in a huff, "this sort of thing happens to stars that come up from 'round the way all the time—ask me how I know. No, I'm not buying big stuff like you do, but it's all relative. You drop fifty thousand when I give my cousin fifty bucks—but it feels like fifty large to me, brother. So since you've come all this way, and the big boss ain't here to kiss your celebrity behind and tell you what you want to hear, you might as well put your butt in a chair and hear some truth for once, being told by somebody who doesn't care who you are."

She spun and pressed the intercom console buzzer to keep from passing out. "Betty, you got that man's tea yet, so he can chill?"

He sat slowly, a deep chuckle finding its way past his diaphragm and into his throat. It was the first time anyone in business had hit him like that, right between the eyes. And, man-oh-man did that woman have fiery, gorgeous, deep brown eyes that flashed and got wide with audacity, rimmed in thick black lashes, and a French braid down her back that needed undoing.

She talked fast and furiously, reminded him of home . . . full lips, head bobbing, hand on hip, unashamed of who she was, but with a professional polish that was dazzling, if not somewhat disorienting. Body, unreal . . . he'd seen it from behind, all that firm womanhood trying to fit into the too-structured uniform of a business suit, but her fantastic, round behind and deliciously thick thighs needed to be in a bright beach sarong, and free. She was sipping air in quick spurts like a flustered bird, petite breasts rising and falling beneath her plain white blouse and pearls. *Uhmmph, uhmmph, uhmmph* . . . yeah, he'd sit down before he fell down.

An older woman poked her head in the door with a nervous look on her face as she advanced with a cup of tea and a saucer and set it down before him along with two packets of raw sugar, a napkin, and a silver spoon. Karin Michaels thanked her first, a hint of an apology in her voice, and he also followed suit and thanked the harried woman who had delivered his herbal tea, and he did so as politely as possible before she scurried away.

For some odd reason, it had suddenly become important how Karin Michaels viewed him. He had some home-schoolin'; his momma ain't raise no fool. Truth resided here in a way he could never pay for. Miss Karin obviously didn't brook no B.S., and he'd traveled the world looking for someone that didn't to be in his corner. He added the sugar slowly, thinking about it all, stirred his tea with precision, and then lifted the cup in a short salute to her and took a sip.

"So, Miss Karin, tell me. How bad a trouble am I in dat you can fix?" He'd intentionally allowed his words to slip into the comfortable patois, since they were getting familiar, and she'd done no less by blasting him East Coast, Philly style.

She just stared at the man for a moment. The way he'd tossed his immaculate locks over his shoulder and sipped the tea with a mischievous smile, winked at her and let her name spill out in a long, exotic, baritone drawl seized her breath, this time for real. Two syllables, Kar-*rin* . . . long rolling *R* in the middle, not shortened by a Northeast Corridor accent that always made her name sound like "Karen" on the lips of the uninformed. He said it like she'd always wanted to hear it; deep, and low, and sexy . . . pronounced like *KarRIN*. Whew!

"Uh, well. We have to, uh, really take a look at all that's come in and get an honest accounting of all you've given out as gifts, which could have repercussions on the people who you've given stuff to, if they didn't pay gift taxes, and if you paid your entourage people by—"

"Karin," he said, his megawatt smile widening as she ceased stammering. "I tink I'ma go wit your firm— only on one condition."

She blinked, but couldn't speak.

"If you are the one to go over my books, and you tell me the truth about what you see, then I will come here—but I don't want no old thief in me pocket. I trust you, 'cause your vibe is real. Dem others, no."

"All right," she said quietly, her voice feeling like it

might crack. "But here's what I'll need from you. You can lie to the world, but you tell me the truth. I can't fix it, massage it, and make it clean and legit if something leaps out from under a rock and bites us both in the behind later. I'm going to need time to look at what the other firm prepared in audits and then sit down with you to ask you what you really did do, or wanted to do. Okay? I can help you, but if you lie to me, I'm done. This is just a job for me, and not worth losing my certification or ending up in prison. I'd rather wait tables and be free than get caught up in some nonsense."

He nodded, fully appreciating where she was coming from. "For me, freedom is everything. I know. I have to be free to be an artist. I'm a Sagittarian, and if I cannot be who I am, I will die."

He let his gaze go out the window and considered the steel gray sky. "Truth—I just wanted to give some people who never had anything, something . . . folks who worked hard all their lives, a little bit, you know? They were dying in jobs that wouldn't let them be who they were, and even when I knew sometimes they'd take advantage, or I really didn't need their services, I'd make up something for them to do. I didn't care too much because I was blessed and had more than I could spend. So . . . okay, yeah, I shorted the tax man a little and gave my people some of what the grim reaper, Uncle Sam, wanted off the top." He chuckled and took another sip of his tea, issuing a sheepish glance at her as he did. "Now I'm in tax trouble for just being generous. There's something so wrong with that."

She nodded. Everything the man said was true about freedom and the world not being fair, and there was a lonely, wistful tone in his voice that drew her. Although he was a big music star, she could see that it had all happened so quickly with sharks all around him, that there was nowhere safe for him to turn. His parents, no doubt, hadn't lived like he now lived, and could only guide him from basic common sense, which was not enough of a weapon against real financial predators. Those around him had been telling him what he wanted to hear to keep the gravy train rolling—she could see that from the crazy expense sheets she'd glanced at. Those who were supposedly his management were as slick as greasy dishwater. And yet this man, who'd clearly come from very humble beginnings, was just trying to spread the love. Problem was, the tax man cometh and the tax man taketh away, if you didn't follow the rules.

Karin let her breath out hard. "Listen. Just because it's ethical doesn't mean it's legal—which is the tricked-up part about all of this. You don't know me from a can of paint, but I'll do my best to unravel this mess you're in, if you'll let me."

She waited a beat and was rewarded by his slow nod and mellow expression.

"All right," she said, gaining confidence as he stared at her with a steady, open gaze. "You will probably have to pay some serious fines and back taxes, but at least if we're actively working on it while communicating with authorities, they won't haul you in for tax evasion and we can avoid a media travesty—you deserve better than that. So does your family."

He set his cup down and laced his fingers together, making a tent under his chin, his expression solemn. "Thank you. For the first time in as long as I can remember, I'm talking to someone who sounds like they care." He smiled sadly. "It was the way you said, 'we.' I like that."

She smiled and glanced away, her face feeling hot. "I

don't like to see honest people messed around with and taken advantage of. Makes me want to fight harder . . . especially when I see the corrupt-but-connected walk away from worse issues for much more selfish reasons, scot-free. Frankly, it makes me sick."

"So I have myself a true champion." He chuckled and leaned back in his chair. "I'm glad you're on my side. You must be hellfire going against an opponent. . . . You sure you're a CPA, not a litigator?"

She laughed and tried to ignore the dimple in his cheek as his smile broadened. "I didn't have money for law school. I got my B.A. and got out, and studied for the certifications really hard and went that way."

"I'm glad you did." He glanced at the clock and then leveled his gaze at her with a dashing smile. "I take it you can't do nothing with these bullshit reports my previous firm had? You need originals and what-not, right?"

"We can use what they had as a loose guideline, but it would be better if you have access to original receipts, checks; anything I can use to retrace the steps to be sure nothing was overlooked or incorrectly categorized."

He stood. "Then we should eat lunch. My man is downstairs with the car, and I jus' have to page him. Can't do nothing today 'bout it. Got a gig in Philly tonight down at the Wachovia Center—will give you tickets and backstage passes. Tomorrow, I gotta crash and burn and get some rest, den I can take you to where I keep everything."

She tried not to smile too hard, tried to remain as stoic as possible. She was on a mission, had to help this guy get his life straightened out so he could keep doing what he did best, sharing his music with the world. Her boss would lay palms at her feet; girl-friends were gonna pass out, if she didn't first.

"Okay," she said, as calmly as possible. "But where's your office? Because I'll have to prepare reports for Kincaid, give him an outline of tasks, and—"

"St. Lucia, luv. I keep everything offshore, at my main house. Don't trust the freaking authorities here. I may be many tings, but crazy, I'm not."

She stared without blinking. Had he said St. Lucia?

"Expense is no issue. Even in tax trouble, I can afford your firm, still. They haven't frozen my accounts yet, so I'll burn it all and rather give it away, before the Man gets to it. I'll tell you everyting over lunch," he said, pulling on his coat.

"I'd have to get clearance from my boss and fill out a trip request—that may take time to get the approvals nec—"

"I'll take you there," he said, interrupting her as she stood wringing her hands. "Don't worry about packing too much—just bring your brain and your calculator and tell your boss he can keep his old, frontin' ass home."

Chapter 2

Her heart was beating a mile a minute as she casually stood, depressed the intercom buzzer and informed Betty she was taking Mr. Kincaid's client to lunch. Jacques Dubois had a pleasant look on his face that bordered on amused, but he didn't say a word and just seemed to be observing her the whole time as she gathered up his files.

She had no idea where to take this VIP, or if her pitiful little debit card could handle the strain given that payday wasn't until Friday. She didn't have access to a company American Express card; only the big bosses got to carry those. Her mind raced as she led the CEO of Def Island Sounds away from the conference room, careful not to drop the files she clutched. She hadn't thought to make reservations, either, and this guy undoubtedly would be perturbed by any sort of wait. She also hated to use her credit cards, which were nearly maxed out, unless for serious travel. Did the big restaurants even take a debit card? she wondered as Jacques Dubois followed her to her cubicle so she could briefly collect her purse and briefcase, and then to the lobby, curious gazes on them as she passed her coworkers and went to the closet to get her coat.

Karin could have kicked herself. How stupid could she get! She bent and shoved his files into her no-name briefcase and secretly cringed. A bad case of nerves had made her not ask Betty the essentials, like where to wine and dine a heavy-hitter, or even ask Kincaid's wonderfully efficient secretary to call ahead, if she'd been on top of her game. Plus, she'd done the unthinkable. She should have made the VIP wait in the lobby, and then gone to the back to get her purse so he wouldn't have seen her paltry, junky desk. After passing all the huge window offices, and then arriving at her little postage stamp of a work cell, he now knew for sure he was dealing with a grunt, as opposed to a bigwig, hotshot CPA.

She sighed. But she was proud of herself when she didn't faint dead away while the man actually helped her on with her conservative, black wool chesterfield that was in serious need of delinting. She was just glad she'd at least sewn the loose button back on it, but so wished in that moment she could have pulled an exquisite Burberry out of the closet.

Karin discretely glimpsed down at her vendor knock-off Coach bag as they made their way to the elevator, also wishing that were real. Would a fairy godmother just sprinkle some magic dust on her and exchange her Payless, basic-black pumps for a pair of chic Pradas, please God? Couldn't her ten-dollar off-the-street watch transform into a Movado or something, too? She didn't even want to consider the sale suit she'd gotten from Dress Barn or the little fake pearl earrings that she'd acquired at a bargain for five bucks.

Her mom and girlfriends had told her to always dress up for the job she wanted, rather than the job she had. But Lloyd had told her to be practical and not waste money on the exterior, given that this was just a job, not a career anyway. Unfortunately, today the job had instantly transformed into a golden career opportunity without warning, right before her very eyes.

Besides, even if she'd wanted to put a few good pieces in her wardrobe, the problem was that a junior employee with hefty student loans couldn't always do that and still pay all her other bills on time. Now she was standing next to the client of a lifetime and looked like a rag. If she could have disappeared on the spot, that would have been fine by her. Unfortunately, at the moment, she had worse troubles than being severely underdressed. She had to figure out where to take a very picky eater, without reservations, no money, near noon, and keep him engaged, and dazzle him with knowledge and details she probably didn't possess. And to think that she'd lambasted him for being fraudulent when this was frontin' at its best!

He stood beside her totally in awe, rendered mute by her presence. This was the most down-to-earth, real sister he'd met in a very long time. Not only was she obviously smart, but so confident that she didn't go in for all the normal trappings or play silly games that other women did. She didn't care that he saw that they'd given her a teeny little office and a pile of work. Miss Karin had strode to it like it was a corner office with a view, head held high. Deep. And judging by the pile of work on her desk, they apparently knew who could get the job done. But he hated that they were dogging a sister. She should have been phat-paid.

His mind raced to come up with some witty small talk, but came away wanting, so he just stared at the elevator doors, glimpsing her from his peripheral vision.

Her skin was gorgeous, flawless, and only had the barest hint of makeup. Natural, and not overdone. Nails natural, not long, glittering talons, but her hands were soft and well-kept; a woman who worked hard for what she had and lived within her means, and was clearly unashamed to do so. Hair neat, not lacquered to her skull or lengthened by nylon or all over her head like a banshee's and sprayed hard to stay that way.

He gave her a long, sideline glance. A naturally curvaceous figure, too, not padded by silicon. Real. A sister who could look him in the eyes without blinking, get in his face and not care, and not be angling to get in his wallet. *Man*, she reminded him of home. No overpriced, gaudy designer anything. Just plain, neat, and very, very pretty. A melodic voice, too; that hadn't been lost on him. *Uhmph.* He especially liked the sound of it when she fussed. He smiled. But he'd also deeply appreciated it when it had softened on his behalf when they finally came to a verbal truce.

He wondered if she were married or had kids. Why that curiosity had leapt into his head was beyond him. But he did notice she didn't sport a rock, so. . . . He banished the thought. This was business; besides, someone as stable and as pretty as she was had to have a man. Miss Karin was clearly the committed type, and no doubt there was somebody somewhere in her life that was planning on making this sister his wife. Abstinence from the groupie circuit and gold diggers was obviously making him act stupid. Focus. This was just business, and needed to stay that way.

A potential paparazzi rush in the streets gave him pause. Where would he take this gem to lunch to talk about his private affairs without eavesdroppers being all up in his business? It wouldn't do to have her pull his files out at a public restaurant to begin the hard discussion—a telephoto lens from behind any given fern could put all his mess in a tabloid. He quietly sighed as the elevator doors opened.

"I was thinking," he said, glad that no one else had gotten on the elevator with them yet. "Maybe we could go back to the hotel and have a more private lunch in my room?"

The moment the suggestion left his mouth he could tell his intentions needed more clarification. She blanched, her eyes widened, and he casually stepped back in case she took a swing.

"Because the paparazzi are everywhere right now," he added quickly, trying to disarm her before the offense took root. "They're everywhere because they know me and the band are in town—we have a show tonight—and to have you flipping through files and sensitive conversation in an open restaurant might not be the ting to do. That's all I'm suggesting."

He watched her shoulders drop two inches in poorly disguised relief.

"Oh . . . yeah. I didn't even think about that."

He had to laugh as he paged Rockko for the limo. "I know my reputation probably precedes me, Miss Karin, but this is business."

She shyly looked away and smiled hard. "I was just taken off guard," she said, obviously trying to save face. "I had asked you to lunch and—"

"No," he said still chuckling. "As you recall, I invited you, so it's my treat."

She looked at him as the elevator slowed to allow more passengers on. "But protocol dictates that our firm hosts you, sir."

He wouldn't argue in the elevator. They were going to the hotel. The bold stares he received from the passengers who'd newly entered the elevator told him a regular lunch wasn't going to work. So he held his peace until they got off at the lobby level, quickly ushering her past the first-floor security guards as he spotted the black stretch through the One Liberty Place revolving glass doors.

"You gwan hafta learn to keep up, Miss Karin, if you gonna hang wit me," he joked as Rockko opened a limo door and body-shielded them as the media swamped the vehicle. He got in behind her quickly and yanked the door shut before Rockko could slam it, simply glad to be behind blackened glass. "You linger too long, and you'll get bum rushed and eaten by the sharks."

Karin gaped as flashbulbs went off. A mini-traffic jam ensued, but the driver was finally able to round the corner and head toward the hotel.

"God . . . Do you *always* deal with this *everywhere* you go?"

"Pretty much," he admitted sadly, looking at her intensely. She really didn't understand, and he was glad that she was innocent of the celeb life. "So now you believe me when I say I wasn't trying to be fresh by asking you to have lunch in my room?"

He watched her blush as a wide grin came out of hiding on her pretty face.

"I'm sorry I even went there," she said, not looking at him and now appearing nervous as she tried to settle herself against the expansive leather seats. "I'm just used to our more traditional clients in more traditional settings."

"Well then, you're in for the adventure of a lifetime," he said, laughing, "because me and the band ain't traditional by a long stretch."

She looked at him and giggled. He loved the sound of it . . . deep, resonant, earthy, real.

"I bet you guys are a trip," she said, mirth glittering in her eyes.

"Oh, we ain't so bad, Miss Karin," he said sheepishly.

She replied with a pleasant scowl and a small grunt that made him laugh harder.

"Okay, okay, we have our ways, but we don't do no harm."

She nodded toward the hotel that was coming into view, noting the swarm of reporters outside. "Now I see why you were late."

Her comment tickled him. He had been almost an hour late, and hadn't called her as professional courtesy dictated. "My apologies, but I had to give them something to feed on this morning so they'd thin out. Right now, they're probably latched onto the other members of the band." He glimpsed back at her. "You need to tell your parents and any boyfriend you got that you could show up as my latest lover in the tabloids, but they shouldn't believe the hype. I hope your boss has a good sense of humor, too."

"What!" she shrieked, her knuckles going taut around the handle of her briefcase.

"Listen," he said with an amused sigh. "That's where half of my notorious reputation comes from. Meetings, business; if the person is female, you would be surprised at the yarn that gets spun in the newspapers about me." He gave a nod toward the curb as their vehicle approached it. "I met with a sister about possibly doing a clothing line, and she suddenly became my latest woman. I went to visit my cousin up in the Bronx, and she was also my paramour, according to the tabloids. I was trying to hook my mother up with a sister in New York that does all-natural body lotions and essential oils to see if maybe it could be a nice little business for me mom, and what next, I hafta be doing the sister, according to what they said. So dat's where half me bad rep come from."

She peered at him, astounded, and for some reason very contented by his admission. "So where did the other half of your bad reputation come from?" She laughed, the question was bold, but she had to ask, given his good mood. His voice had done her in.

He opened his mouth, closed it, and then held up his hand, laughing. "Now see, woman, you getting into me very personal business that no gentleman would dare put on paper. Suffice to say that some tings happened in me youth dat I cannot retract . . . but I don't go there anymore."

"Uhmm-hmm . . ." she said, still chuckling as the private divider window lowered.

"You ready for the onslaught, boss?" the driver asked.

"Yeah, mon. Let's do it."

"The little lady ready?" the driver asked, seeming concerned that she wasn't.

"How about if I take my time to wade through the crowd, and you escort her up to my suite through the back elevators, feel me?" Jacques glanced at Karin and gave her a wink. "She probably got a man dat wouldn't understand this at all, and might not take kindly to a business meeting that got twisted in the papers. No sense in getting my ass shot in the Wachovia Center over a li'l misunderstanding."

The driver nodded and depressed the button to make the window slowly rise. "Will do, boss."

Stunned silent, Karin stared at her new client. She wasn't sure if she were more flattered by him thinking anyone cared enough about her to bear firearms in her honor or frightened by the prospect of needing a personal bodyguard to escort her to his suite. The whole thing was so foreign to her reality that all she could do was go along with the adventure.

"Okay," Jacques said, taking a deep breath and steeling himself to exit the vehicle. "You stay out of sight, Rockko will get you up to the room, and I'll wade through the piranhas, give them a few hunks of flesh, and we'll meet you in the room. Cool?"

Karin just nodded and made herself small as he exited the vehicle to a hail of blinding flashes. What had she gotten herself into?

The curbside spectacle and the grace with which Jacques flowed into the hotel trailing media blew her mind. However, instinct made her hand reach into her purse for her cell phone to call the office. Kincaid had to be kept abreast of the fast-moving developments. She rattled off the facts to Betty as quickly as possible while the limo rounded the corner to get away from any potential media and fan stragglers.

"Betty, ohmigod," she said breathlessly as soon as the line connected, keeping her voice low in case the driver might overhear her. "Tell Kincaid we definitely got Def Island as a client. The media was so bad that we have to have the meeting at the Ritz, but not to worry about the expense, as the client insists on picking up the tab. I don't know how I'll get Kincaid a full report in the morning, because I have to go to the client's concert tonight to stay in political favor— because he's going to give me backstage passes and everything, and I don't want to possibly seem uninterested and make a bad impression. But I'm gonna need tickets to go to St. Lucia, stat, two days from now, because Mr. Dubois wants me to review his original files there—I know the boss is gonna have a cow, and he can speak directly to Mr. Dubois about it, if he doesn't believe me—I wasn't trying to overstep my bounds and didn't insist or try to pull a fast one . . . the guy trusts me, and, uh, oh, Lawd, Betty, I don't know what to do!"

"What!" Betty screamed into the receiver.

"I know, I know, and Kincaid will flip. But this guy doesn't trust Kincaid and insists that I stay on as his primary contact, even if Kincaid does the real sexy work—I'm no fool and know I don't have the level of experience this client needs, and I'll be sure to tell him that he has to let Kincaid—"

"You betta work it, girl," Betty whispered, her tone suddenly very protective. "You keep doing your thing. Go to the concert; I'll stave Kincaid off and tell him what he needs to know. *I'll* get the tickets; Kincaid can hear that part after the fact. Bunk him. I'll tell him it's a black thing and he wouldn't understand, and the client was blown away by your professionalism, skill, and sophistication. Pullease. . . . I've been waiting almost twenty years to see something like this happen to that old fart."

Karin closed her eyes. The limousine had stopped moving. Betty made her want to cry. Insecurity made her want to scream.

"Betty, thank you so much," she whispered. "I'll probably lose my job behind this. I'll bring everything I learn back to the office so the more senior guys can do this client right. I don't have the experience, lady . . . and I'm sorry I sounded sharp when I asked for his tea. . . . I know I'm rambling, but . . ."

"But you're scared, rightfully so, and this is an opportunity of a lifetime. *Carpe diem,* seize the day, and don't let anyone who ever thought less of you enter your brain. Obviously this client felt comfortable with you, which is half the battle. And why wouldn't he?

You're nice, reliable, and honest. Period. All of them started the same way," Betty soothed, ignoring the tea request incident as though it didn't exist. "They got a shot, a chance to prove themselves early on, and had more senior guys to work behind the scenes to coach them along. They learned on their first big account, like you will—and I see no reason why the rules of advancement should be different for you, sweetheart. That's not fair."

Karin nodded with her eyes still closed, pressing the cell phone to her cheek. It was the first time that anyone had really gone to bat for her so sweetly. Betty was putting her job on the line to do this, believing in her more than her own mother or boyfriend ever had. Real tears wet her lashes, and she blinked them away. "I'll do the very best job I can on this," she murmured. "I promise I won't let you down, and I so appreciate this chance."

"That's all anybody can ask of you, honey. I've been watching you, chile. I see how hard you work, how late you stay, the kinds of accounts they've given you, the little perks the others got right off the bat, but they said you had to earn. I know what everyone else's expense reports look like, too, and how you can't spend a dime. Humph. It ain't right, especially when you're twice as smart as they are, got higher grades and better scores and your work is clean as a whistle, reports on time or early, and you take care of even the smallest client like they're a VIP."

Karin's eyes opened wide. "My other clients! Who will—"

"They will," Betty chuckled. "I'll oh-so-casually walk around to the supervisors and drop that crap right back on their desks for redistribution—since you're now working a major account. Just like they did you, okaaaaay?"

"They'll die," Karin whispered, chuckling.

"Yes, they will, especially when they find out the client is treating you to lunch—which I'll casually mention was necessary because they'd failed to provide you with a company American Express, so the client took issue with their cheapness. Oh, yeah, and I'll explain that for political reasons, it was necessary for you to travel to the client's event and take front-row seats at a sold-out concert to appease this VIP, who also wants to discuss more at his private office in St. Lucia, after I purchase nonrefundable tickets. Hmmm . . ." Betty said, laughing. "What else can I do? Oh, yes, I know, I need to run out to acquire you a top-of-the-line laptop, because upon Mr. Kincaid's orders, you must stay in e-mail contact with him. And this afternoon, I'll get a travel advance of say, two thousand dollars, processed immediately, and you must rent a Mercedes while there to take your VIP client around right. . . . Might I suggest you buy some clothes for the occasion, while you're at it?"

"Betty, they'll fire you!" Karin wheezed.

"Darlin', I've got twenty years in at this firm, my house is paid for, I do catering on the side and can live off that, and have my retirement already bankrolled from watching the fellas invest and putting up my two cents for a rainy day—and if Kincaid fires me today, he'll rehire me tomorrow. If I'm not there, he wouldn't be able to find a single thing, *trust me* on that." Betty sighed, her tone mischievous. "Besides, vital files have been known to accidentally get shredded, so that old bastard *does not* want me for anything but his best friend and confidante. He and I came to terms a long time ago. Any ole way, how you think he got the tip on the account?"

Speechless, Karin whispered the truth as the driver got out of the vehicle and approached her door. "I don't know. How?"

"The New York firm's secretary was pissed off at her boss. She and I just so happen to go way back. Word that the New York firm was robbing him blind got to the secretary of Mr. Dubois's best friend, who told him. His best friend is one of our clients."

Betty snorted and made the distinctive sound of a woman sucking her teeth into the receiver. "Kincaid knows that Def Island Sounds was my find, and that I delivered that client to him on a silver platter. He ain't about to mess with me on this, so you go on and have fun. For once, his surly behind can stay in the office and do the grunt work while you go get the necessary information and throw it back over the wall to him. How's that for a little comeuppance, old-school?"

"Betty . . . I can't even begin to thank you enough." Karin peered up at a hulking bodyguard wearing a black designer suit, black shades, and a wire in his ear. All of it exaggerated his already menacing presence even more.

"Ready, Miss Michaels?"

She nodded at the man she'd only heard called Rockko, and began to scramble to her feet and to collect her belongings. "Betty, I have to go, but I'll call you from the road. Bless you."

"Just relax and do your thing, honey. I've got you covered back in the office."

The call disconnected, and a firm grip on her elbow practically lifted her from her feet before they hit the ground. She struggled to keep up with Rockko's long strides, her feet barely touching the pavement with each footfall as he quickly ushered her into the hotel, through a VIP side entrance and avoided the lobby throng.

A concierge-blocked private elevator offered temporary sanctuary. What felt like a thousand thoughts slammed into her mind, the first of which was a renewed respect for executive secretaries, the real power brokers. That one had taken her under her wing was more than a mere blessing, it was a gift from God . . . very much like the whirlwind adventure that had broken through her gray, cold world this morning with a bright splash of island color. Surreal.

She watched Rockko talk to his boss through the wire in his ear as the elevator went up to the suites that required a special elevator key to access. Apparently Jacques Dubois had made it through the lobby on his own recognizance and was just fine. But what he'd done was beyond chivalrous. The man had given up his bodyguard, dealt with the crowd alone, all so her face wouldn't be plastered across some seamy tabloid. He didn't have to do that, or care about what happened to some chick from an accounting firm, but he did. That was the point.

Oddly, Rockko's steady presence made her relax a little. It was like walking beside a mountain. Although a man of few words, he always seemed to give a cue about what he was going to do before he did it. Like the way he just didn't stop the limo and yank open the door. He announced his intent, just as he stopped at the suite door now, knocked even though he was expected, and then inserted the key. Dignified.

She wondered what it must be like to have to have someone constantly shielding you, or to always have to think out your route or activities, plan the simplest tasks— like going to lunch, the supermarket, or shopping—

and then act? For someone who apparently loved life and freedom as much as Jacques Dubois did, the whole reality probably felt like a living nightmare. The new awareness hit her; no wonder the man just went buck wild with his finances. Perhaps that was his only real freedom . . . that, and his music. Everything else around him most likely had to be carefully controlled. Karin almost covered her mouth with her hand. A bird in a gilded cage.

"So you made it, without incident I hope?" Jacques stood up from the leather sofa and beamed at her as she and Rockko entered the suite.

"Everything's cool, boss," Rockko said. "Need anything else before I head back downstairs?"

"I'm good. Although Miss Karin looks like she needs a Valium," Jacques said, laughing.

"Ohmigod, no!" she said before her mouth could consult her brain. "I don't do drugs."

Both men laughed.

"House rules," Rockko muttered. "Nobody on the staff is allowed, or you're off the team. The boss don't play that, says drugs make you stupid." He issued a lopsided smile to Jacques and then turned and left the room.

Karin stood in the middle of the floor, her purse pressed to her side, gripping her briefcase so tightly that the leather handle had bent. "I didn't mean to offend the man—or you—I wasn't trying to say that . . . I mean, listen, the music industry is, uh." She lifted her chin and closed her eyes. "I was a little nervous downstairs, but I don't need a Valium, thank you."

"Girl, I was just playing with you. How about a glass of wine to take the edge off while we eat?"

She opened her eyes but didn't move, for the first time really taking in her surroundings. Deep golds, exquisite ivory, elegant royal blues and enough

leather and wood appointments to have cleaned out
a showroom greeted her. The view of City Hall was
crazy. Oh, no, she couldn't move for a moment; her
legs were jellied. She offered him a weak smile. She
wasn't supposed to drink on the job, not while with a
client.

"Maybe an iced tea?" she finally said, suddenly feeling the strain of looking at him in the new environment. In the office was one thing. Why being in a suite
alone with him for a business lunch seemed to magnify
how fine he was or amplify his charisma, she wasn't
sure. All she was sure of was that she had to push all
that aside and deal with this man's tax troubles.

"All right," he said with a slight chuckle. "Then may
I offer you a seat? You can take off your coat and put
down your bags to look over the room-service menu,
ya know. I promise I won't steal anything if you leave
your belongings on the chair and sit down."

She glanced at the bags she clutched, feeling foolish. "Oh. Yes. Thank you. No problem. I just didn't
wanna presume on your space," she stammered, removing her coat, but forgetting to set down her briefcase and purse first, like a klutz. She might have been
able to coordinate her movements a little better had
he not come over to help her off with her coat. Now
she was all tangled in the sleeves and purse strap and
had to look like a crazy woman!

"Miss Karin, why would you presume that I'd have a
woman eat lunch in her coat?" he said good-
naturedly, trying to help her untangle herself and getting the briefcase out of her hand with effort. "Good
Lord, woman. Whatchu been reading about me dat
has you spooked?" He laughed harder as she became
more flustered, thoroughly enjoying the spectacle.

"Me? Read? I don't do that," she said, finally

extricating herself from her coat, and openly cringing as she glimpsed the tattered lining.

"Now I am concerned if you are telling me that as an educated woman you don't read."

She froze. "No. I read. I mean, I haven't read anything bad about you . . . I mean, nothing you could really believe, anyway."

He walked away, trying to swallow a smile as he folded her coat over a Queen Anne chair and placed her bags on the floor beside it. He'd been teasing her, and she'd gone stone cold serious on him, so he'd stop messing with her for now.

But he liked her, liked how she reacted to things. Every response was raw, fresh, honest, no pretense, even when she got tangled up in her coat. It was the most endearing thing he'd ever seen. She had no idea how many women had slinked into his suite in the past, coolly, professionally dropped their full-length fur coats at their feet to leave them naked, and ridiculous mess like that. Or could disrobe with one hand while doing what he wouldn't think too hard about right now with the other. But to have a gorgeous sister in his room, clutching her purse and briefcase as though she might brandish it like a weapon, decline drugs—a test—decline alcohol—another test she'd passed with flying colors—and hang onto her coat like it were a shield, blew him away. Yeah, he definitely liked some Miss Karin Michaels.

He bid her to sit on the sofa with a wave of his hand and went to the minibar and fridge to fetch her the iced tea she'd requested. "Got a Snapple in here— plain lemon, I think. Might have some other flavors; I haven't really had time to case the room yet."

"Whatever you've got is fine," she said quietly.

Whew . . . really? He could not process the statement

the way he knew he'd wanted to hear it. It had been way too long since he'd had a woman in his company that interested him this much. He turned his attention to the task at hand, and brought her the iced tea with a short rocks glass and some ice. Maybe he also should have sat down a little further away from her, as would have been more appropriate for business. However, it was too late; he was already committed to where he'd plopped down and could only hope she wouldn't react badly to his proximity.

She accepted the bottle of iced tea and the glass that had been offered right on time. Her mouth was so dry she could barely speak—and she was supposed to make small talk until lunch came?

"Thanks so much," she said trying to open the bottle without setting down the glass.

He just watched her struggle for a moment, bemused at her decision to temporarily put the glass between her knees and then pop the bottle cap, rather than set it down on the table. The brief interaction did something to him. Again, it was a glimpse of home, something you'd do sitting outside on the steps, not in a luxury suite of a five-star hotel. . . . Just seeing the glass filled with ice between her knees had given him an instant erection. Oh, no, over the top. This was business and he needed to chill.

The unplanned reaction to one Miss Karin made him decide to give her some space so he could breathe. He shot up from the sofa, rounded the calla lily–adorned table at the far side of the room, and began rattling off menu choices.

"Okay, since this is a working lunch, and you have to get back to the office and I definitely gotta get some rest before I go on stage tonight," he said, talking faster than he intended, "lemme see, they have the pepper-crusted salmon, all kinds of salads, uh, steaks, chicken breast, you can have a look or whatever, but I'm gonna get some wine—I'm tired, ya know I have to get de music in my head straight for the show later on." He glanced up at her to see her simply staring back at him, holding her glass of iced tea mid-air.

"You came in on a red-eye flight," she said, her voice sounding very far away as though deep in thought. "This was a very kind offer and a business protocol you don't have to feel obligated to keep. I can only imagine that the concert takes a lot of preparation and a lot out of you. I can leave now, we don't have to do lunch, and that way I can more thoroughly go over your files, debrief Mr. Kincaid, get prepared to—"

"No, no—it's cool. I always start bugging the day of a concert. Before a big gig, I go through changes, but when I get on stage, I'm in the zone."

What was he saying? He was babbling for this woman! He wanted her to stay, even though it was probably best that she didn't, right now. Her voice felt like easy silk flowing over his senses, the way she'd tried to diplomatically exit, all on his behalf. Again, this was a first; most pressed and whined to stay. But this one had gently set down her glass and was about to stand to leave. It had to be pre-concert adrenaline that was causing wood. All the girl did was put the short rocks tumbler between her knees for a second to open a bottle. Why revisiting the image was making the throb in his groin worse, he wasn't sure. Maybe it was her soft, understanding smile that was adding to it.

"Mr. Dubois—"

"Jacques. I've already taken liberties and called you Karin several times, right?"

She smiled and looked down at the floor. Either her

contacts were lying, or the man was hung like a Georgia mule, something she also hadn't noticed back at the office. If that's what he was packing while relaxed and uninterested, it was probably best for her to leave now before she allowed her mind to wander any further.

"Okay, Jacques," she said, trying not to breathe out his name, but simply say it. "I have a lot of respect for the artistic process, and don't want to hinder that. I can imagine you've been under a lot of pressure, and I want you to be completely in the zone tonight."

He needed a drink. *She* was worried about *his* gig and the pressure *he* was under? She would actually leave so that he could do his thing, get his head right . . . a woman who knew how to give an artist space? His mouth went dry. *And* she was good in business? *Plus* fine? "Uhm . . . I have to eat anyway, and sharing a meal with good company helps put me in the right frame of mind."

She hesitated. "Are you sure?"

He nodded. "Can we just not talk about the tax madness, though? Strange request, but it's stressing me. I just wanted to feel your vibe, see if you were someone I could trust to handle my business. After I perform, we can get into all the details. Is that cool . . . I mean, can that work for you?"

She relaxed, picked up her iced tea, and closed her eyes as she sipped it with a nod. God had heard her prayers. She didn't have to be on and know every tax-code cold, as though going into a final exam all through lunch. She had time to study and bone up. And as far as vibes went, she definitely liked his—easy, open, honest. Yeah, they could do that.

There was something so sexy about the way that woman brought the glass to her lips, closed her big, gorgeous eyes slowly, took a deep swig of iced tea, and then allowed the glass to come away from her mouth, leaving it wet—so sexy that he didn't know what to do with himself. He had to remember to breathe.

"Then you'll stay?" he said, almost murmuring the question.

"I'd love to, especially if we can just laugh and get to know each other . . . since we'll be working side by side for the long haul."

No truer words had ever been spoken so sweetly. But since his condition hadn't changed, he didn't step forward to hand her the menu.

"Do you know what you want?"

For a fraction of a second she just stared at him, and immediately grappled within her head to pull it together. Hell yeah, she knew what she wanted, but it was wrong, wrong, wrong, and way out of order. "Just a salad," she said.

"They have five different kinds," he said with a smile.

"Caesar, with shrimp, if they've got it."

For a moment, he just stared at her. He had to pull it together, but a part of him already knew he was gonna spoil her rotten down in the islands. "You like seafood?"

"My weakness."

He swallowed hard. "Mine, too. But I have to warn you, once you have it down home, you'll get picky when you come back to the States."

She had to mentally rethink what he'd just said, because her mind had completely processed his statement in a very wicked way. "Kinda like the blue water, I bet. Like after that, you're ruined for the gray water at the Jersey shore."

He smiled. "Same with the beaches." He had to stop looking at her like he knew he was: too hungry. "So, a

Caesar with shrimp for you, a plain one for me. You want dessert?"

She smiled. "Too early for me to decide. I have to eat lunch first."

"Oh, yeah, true dat," he said, becoming immediately embarrassed. Whether what she'd said held a double meaning or not, he was way out of order. He'd definitely been focusing on dessert. "But you want anything on the side?"

"No," she said, laughing and flopping on the sofa. "My butt is already too big. It doesn't need any help with dessert, fries, or whatever—so I've been trying to stick to the main courses and that's it."

He almost blurted out that her butt was fabulous as is; however, he thought better of commenting. Tight, high, round—oh, Lord, yes, it was righteous. Rather than really mess up with a foolish remark, he chanced walking to the phone to place their order, awkwardly trying to keep his back to her until the damnable hard-on died down, all the while wondering if what she'd said about sticking to main courses was a clue or insight about anything else in her life.

Now he was *sure* he was bugging.

Chapter 3

His voice was a wonderful, intoxicating combination of maleness and island sensuality that registered somewhere between Billy Ocean's and Sean Paul's exotic blends. His laughter flowed out over the table like gem-studded Caribbean waters, broken up occasionally by deep booming belly laughs, or offering a sexy chuckle instead. But for all the obvious stress he was under, when talking to her earlier . . . his eyes, they took everything in with an open level of serenity that she'd never witnessed in any man before. It was as though she could actually see into his head, and watch him compose on the fly as he spoke, paused, looked off into the distance through the window, and then came back to a point to excitedly conquer it or convey what he was feeling.

Uninhibited was the only word she could summon to capture what he represented. A free spirit in love with life and enraptured by the sound of everything around him. That was definitely new. No matter what happened with him as a client, he'd already paid her in full, just by sharing the gift of knowing that every job and every profession didn't have to be drudgery.

She had to remember to keep a steady rhythm to appear nonchalant as they ate lunch, repeatedly telling herself, *Stab the salad, lift it up, put it in your mouth, girlfriend, and chew—then swallow.*

"Can I ask you a question?" she said quietly, feeling relaxed by his affable presence.

"Sure, luv. No secrets between me and you, or you drop me rusty behind, right?"

She laughed, set down her fork, and gazed at him intently, trying to really understand this enigma of a person. "How did you do it—I mean, just find your passion and then become so free?"

"Ah . . . the fifty-million-dollar question," he said, jokingly. He abandoned his napkin beside his plate, sat back in his chair, and put one finger to his lips, appearing to give her question heavy contemplation. "I wasn't always free," he admitted.

"I find that hard to believe," she replied with a wide grin.

"No. For real," he said, beginning to talk with his hands again. "I have one younger brother who was me da's pet. Jean can fix anyting, and became a master builder. Dad was so proud of him; I was the clumsy one, couldn't drive a nail to save me life, and would burn a house down by accident if they left me to strip it wit a heat gun."

He laughed hard and shook his head, raking his fingers through his hair. "Den, me two sisters are professionals. Annette is a nurse—a good one, too. Ginette, she's a professor. You can imagine how me parents felt with their firstborn son running around, smokin' spliffs, playing in a wild-azz band, staying out all night in clubs and whatnot, and sleeping all day, and chippin' every piece of me ma's china cause I was banging a spoon against it at the table with beats in me head driving her crazy." He gave her a sheepish grin. "I don't do the spliffs no more, though. Ting of the past. Had to let it go if I was gonna get serious with me craft and also travel through customs all over."

She chuckled softly, sensing a tender wound that he'd covered over with mirth. She did indeed know what it was like to be compared. She watched him pick up a piece of silverware and begin tapping it against his wine glass as his eyes slid closed.

"When you are a musician, music is everywhere. It's like air dat you have to breathe. Listen to the sound coming off dis glass when it's half full," he said, and then began tapping the side of the plate in a different tempo. "Different, right?"

"Yeah," she murmured, mesmerized as he gave her a quick glimpse of his muse.

"I never fit into the boxes, Karin. I play axe and keys, so I don't bust up as many dishes," he said with a self-conscious chuckle. "But the guys on drums, they wear a house out."

She laughed with him softly and saw the performer begin to eclipse the vulnerable side of the man. "I admire that you fought and held your ground to do what you wanted to do—now we're all better off for it."

His smile faded as he stared at her, and then became brilliant again. "Ah, but the public is fickle, luv. Last few years me and my band have been hot. Next year, who knows. It's a crazy business. You scrap your way to the top, stay there for a flash in de pan, den it's over . . . but you've still got the music in your soul."

He set down the silverware and all the mirth left his face. His voice dropped to a solemn whisper. "This is why I have to get my business straight, so I can remain free. There's only a few cats who are the real greats, the ones who lasted a lifetime doing this . . . Stevie Wonder, Elton John, Ray Charles, Q, a few more—think about it. Everybody else is doing movies, got clothes, or is producing other artists now to keep themselves a little bit free. But they've become businessmen, and the music, their first love, is by-the-by. That scares me to death."

Impulse made her reach across the table and grasp his hand. It was such a sudden but necessary thing that they both just sat quietly for a moment to take it in.

"I know what it's like to have people all around you telling you that if you don't stay within the painted lines, you'll crash and burn," she said in a soft tone. "And I also know what it's like to be compared to people who have different gifts that seem to fit everyone's expectations—trust me, my mother is a pro at making you feel like you could have always done better. From cousins to girlfriends to her friends' children, I was always just a pace behind, according to her, and it hurt."

"No offense," he said, his eyes searching her face, "but the woman must be blind, because the one gift you own, besides being very smart, is hearing what hasn't been directly said."

The statement was so profound and such a compliment that it made her gently withdraw her hands and ball them in her lap. It was beginning to be very difficult to continue to just see him as a client, but she had to for both their sakes.

"You keep flying high and just let us spot you on the ground. . . . Let us put a safety net under you to catch you for when the winds change, or the public gets fickle. I can't pretend to be as courageous as you, or to know exactly what you're going through as a human being . . . but I can try to help by doing the only thing I know how to do—since I took the path of least resistance and became an accountant."

She smiled and picked up her melting glass of iced tea to keep from reaching for his hands again. He picked up his glass of chardonnay and clinked it to the side of her glass.

"I'd better go get working on those reports so you can get some rest for tonight."

He reluctantly nodded and set his glass down with a sigh. Where had this beautiful champion come from? A woman who had such surface discipline but a depth of character that one couldn't paint on or pretend? Wounded in her own right, but also very strong. And her words had been the sweetest melody beneath a constant refrain that he couldn't get out of his head: *Baby, do your thing. I've gotchure back.*

Karin Michaels stood with grace, and it took him a moment to come out of the haze to walk her to the chair where she could collect her belongings and prepare to leave. As he paged Rockko, he felt an irrational loneliness overtake him. Although there was no earthly excuse he could devise to keep her in his company any longer, he wasn't ready for her to leave. No one he'd ever met had gotten to his core so quickly, or had seen beneath the laughter he wore as a public shield. She'd seeped around the façade and under his skin like warm palm oil, smooth . . . fragrant, making the hard, ashy areas within him suddenly return to life.

"Thank you for a wonderful morning and lunch," she said, extending her hand.

He shook his head, smiled, and declined the hand, giving her a hug. "I do business with family and friends, and we don't shake, we hug."

She chuckled and hugged him back, but that was

definitely another level of his undoing. Even though he towered over her, the way her soft, curvaceous form fit against him within the platonic hug shot quiet want through his system. It was more than the curves of her female body. It was the warmth she exuded—not physical, though. He broke from the embrace, confused, unable to place it in his mind or analyze it as he came out of the union.

Almost stammering, he paced away to get his head together. "I forgot. You won't be able to get into the concert without these," he said, talking a mile a minute as he dashed into the other room, ransacked his suitcase, and returned brandishing concert tickets. "We always get some front rows and backstages, but I rarely use mine up any more. Most times, I just give 'em to the rest of the guys or to Rockko, ya know."

"Oh, I forgot!" she exclaimed and rushed over to him. "Thank you!" She accepted the tickets with a joyous squeal, hugged him tightly, and then raced for the door, shoving them into her briefcase. "All right, I admit it; even though I'm your accountant, I'm also a fan." She winked, at him, laughed, and then slipped out the door.

He just stood there rooted to the floor and watched her leave—the passionate change of temperament, the sound of her voice, the rush of the hug, the sexy wink, all of Karin Michaels blowing him away.

She couldn't wait for Rockko to put the privacy window up between them, even though she was so happy that she could have kissed the man in the street. She snatched her cell phone out of her purse, flipped it open, and hit Lloyd's number without giving it a second thought. They had front-row seats at a Def Island concert!

"What is it with you today, Karin?"

"Guess what?"

He paused and blew out a disgusted snort into the phone. "I'm working."

She refused to allow his terse response to ruin her surprise. This would definitely lift his spirits. "I've got two *front-row* tickets to the big concert at the Wachovia Center tonight—plus backstage passes!"

"Karin, tell me you didn't waste your hard-earned money on some thug concert. I know you cannot possibly think I'll go to some—"

"It's business," she said, her tone instantly icy as true outrage set in.

"What do you mean, it's business? C'mon—"

"I just landed a major account, Lloyd."

He hesitated. "And they gave the new black girl thug-concert tickets. I'd think you'd be offended, not bouncing off the walls with joy."

She chose her words with care, making each one nearly snap with precise diction. "My major client is Jacques Dubois—a very eloquent, talented businessman. I represented the firm and he is coming to us for some work. He gave me the tickets as a thank-you. I thought you might like to go as my escort, since you are always telling me that I should get more involved in the political aspects of networking for the job. However, if your weekly tennis match is more important than my career advancement, then I understand. I really, *really* understand it all now."

"You're taking this the wrong way, Karin. Anyway, not much serious networking goes on at those types of ghetto affairs. Backstage passes mean a groupie-fest, and I fail to see the merit of—"

"Fine," she said quickly, cutting him off. She didn't want him to go; in fact, she didn't want him anywhere near her new opportunity. Rage had nearly closed her throat, but not before she got in a sarcastic dig. "Then, I'll see you when I get back from St. Lucia and—"

"Hold it! St. Lucia?"

"Yes. For business. The firm is sending me, with a new laptop, a two-thousand-dollar advance, a luxury rental and—"

"When did all *this* happen?"

Karin settled back into the plush leather and smiled as she looked out the window. "This morning . . . after I called you and you hung up on me without as much as a good-bye, because you were working. My boss got sick and I had to step in for him with an important client. My boss trusted me to do what was necessary to land the account, and I did," she said, adding a bit of embellishment to the story for theatrical effect. "So I understand that you can't make it tonight. Maybe I'll see if another colleague from the firm can go, like perhaps Brenda or—"

"No, no, wait a minute, K. You didn't give me the full details when you first dropped this on me, and I've had a harrowing day around here, so let's not jump to conclusions. If this is really a part of your job, then . . . all right. I can move some things around and make myself available."

"Don't stress yourself," she said coolly, enjoying being in control of the dynamics for the first time in their lopsided relationship.

"Just as I would expect you to escort me to a networking function at the hospital, I think it's my place, if not my right, as your significant other to do likewise."

"That's why I called you, Lloyd," she said flatly, truly beginning to dislike him. She let out a long sigh, wishing she'd never even told him. Brenda deserved to go more than anything, and she also had a couple of solid girl-friends from way back that she also could have called.

As the tension of silence crackled on the line be-tween them, she realized just how many really good old friends she'd abandoned for him. The new ones she'd replaced them with, the ones *he* approved of, weren't really good friends at all. They were *his* friends, the significant others of *his* colleagues, not hers. It had happened so slowly and so insidiously that she hadn't even noticed until now.

First, he'd complained about her girls, or would make snide, haughty comments around them that would make an evening uncomfortable. Then, slowly but surely, every time she wanted to get together with her best friends in a group with his buddies, or there was a party invitation, he was mysteriously always un-available, citing work as a reason. Then, finally, the invitations ceased, the calls between her and her old-time friends became fewer and fewer, until the rela-tionships dried out and turned to dust.

"What time is the concert?" he asked in a weary, bored tone.

"Eight o'clock, so we should leave at seven, if you're going."

"I said I would," he snapped. "Parking will be a nightmare."

"Yes. The whole evening probably will be, too."

"What's *that* supposed to mean?"

"Nothing," she said, all the joy of earlier today evap-orating. "I'm just agreeing with you."

The only thing that lifted her spirits was the buzz in the office the moment she stepped off the elevator.

Coworkers came out of cubicles, secretaries flocked, and the reception area was filled with unusual mayhem. She was one of them, a grunt, but she'd been gone for two hours on a real power lunch, and to their way of looking at it, she'd come back to the firm as the conquering hero.

"I got your laptop and advance check, Karin," Betty said with a wink. She glanced at her buddy in the controller's office.

"Yep, went through without a hitch," Doris said.

"Just like the plane tickets, hotel," Eileen whispered. "Now tell us *all*, chile!"

Unused to so much attention all at once, Karin laughed as her face warmed. What could she say to them to properly convey who and what this person was? He was more than a client; he was thirty, and fabulous, and brilliant, and artistic, and soulful, and had a soft side, and a great family, and wow! But she also felt strangely protective of this new person, client, friend, so she wasn't about to divulge too much.

"He's a consummate businessman. Very astute and was forthcoming. He made some blunders, financially, but I think the firm will be able to address them in time. He needs a good bookkeeping structure to track his erratic travel and lifestyle, and some guidelines to help him navigate the tax terrain, plus a more centralized control of how his bills get paid and expenses disbursed, much like our comptroller depart—"

"Girl," Brenda said, her voice a vicious whisper, "what's *the man* like?"

A cacophony of laughter surrounded Karin and caught her off guard, especially the source that had generated it. The tickets were burning a hole in her pocket, and she so wished that she'd just come back to the office without calling Lloyd. Stupid. She'd already had the perfect out; he'd be playing tennis and didn't break his commitments, per the words out of his own mouth. But she'd missed that opportunity, too. So the best she could do was give into the sway of her coworkers and friends and simply tell them the truth.

"The man," she said, drawing out her words for dramatic effect, and making the whole lobby go still. She dropped her voice, glanced around to be sure no supervisors were in earshot. "He's *awesome*. So freakin' fine I had to remember how to eat my salad."

Every female in the lobby swooned to bring another round of laughter to erupt in the normally staid environment.

"Girl, you are living the life that we have all dreamed of," Brenda said in a wistful tone, gaining nods from the others. "Who in here hasn't wished that a gorgeous, rich, eligible client might one day come in here and whisk her away?"

"Oh, pullease, y'all," Karin said self-consciously, embarrassed by Brenda's assessment. "He hasn't *whisked* me away, and that will *not* happen. Last time I checked, I still had on Payless shoes, and my check hadn't changed. He's the millionaire, not me, and if I don't get his books right, I'll be hunting in the newspaper or standing in the unemployment line looking for another job."

Again, everyone laughed and nodded, slowly disbursing as reality set in.

"One can dream, though," Brenda said over her shoulder as she shuffled back to her cubicle.

Karin let her breath out hard and made her way back to her desk as the group broke up. Yeah, right . . . but what would a guy like Jacques Dubois want with her short, plain, run-of-the-mill self? It didn't make sense, and crazy fantasies like that were more than foolish, they were dangerous. Anyway, the man was a notorious player. There were women in his videos alone that were so perfect and so fine that they'd make a normal female's eye twitch from sheer body envy. Not to mention she was already attached, and a guy like J.B. probably had a long-stemmed beauty tucked away in every port of call. Plus, he hadn't shown the least bit of interest, even if she'd been looking for any—which she wasn't. The man had been nice, courteous, and civil, and he was a new client, and that was simply the end of it.

The fact that Lloyd had been right didn't improve her mood. Traffic was a logjam leading to the concert, and the parking process was also a long, arduous, creeping inch of bumper-to-bumper vehicles.

It also hadn't helped that he'd criticized her outfit. She'd chosen a pair of crêpe wool, black, flare-legged pants, strappy black high heels with little rhinestones across the top, and a black-beaded camisole to go under her raw silk, midnight-blue jacket that had an iridescent black finish to it, and had carefully selected her favorite snakeskin belt with rhinestone studs and a small beaded clutch that hung from a long silk strap. But, according to him, she looked too concert-gaudy.

He hadn't noticed that she'd spritzed on her favorite perfume, "Angel." Nor did he seem to notice how she'd taken time to rim her eyes with kohl and midnight blue and used a deep plum for her mouth, with a matte finish. He didn't notice that she'd swept her hair up into a narrow, rhinestone-studded band, and had painstakingly created a profusion of curls to give her a sexy but controlled appearance.

So what that he came wearing a blue business suit and, as handsome as he was, seemed out of place? Until he'd started picking away at her choices, she'd felt pretty. She'd dressed to the beat of the boogie, happily blaring her music throughout her one-bedroom apartment to put herself in the concert-going mood. She'd gabbed with her coworkers and squealed with delight. Now all she felt was nervous and self-conscious, but he'd arrived exactly at seven and didn't seem patient enough to allow her to make a change. Damn him for always being a joy thief.

She said nothing as she sat quietly fuming and stressed out in his immaculate silver Beamer. Everything about him annoyed her to distraction . . . and after hearing her name finally pronounced correctly by a man, Kar-*rin*, spoken softly with a melodic edge, not "Karen," as Lloyd always said so nasally, she didn't want to hear a thing her so-called boyfriend had to say.

"And I suppose I'll have to part with the twenty to park in this mayhem," he finally snapped. "Do you want the receipt so you can reimburse me later once you file your expense report?"

"No," she said coolly, rummaging in her purse without looking at him. "Just flash this and put it on your dashboard so you can park in the VIP section for free." She handed him the pass and kept her line of vision trained out the opposite window, but did glimpse his surprise as he inspected what she'd given him.

"Guess it pays to know people on the inside," he said curtly, but he couldn't completely hide his amazement as the parking attendants with light wands waved him through toward a restricted section.

She refused to dignify the comment and fastened her gaze on the mammoth building ahead.

"So, what next? You know how these black events are. They never start on time, and we'll—"

"Be going in the back to the green room for hors d'oeuvres, once you park and get out of the car."

"Oh."

She shot him a glare and opened her door without waiting for him to do so the second he turned off the ignition.

They said nothing as they made their way up the wide cement steps to the back entrance, and she held the tickets as though they'd come from the state lottery, beginning to feel butterflies coming alive within her, despite her surly escort.

"Have a great evening," the security bouncer at the back entrance said. "Present your passes to the elevator attendant and you'll be escorted to the VIP refreshment area. Enjoy the show."

"Thank you," she said with a tense smile. If she'd been with anyone else, she would have given her partner a high five the moment they got in. But she was with Lloyd, and that quelled the natural response.

Still refusing to look at him, she fastened her gaze on the elevator buttons, watching them light up as they again flashed VIP passes at the guard and made it to the next level of being on the inside.

"Just go down the hall to the walnut double doors and present your passes. When the show is about to begin, someone will be seating all front-row guests."

She needed to pinch herself as the elevator attendant in a chic black suit and gold name tag spoke, but she remained as calm as humanly possible. She was with Lloyd.

However, she could feel him trying to get her attention, to lean in and make a comment. She ignored his attempt, feigning obliviousness. Screw him. He was not going to make another dig and steal another moment of joy from her evening.

As they entered the room, it was all she could do not to gawk. On one side of the room there was a veritable slaughterhouse of meat choices, everything from chicken to small ribs and a beef-carving station, while seafood of all varieties spilled over platters and silver stands in such abundance that it bordered on decadent. Bottled water, wine coolers, expensive wines, champagne, nonalcoholic beverages completed the spread. It seemed as though every microbrewery and all the majors had loaded the place down just to be at the party for publicity.

The local celebrities were out in full force, and she recognized all of the hot DJs, talk radio personalities, and a bunch of people that had to be their family and friends. Politicians, businesspeople; so many faces were in the large room replete with comfortable leather sofas and chairs that she didn't know what to do.

From the corner of her eye, she glimpsed Lloyd, who for the first time literally seemed stunned silent. Good. Something childish within her wanted to whisper, "How you like me now, brother?" But she didn't. Her mind seized upon witty little jabs she could deliver to him like, "*This* is networking, okaaaay?" But she held her peace and simply smiled and made her way to the buffet for a cracked crab leg.

"Those are messy to deal with," her date whispered as he sidled up beside her. "You don't want to be shaking hands and smell like fish. Same with the ribs and chicken wings, and fare of that nature. I'd suggest something easier to navigate with a plate in hand, like the mini quiche, or some veggies. Just a suggestion." Then he moved away from her the moment he apparently saw some people more important than her.

Fine. Karin looked at the seafood in despair and selected a few shrimp, just for spite, and popped one into her mouth. The man even made a beautiful buffet feel inaccessible, and a slow, roiling resentment made the sweet shrimp go down in an acidic swallow. Her stomach rumbled from hunger, but she went to find a glass of wine and gave up on attempts to enjoy the food. She was already nervous enough, and the last thing she needed was to peer across the room at Lloyd's disapproving scowl.

Oddly, even in a room of nearly seventy-five people, she felt like she was alone. She wondered if that was how Jacques felt at times, while on stage. She selected a glass of chardonnay as a server passed and offered it to her, remembering how his mouth looked as he'd sipped it casually in his room. The man had an easy quality about him, no pretense. He'd picked up croutons with his fingers and popped them in his mouth, laughing and talking a mile a minute, regaling her with wild stories from being on the road. As much as he had in terms of money and fame, for some strange reason, he also had a disarming way of making her feel like she did fit into his world, like she was acceptable as is, and there was no need for further refinement.

Jacques Dubois thought that she was smart, that she knew her stuff, and he laughed at her jokes—not in a strained way, but with genuine, deep down, raucous laughter, as though she'd tickled him. Karin smiled a private smile, sipped her wine and began to absently mill through the crowd. Everyone else seemed to already know each other; she had no clue as to how to break into those conversations, and Lloyd didn't seem eager to help with the dilemma.

Growing bored, she glanced at her watch, wishing that the show would begin. Time was creeping along like a snail. If the show would just start, she could then be blanketed by the darkened stadium, the only lights those on stage, and the roar of the crowd and blaring music providing anonymity.

It would be impossible to talk while the performances took place; thus, any snide remarks would have to wait until the opening act was done, and then those negative vibes could be shunted aside again when the main act came on, Def Island. Then she could close her eyes and dream for just a little while during what she knew would be the concert of her life, or jam until her feet hurt, shake her booty until Lloyd passed out from shame, and not care. Tonight, she was gonna party. Tonight, she was here to have a good time at *her* client's request. Tonight, it was not about what Lloyd thought, it was about what she knew—Jacques Dubois was all that.

After the longest half hour of her life, the announcement was finally made that guests with passes could either take their front-row seats on the floor now or wait in the green room and continue to enjoy refreshments until the main act started before going downstairs. Although one could see the stage from the large window inside the VIP lounge, and monitors and speakers offered a way to enjoy both, she was out.

Diplomatically nudging her way through the small groups of people, she found Lloyd engaged in heavy networking.

"Do you want to go downstairs now to see the first act?" she asked as casually as possible, once there was a break in conversation. She waited for him to introduce her to the people he was speaking with, but he didn't.

"Why don't we wait until the main act comes on?" he said, blowing her off and going back to the people he was speaking to.

She smiled, opened her purse, and handed him his

ticket. "Okay. See you in about an hour." She then calmly spun on her heels and sought out a security escort, knowing full well that Lloyd Jacobs had too much pride to follow her after the mild public scene she'd caused. She also knew she'd hear about it later, but didn't care at this point. Being near him made her claustrophobic.

Only the bigwigs stayed behind, and she left with all the so-called little people—probably the cousins, friends, family, and lovers connected to the opening acts. But they were real. They exuded excitement and laughter. They weren't networking or doing business. They, like her, were obviously there just to have a good time and take in the first-class moment of it all.

The volume of the crowd was shattering, but fun. She loved every moment of being in a small huddle of people who talked to her even though she wasn't anyone in particular. They were all gabbing and laughing, and as they made their way to the front, one overly madeup, heavyset woman turned to her and exclaimed, "Girl, ain't dis da bomb?"

"Yes, girl!" Karin shouted, laughing and glad to be in good company.

"Who you get your tickets from?" the woman asked, her cronies all gathering near as they walked down the sidelines to the front. "We got ours from Power 99 FM. I won the call-in, chile. It don't get no better than this!"

Karin laughed, "Sho' you right, sis!" But she reserved comment on her source. It didn't matter anyway; the small group was so excited that they hadn't noticed.

There was no need for seats, really. No one sat down as the first group came onstage and hailed Philadelphia with a "Yo, yo, yo, how you livin' Philly?" From that point on, it was pandemonium. Speakers bigger than her drowned out her voice as she screamed with the best of them and the bone-jarring music became her pulse. She was jamming her natural butt off, didn't care about sweat, makeup, or whatever. Her row-mates were having a blast, slapping five and pounding fists each time a new song came on.

When the chaos finally ebbed and the house lights came up, Karin made a mad dash for the ladies' room with about five thousand other women. This was the time to repair all damage, get it back together, and correct oily T-zones, just to do it all over again. A soda had her name on it, that she would get for sure, and she'd spend an hour of pure delight, dancing her heart out in the aisles. Lloyd Jacobs could kiss her behind. She quickly reapplied lip gloss that had been screamed off.

Unfortunately, when she got back to her seat, he was there, his expression angry and disappointed.

"How could you pull a stunt like that when you're supposed to be working?" he snapped, moving over so she could take her seat. "I was talking to the director of HR over at Children's Hospital, because they'd been given some complimentary tickets for their staff and some of the children in the Sunshine program."

"I wouldn't have known who you were talking to," she said, her gaze directed toward the stage in anticipation. "Since you didn't introduce me, how would I have known which VIP had your attention?"

"Karin, please," he scoffed. "You know that during opportunities like this you listen, stand close, and then insert yourself where appropriate—I can't babysit you, or hold your arm and take you around if you're too shy to extend your hand and meet people."

Now he had her attention. She cut him a sideline glare.

"If I were your wife, wouldn't you say, 'Oh, Mr. So and So, this is my wife, Karin,' or would you just wait for me to insert myself? You could have said, 'This is my friend, or *girlfriend*, Karin, who works for Broderick, Kincaid, and Barron,' but you didn't."

"I'm not going to get into this here, of all places."

"Good," she snapped, returning her focus to the empty stage. *God, just make him shut up!*

"But you missed a perfect opportunity to cultivate several other truly legitimate clients in that room, where you could have scored business cards and contact information for follow-up later. Every major radio-station exec was there, several corporations' VIPs, sports-team owners and their wives—but you chose to be on the floor like a party girl, shaking your booty for a second-rate rap group. *That* is disappointing, Karin. However, it's your career, not mine. I was just trying to help."

She was so angry that she simply closed her eyes for a moment, counted to ten, and opened them as the house lights went down. The crowd's volume hit an earsplitting decibel that made it nearly impossible to hear herself think.

She wasn't sure which part of what he'd said had slapped her face more—the fact that he did have a point about the missed opportunity, or the sly dig he'd made about "truly legitimate" clients, as though Def Island weren't, or the way he'd diminished her need to release tension after all she'd gone through today. She wasn't sure, and it didn't matter. Her song was on, and within moments, her client who felt more like a good friend would hit the stage and banish Lloyd's contempt for a couple of hours.

The high-pitched whine of electric guitar combined with the low, strobe effect of bass went through the floor; drums put pinpoints of light behind her eye-balls; keyboards sent chills down her spine, and the crowd went nuts. It almost seemed to be happening in slow motion, the way Jacques walked across the stage. *No shirt.* Multicolored hot lights forming beads of sweat that she was close enough to almost touch. *Ohmigod* . . . Black leather pants with rips everywhere, low slung on narrow hips, crazy snakeskin boots with silver-tipped toes, and a black bandana tied around his head holding back those gorgeous locks.

Jacques scanned the screaming crowd and threw his head back and laughed. "Philly in da houze, mon!"

It felt like the Wachovia Center lifted off the ground two inches and slammed back down, the crowd was so off the hook. Karin was out of her seat, hollering with the best of them, ignoring her date's tug on her jacket hem to sit. Sit? Was he out of his danged mind? Pullease!

"We gwan ratchet dis party up till y'all take me there . . . den we gwan slow it down, and get wicked-nasty, and serve de ladies some romance, we good?"

A one-voiced crowd screamed back, "Yeah!"

Individual shout-outs pelted the stadium.

"Take me there, baby!"

"Get your groove on, J.B.!"

"Holla!"

Karin covered her face and laughed into her hands. If only Brenda and the girls could have been there. This was madness, and she was so glad to be in the front row losing her mind. Island funk had her doing everything from the Beyoncé butt shake to the West Philly wiggle. So what that her date was dying a thousand deaths, too mortified to move. The man on stage could throw down on the guitar, and could run that reggae rap so fast and so smooth that it hit her vertebrae in a ripple, dominos dropping her spine on the floor. Jesus, the way he rolled that mess off his tongue without taking a breath and danced at the same time. Lawd smack her!

Five songs in a row, and he wasn't even breathing hard, she noted. Other thoughts entered her mind, stamina being one of them, but she shook it away as she danced. *No, chile, don't be real crazy—this is just a performance.* But why'd he have to come to the front of the stage, lean down and do a double-take and visually acknowledge her with a nod?

Karin froze. J.B. smiled, pointed at her, nodded again, and stood up, then hit another cord on his axe.

"Y'all taking me dere real fast and real hard tonight. Jus' saw a lovely lady dat's gwan make me back down this party to some slow, funky groove. Ya know how it gets when it's hot and you can't do nuthin' 'bout it, mon, but *swelter*. Dat's what we getting' ready to do up in dis here Wach Center tonight."

Her hefty, previous row partner grabbed Karin by both arms and screamed in her face, "Girl, he was talking to you!"

Now Lloyd was on his feet, but he couldn't get to Karin for all the hysterical female bodies blocking him. She had been spirited halfway down the aisle by a tide of excited ladies, hoping to bait the superstar to that side of the stage again using Karin as a lure. Truth was, no male, probably not even a bouncer, could have made it through the chaos that required a riot squad.

Jacques Dubois nodded, and handed off his guitar as his signature baby grand piano was brought forward. The lights dimmed, but not before he fixed his gaze on Karin, sending another ricocheting tide of screaming thunder through the stadium. She froze as he adjusted the microphone at the piano and the lights went down to blue starlight, making the crowd erupt again when he sat.

"Dis is for de all-natural beauty in every woman, particularly Miss Kar-*rin*," he murmured, and went into the ballad with sudden authority, issuing a level of intensity that made her have to lean on two ladies she didn't even know.

Limp, she let the music take her to a place she'd never dreamed possible . . . a place of hope. He'd said *her name*, on stage, and didn't care that at least twenty thousand people had heard it, too. Every lyric resonated through her like it was welded to her pulse. Even though she knew it was all probably done just for the sake of performance, for this deeply personal but very public moment, she'd been made to feel like she was the only woman on the planet.

The way he crooned felt like it was just for her, and from now on, every time she heard any of his songs, she knew she'd put them in her secret treasure chest of dreams.

> *Be mine, all-natural, girl, 'cause I'm missin' home*
> * so bad.*
> *Hate the road, 'cause it takes me away from you.*
> *All-natural girl, you more woman than I deserve,*
> *but I'ma make it all right, any ole way. . . .*
> *Let me show you how, real slow.*

She closed her eyes near faint as his deep, exotic voice filtered through every cell in her. When the last beautiful melody rippled down the keys from his graceful hands, only then did she breathe and open her eyes. She peered up, mesmerized, to be greeted by his megawatt smile. She placed her hand over her heart, trying to stave off a heart attack. Jacques jumped up from the piano as though a bee had stung him, and motioned to his band to strike up a faster song.

"Naw, y'all, we came to party, and see, I can't stay dere in the love zone, doing the slow songs like dat too long . . . mess a brother up, feel me?" He snatched off his bandanna and, theatrically mopped his brow with it, then took a deep swig of bottled spring water and walked around on the stage in a circle for a moment, only causing more screams from the audience.

"Take your time, man!"

"Been there!"

"Serve it, brother!"

J.B. raked his fingers through his locks, nodded, picked up his guitar again, and looked at Karin with a wink and a huge smile. Then he did the unthinkable: came to the front of the stage, called her forward, and dropped the bandanna for her to catch.

Chapter 4

Karin only glanced back down the aisle at Lloyd as the last song of the night began. He was puffed up so badly that the poor man looked like he'd explode. Whateva. The jam was coming on, a truly git-down tune that she dared not play around him or her momma. Yeah, the lyrics were foul, but hey, they were also funny as all get out. All right, maybe they had a point; "Sukiyaki" was a *nasty* little song. But a good one.

It was also the kind of song with the right bass line and hook that made you have to sing it, and sing it loud. Lloyd probably needed an ambulance, or smelling salts at the very least, when something came over her and her hands went in the air, and she was belting out the refrain like everybody else in the house.

Yeah, gimme dat Sukiyaki, girl!
Wet and greasy, slide it in easy.
Oooh sweet thang, show me how ta eat it.
Wurk that stuff, 'cause I know how ta treat it.
Sukiyaki to me, baby, all night long!

Okay, so the song was over the top, and so was J.B.'s onstage performance for that particular cut. But it was *the jam*. Dude had changed for the third time, coming out in the last number doing all white, with mad-crazy female dancers in white thongs and not much else blowing up the stage, pyrotechnics and whatnot, the bass off the meter—what could she do but a little "Sukiyaki" in the aisle herself? She hadn't partied like this in *years*. Uhmph, humph, humph! Sukiyaki all night long, have mercy!

Despite the call for more, the band wrapped up the evening by throwing white roses and said good-night. She could see Lloyd cutting a swath towards her, but bouncers had entered the fray to escort red and yellow VIP ticket holders backstage, so he had to go with the rushing human current. She burst out laughing, knowing there'd be a heavy price to pay later—but that was later, and this was now, and she'd gotten her party on so hard that her hair was a wild wreck. She didn't care.

The sorting of bodies at the stage wings was a crazy process guided by mayhem, but somehow, efficient security that had been through the drill a hundred times separated the wanna-get-backstage folks from people who had legitimate passes. By the time everyone who was supposed to be back there got corralled into the inner sanctum, she was at least twenty-five feet behind Lloyd.

Then, from nowhere, she spotted Rockko and instant recognition gave her a leg up. The huge bodyguard nodded, whispered something in another bouncer's ear, more nods were exchanged, and then a hollered announcement came.

"Yo, yo, yo!" one burly security guard said. "Listen up. Def Island will be signing autographs for everybody with a yellow ticket. Hold 'em up, people. We got T-shirts for y'all, the new CD, and a gift bag filled with stuff from the label, but you have to chill. Anybody pushing, rushing, or trippin' out here when the band comes out gets bounced. J.B. is gonna sign everybody's shit, no worries. It's all peace."

He glanced at a team of ten black-shirt-wearing security guards, and took another deep breath so he could belt out the next round of instructions. "Now, I'ma need you folks to step to the left, and let the people who have a red ticket—I said red, not yellow, *red*, come through. They're media, and unless you are media, like we said earlier, you have to chill. We cool?"

Heads nodded and people moved over, glad to just be standing on the inside, and not wanting to be put back on the outside of the excitement. Karin glanced down at her ticket and clutched it tighter. It was red.

A much smaller retinue of individuals filed by, but her rowmate gave her a bright smile and tugged on her sleeve.

"Who you, girl?" the large woman said, starstruck. "What station you wit—I coulda got your autograph all that time!"

"Let the lady through, sis," Rockko said, coming to Karin's rescue. "You slow, you blow."

With that, he had Karin under the elbow, providing a body block for her as new people gaped and some of the veteran radio station personalities glanced at her in confusion mixed with curiosity. Tonight, she was somebody. Who? She wasn't sure. But definitely somebody.

Only once in the real inner wings was the group small enough for Lloyd to get to her side. But even so, there wasn't a private enough space for him to launch into a tirade, so he had to hold whatever he wanted to say zipped behind his tightly pursed lips.

They all followed Rockko down a long corridor that emptied into another lounge. There the band was already sprawled on chairs and sofas, sharing fist pounds, guzzling bottled water, and in the midst of an outrageous post-performance natural high. Gorgeous backup singers, video queens of every hue with voluptuous figures, even made Lloyd gawk. Just looking at their toned female bodies and perfect hair and nails, not to mention their designer outfits, strangely made Karin simply want to hide. She was definitely out of her league.

All of the red-ticket holders obviously already knew the band and J.B., and hugs and back slaps got passed out like it was a veritable family reunion. Radio jocks teased each other and wisecracked with the band. Cold beers got passed around, food got munched, and Karin watched it all from a very remote place in her mind . . . waiting. Okay, maybe Lloyd had a point. But how did one insert oneself into something like *this*?

"Hey, Miss Karin!" Jacques hollered from across the room, making her want to die a thousand deaths as everyone turned to stare at her.

"There really is a Miss Karin?" one radio jock teased. "I'll just be damned!"

The DJ sauntered over to Karin, who had only weakly waved hi. "You look too innocent to be traveling with this character. This man is trouble on two legs. Your momma know where you are?"

Although the joke had a complimentary element to it, it still made her want to just disappear into the nap of the carpet.

"All lies—tol' by da media!" Jacques shouted over

the laughter, moving toward Karin and giving her the eye to remain calm. "Dis little lady is gwan set me world right. After traveling wit dis buncha renegades, gotta get me house in order."

Again, it was the truth, but it didn't fully explain her role, and the comment could have been taken any of several ways. The way he'd delivered the statement had also made Lloyd turn a shade of gray that would have troubled an undertaker. Plus, the way Jacques gallantly strode over, still exuding his J.B. stage persona, and took her by the arm to bring her to meet the band, left little room for argument, especially in public.

"Now, Miss Karin, dese are who you watch out for, not me," Jacques said, beaming. "Dat's my boy, Blind, on bass, otherwise known as Claude. You will notice that he got his name from the fact dat the man don't take off his sunglasses day or night."

"Whassup," Blind said, smiling. "J.B. said you was good people, so you a'ight wif me."

"Puff, also known as Donovan, dat's da man on second keys—but don' ask me how he got his name. We also got secrets dat can't leave Cancun."

Puff laughed and pounded J.B.'s fist. "Word. Glad you in the house, Miss Karin. Don't pay my boy no mind."

Jacques chuckled and shook his head. "Dat's Sweet, Cyril, on drums. Chewy, alias for Julian, on bells and percussion. Frank's on the mixing boards and keeps our tech tight."

A unified, nonchalant, "Whassup," rippled through the lounging band.

Karin smiled, offered a little wave, and simply said, "Hi, guys."

Now what? She knew she should say something, but media had already swamped him again, asking when he'd be back in town, if they wanted to go out and party after the band changed, and if morning drive time interviews were possible. She watched the man gracefully negotiate the chaos, and almost jumped out of her skin when Lloyd sidled up to her.

"Don't you think an introduction is in order?" he muttered under his breath.

She swallowed a smile. "The next time I can get to him . . . but you should have just walked up and inserted yourself into the conversation, honey. I can't baby-sit you while I'm working."

Who was the joker in the suit, was all he wanted to know. But Jacques kept glad-handing and flowing around the room in conversation, still feeling the adrenaline from the performance. That could not be Karin's man. Had to be a brother, cousin, coworker, family, whatever. She'd transformed from the shy mouse he'd met earlier that day into a completely ravishing beauty. And the girl could party, had almost messed up his concentration during the performance when she'd thrown her hands in the air. He loved the transformation; a woman who could be all business by day and so much more at night.

Just in case it was a family member that she'd dragged along, he decided not to ignore the guy. That would be bad form, to be ignorant to her peeps. No. So he made his way back to their side of the room, especially since the brother had stolen the beautiful smile from her face.

"Yo, man, forgive me. It's chaotic in here," Jacques said, extending his hand. "You Karin's family?"

"In a matter of speaking," Lloyd said in a tight voice.

Jacques smiled. *So this is the boyfriend.* He watched

Karin's body language become tense. "Cool, mon," he said. "She's awesome. Glad I found her firm."

Lloyd nodded and glared at Karin to make the proper introduction.

"This is Lloyd Jacobs," she said, not delineating who he was or what he meant to her. She knew it was childish, but it served him right. She'd also neglected to put his title in front of his name as an added dig, just to teach him a lesson. In her mind it was fitting, since Lloyd always made it a point to let people know he was an M.D., and she knew it grated him to be around those he thought were less sophisticated but so much wealthier than he'd probably ever be. So she let it ride.

Jacques nodded at the brother, who looked like he was about to choke on his own spit. Miss Karin had a bit of the devil in her. It was the way she'd allowed the man's name to fall out of her mouth with just a hint of boredom in her tone. He'd picked that up right away. He could hear what hadn't been said, and it was in her eyes—that slight cut that she gave Lloyd. This woman was beyond fine, she was fascinating.

"Well, listen, we're probably gonna go back to the suite, kick it a little bit, before everybody crashes out. You all are welcome to come, too." Jacques nodded toward the media. "My bread and butter, gotta give them a good house party before we leave town, or they won't play a brother's CD, feel me?" He looked at Karin, hoping she understood the politics that went with the ordeal, and that she might come back to make it bearable. Truth was, he was dead on his feet, but still had the obligatory afterparty to host.

"I have rounds at the hospital in the morning," Lloyd said before Karin could answer. "There are sick people that require healing, and I have to be sharp when I work on them. But thank you for the offer."

"That's cool, mon. You're a doctor?" Jacques asked, only half impressed. But he had to admit that it gnawed at him a little. Of course a woman like Karin would have chosen a scholar.

"Yes," Lloyd said lifting his chin a tad. "So, we'll have to decline the invitation this time."

Karin looked at her date for a moment. The arrogance. "Uhm, listen, Lloyd, I know you have to get up in the morning, so, since Mr. Dubois is a new client of the firm and I'd like to get to know the other folks he works with better, maybe you should go on to your apartment and get some rest. I can take a cab—"

"Oh, I wouldn't hear of it," Jacques said, cutting her off. "Rockko, my driver, can take you home when you're ready to go. That cool?"

Okay, it was a cheap shot, he had to admit it, but he hated the haughty way the guy had responded to him with his nose in the air. More than that, he really wanted Karin to come along.

Jacques watched Lloyd glance from him to Karin. A brief but deadly silence stood between the threesome. The woman had made herself clear; she wasn't going to be bullied. And she'd sent the brother a clear message to get lost. Either this Lloyd Jacobs character wasn't her man, per se, and just wanted to be, or he must have *really* pissed her off royally.

Not to mention, Karin had let him know that they weren't living together by the little sidebar comment about the man going back to *his* apartment. And if the guy was just a contender, it was also obvious that she had no intention of sleeping with him tonight— something that, until this very moment, he hadn't realized was so important to him.

This was getting deeper by the moment, and it had been a long time since he'd faced a challenger to a romantic interest—and at the same time, Miss Karin hadn't really shown that she was capitulating to him, either. It was more like a don't-tell-me-what-to-do type of thing. Besides, was he crazy? Karin Michaels wasn't supposed to be anything more than his tax advisor.

"Well, since you're obviously *working*, Karin," Lloyd said in a lethal tone, "I'll call it a night. Talk to you in the morning."

"After this late night," she said, her words seething past her lips, "Let me call you. I have reports to prepare for Kincaid prior to my leaving the country. Drive safely, Lloyd."

Whoooowe! Jacques raked his fingers through his locks. Women could be so cold. This was definitely no church mouse . . . and the fact that this had begun to tug on the wrong side of his brain and stoke his libido was another indicator that he was losing his grip.

"A'ight, man," Jacques said, straightening out his patios, half preparing for the guy to take a swing. "It was nice meeting you."

"Likewise," Lloyd said, and spun and walked out.

"Now that was deep, Miss Karin," Jacques said with a sheepish smile. "Later, in private, you'll have to fill me in."

He watched the fire in her eyes dissipate and become pure mischief.

"I don't know what you're talking about," she said, and then left him to go grab some munchies and chat with his other guests.

Four A.M. and they were still going strong, but she couldn't hang. Stifled yawns became wide-open flycatchers, even if discreetly released behind her hand. Finally Rockko, who saw all, came to her side to whisper what they both knew was true.

"Miss Karin, you have to build up the stamina to hang with these guys. How about if I spell you, sis, and take you home."

"Bless you." She almost kissed the man. Fun notwithstanding, she had to get a few hours of shut-eye before the alarm clock went off at six, then would have to pour black coffee into her gullet, demand that her synapses boot up, and come up with a report that would mollify Kincaid by nine A.M. sharp. What had she been thinking?

"Just let me say my good-byes," she said, yawning.

Rockko nodded and waited for her by the door.

Jacques was sprawled out on a sofa, eating grapes, drinking more water, and still holding court with the haggard-looking media folks and too-eager-looking females who were still trying to pull an all-nighter with the band.

"Folks," she said, giving them a group wave, "I can't hang. I'm done."

"I hear you, sis," one DJ said. "We ain't far behind you."

Jacques stood and stretched, and even in her weary condition, the sight of him doing that lit a small brushfire within her. "Aw, girl, com on. You leaving already?"

She chuckled as sly glances got passed around the suite. No, she was not a groupie and wasn't bedding this man. Period. They *all* needed to be clear about that. Besides, it was quite obvious that there were plenty enough women in the suite that would accommodate any of the band's needs. Even though all the girls had been very nice to her, as they'd clearly never registered her as a potential threat, that reality somewhat annoyed her and put a distinct edge in her tone.

"J.B., a sister has to go to work in the morning and get your reports done, okaaay?" Karin said, lifting her chin and smoothing out the wrinkles in her jacket. "Not to mention, I have to give my boss some reasonable explanation as to why he's spending plane fare—"

"Plane fare?" Jacques straightened. "Whatchu mean plane fare, luv?"

Confused and exhausted, she scratched her head in reflex. "Uh, last time I checked, that was the most expedient way to get to St. Lucia."

"You riding with us, right? On the jet, tomorrow afternoon. Didn't I say I'd take you over there?"

She stared at him without blinking.

"You bought a ticket?" He was incredulous. Man, she played by the book.

"Well, yeah. . . . Betty ordered it for me right away."

"Aw, girl. Tell her to cancel it." He sighed. "You book a hotel, and whatnot, too?"

"Of course. Where else would I plan to stay?"

Rockko just shook his head and a couple of the band members leaned forward in their seats as though watching a hot new show on TV. Several of the female eyes in the room narrowed.

"At the estate, girl. That's where everybody who visits stays. Mrs. Orville will put you up in a room. All you gotta do is tell her what you like to eat and when you want it, and that's it."

"But . . . but . . ."

"No buts," he said laughing and closing his eyes, signs of fatigue from the night finally showing as he lolled his neck and rubbed the tension away from it. "If you need to go anywhere, take a car from the fleet." He opened his eyes and looked over his shoulder at the band for confirmation. "Right fellas?"

A sleepy round of "Sho' you right, boss" followed Jacques' statement.

"If Rockko ain't around to drive, or you want to go

somewhere, just go to the garage and take whatever is your pick of the day. Simple. Don' be stressing your boss about that kinda stuff, luv. Den the ole bastard might start hemming and hawing about you coming, might wanna send a senior partner and all that, and I tol' you before, I wasn't feelin' them."

All eyes landed on her. The situation was precarious at best, and by the quiet anticipation that reverberated through the room, she was also very aware that her personal reputation was at stake. So she hedged, making a diplomatic compromise.

"I would love to take a flight over with you, but must insist on keeping my hotel and transportation accommodation as is. I think that would be best for the sake of propriety, and Kincaid can spare the cost of my expenses as an employee doing work on your behalf. But thank you for the generous offer."

There. It had been said. And she'd gone corporate lingo on him to let him know she wasn't playing. It was imperative that the guys, and especially any media around to dish the dirt later, knew she wasn't attached to him, trying to get attached to him, or gold digging in any way shape or form. Most importantly, Jacques Dubois needed to know that. The other women in the room got the message instantly and relaxed.

He smiled and gave her a jaunty nod. "Much respect, Miss Karin. Spoken like a true professional."

"Thank you for understanding," she said, and again turned to the group to make her farewells. "It was nice meeting you all, and the concert was off the hook—the most fun I've had in ages. You ladies and gentlemen get some rest." She offered Jacques a shy smile, "I had a blast, and appreciated the VIP treatment. Thanks. We don't get that much in my profession. See ya tomorrow afternoon."

She walked quickly to the door. She had to get out of there just so she could finally take a deep breath. Having Jacques walk her through the suite twice in the same twenty-four hours, especially after the rousing performance he'd given with her name embedded in it, made her definitely need fresh air. But as all good things must come to an end, if she was Cinderella tonight, it was time to go before everything about this surreal experience went *poof* and vanished.

"The plane leaves at four. I'll hit your cell phone with gate and runway info," he said with a sly smile, leaning on the open door. "But, uh, a brother needs those digits—unless you want me to call the office?"

There was something in his eyes. . . . Maybe it was the fatigue from the show, or the after-party glow, or perhaps the adrenaline was still raging through his nonstop system, but his voice had taken a decided dip toward the sensual, as though the man was hitting on her. She let a smile stand as her response for a moment, not sure if she was reading him right.

"I'll give it to Rockko on the way home."

A half smile came out of hiding on Rockko's stone-chiseled face.

Jacques nodded. "All right, luv. I can live wit dat."

She climbed into the huge black Lincoln Navigator and watched Rockko drive. Yes! She had been to the ball!

As tired as she was, a million thoughts swarmed her mind. True, she had to get Kincaid's report done, but that would have to happen from home—the boss would just have to understand. If he didn't, so what. It wasn't like he could fire her, not now. She had the power!

A private freakin' jet was leaving Philadelphia International with Def Island Sounds aboard, *and her!* Kincaid could say what he wanted, but she was on that particular flight, and to be ready, she would just tell the man flat out that she'd update the report via laptop in the air and transmit when she hit the ground . . . because after all, a sister had to get her hair did, feet did, nails did, pack, and be sharp as a tack for this!

When the vehicle stopped in front of her apartment, she almost forgot that she was supposed to wait for Rockko to get out and open the door.

"Miss Karin," he said in his slow, steady drawl. "Want me to be sure that joker you came with doesn't have a problem with you rollin' with us for a few hours?"

Karin leaned forward in her seat, so taken aback that she didn't immediately know what to say. Lloyd Jacobs a problem that required security? She laughed. "No. He's a doctor, and the last thing he'd do is bust his knuckles over me."

"He's a man, baby, and the brother didn't look too happy that you was hangin' with us," Rockko said calmly. "You're a VIP, and in the family, now—J.B. said. So, uh, lemme do what the man pays me to do. Cool?"

"All right," she said slowly and sat back, trying to wrap her brain around this new lifestyle and reality.

She watched Rockko get out of the vehicle, case her building, and then come around the car to collect her.

"I'll walk you up," he stated flatly.

"That won't be necessary. It's just—"

"What I'm paid to do, sis."

How did one argue with a mountain? Karin sighed. "Okay, but if you want to come up to my messy little piece of the world and case the joint, I'll stand down. Thanks, Rockko. I appreciate it."

"It's my job, sis, and an honor to be sure a nice sister like you is okay."

Again, words failed her. She'd never received the royal treatment in her life, much less all this fanfare for coming home alone from a concert. As Rockko did his thing and went up the steps before her, then walked through her small place as though a SWAT unit might bust out of a closet at any moment, she suddenly realized how much she'd taken for granted.

It was disorienting as she watched him sweep her apartment, and all she could think of was the number of nights she'd entered a dark place all alone, or the nights that Lloyd was in too much of a hurry to walk her up, dropping her off at the curb. It *was* dangerous to be living alone in the city, particularly being female. But there'd never been any other way around that reality, and she'd adapted to it just like she'd gotten used to everything else. Somehow, in one day and one night, Jacques Dubois was making her reevaluate her entire life.

Rockko met her at the door and gave her the all-clear sign.

"Thanks so much for everything," she told him, truly meaning it.

He smiled, and if she were not mistaken, he almost seemed a bit embarrassed by the open appreciation.

"Uh, Miss Karin . . . I can't go back to the suite without those digits."

They both looked at each other and finally chuckled. She produced a pen and paper from her purse, scribbled down her cell-phone number, and gave it to him without a word. Now she knew for sure. Something else was going on with Jacques Dubois. She just had to wait until Rockko drove off before she could cover her mouth, lean on the closed door, and scream.

* * *

The moment she'd left his suite, he felt the exhaustion. Oddly, as long as she was in the room, he had all the energy in the world. But when she'd called it a night, he was ready for everyone else to go, too. The way she'd gone from choir girl to party animal to professional verbal sniper to a fun, easy, around-the-way girl to a corporate businesswoman when he'd made the suggestion that she stay with him, and then shyly lowered her gorgeous eyes and left, had messed him up completely. And the outfit she had on . . . showed every curve . . . and the way she'd danced and been into his rhythm . . . and dayum, she smelled so good . . . hair all on top of her head. If there was ever a woman he wanted to get with, it was her.

He'd had enough groupies to fill a club. He'd had enough women with designs on him, and had to be extra careful not to get caught up in the drama. Either God looked out for children and fools and he'd been both, and thus had been covered, or all his momma's prayers that he wouldn't bring no babies home for her to raise had been answered. But Karin Michaels was a first of many things for him . . . the first woman to tell him no, to decline a serious offer to be spoiled rotten, and to do it firmly and publicly, putting him in his place. This one was beyond smart; she had integrity, and a good soul to go with what seemed like a heart of gold. What's more, she could hold her own. He loved how she'd served that brother who was sweating her the brush-off. Polite, but no-nonsense. A real lady.

She was in his head, fusing with his music, making lyrics enter his skull, was causing him to compose on the fly just looking at her. The epicenter of taking a break from all female madness and drama had suddenly begun to take its toll—that had to be it . . . because if his suite hadn't been loaded with guests, and she'd stayed just a little longer, he might have been bold enough to bust a move that would have gotten him slapped.

He smiled a private smile, not really listening to the boring conversation buzzing through the room. Suddenly he needed space and stood up.

"Okay, people, I'm done. A brother needs his rest. It was a helluva night, though," he announced, and grabbed a beer, walked into the bedroom and shut the door.

He just prayed that Rockko got that number.

Chapter 5

The cell phone on her nightstand sounded like a huge gnat buzzing in the distance as Karin swatted at it twice and then finally coordinated her fingers to clutch it. She never lifted her head from the pillow and refused to consider that someone had called her before her alarm clock had gone off. But there was only one person on the planet so audacious—her mother.

"Karin," her mother breathed out quickly. "I was so worried; you didn't answer your house phone; you have to let people know where you are—even grown, so we don't worry; have you any idea how—"

"Mom," Karin croaked. "It's gotta be before six in the morning because my alarm hasn't—"

"It's five of, and I wanted a few moments to talk to you before you started rushing around telling me you'd be late for work."

Karin groaned and rolled over to click off her alarm clock and to turn on her house-phone ringer. Why she'd been foolish enough to expect Lloyd to be blowing up her line, and had turned it off when she'd gone to bed, was beyond her. "Mom, don't start."

"Don't start?" her mother practically shrieked. "Have you lost your mind? Are you *home*—alone?"

"What?"

"Answer me, Karin; this is no time for games."

Karin allowed the cell phone to press into her cheek as she willed her mind to clear and her tongue to say only that which was respectful. Both feats were a challenge. "I'm home, alone," Karin said in a weary tone. "Why?"

"Well, good," her mother said, and then released an impatient huff of breath. "That's a start, because we were worried that you might have lost your mind."

We? Karin slowly dragged herself up to sit with her head leaned back against the wall. Last time she'd checked, she was an only child, her father had died of a heart attack hauling postal bags years ago, and her mom wasn't on intimate speaking terms with any of her aunts. So, who was *we*?

"Mom, at this hour, you're gonna have to be clear and get to the point. I—"

"Are you high on some of those funny cigarettes and drugs, baby? Did he drug you?"

"What?" Karin scratched her head but kept her eyes shut tightly.

"Aw, Lawd, I knew it!"

"Mom, get a hold of yourself. What are you talking about? Lloyd is a doctor and—"

"Precisely my point! That fine young man told me how you just completely humiliated him on a date, and refused to allow him to escort you home like a lady should. Are you insane, to be traipsing around with some hoodlum and—"

"Hold it!" Karin shouted, unable to monitor her volume as she shot out of the bed and began pacing.

"Are you telling me that Lloyd called you and *told* on me like—"

"Now, Karin, it wasn't like that. The young man was—"

"Outta his danged mind!" Karin shouted. "Ohmigod! I'm done, Mom! I am through, *fini*, it's over, this is too—"

"Now, baby, don't be hasty. And you need to check your tone with me. That young man is a great catch—"

"Translation: I'm not?"

Silence made the static crackle on the line between them. Pure fury made Karin's ears ring.

"Did he tell you, since he was so big into tattling to my mother, that this so-called hoodlum was the biggest client I've ever worked with, the firm asked me to roll out the red-carpet treatment for him, and I'm even getting a business trip out of this?"

"Child, you're talking in run-on sentences—"

"It runs in the family," Karin hollered into the line.

"Don't be fresh," her mother snapped, but with a bit less bluster in her tone.

"You listen to me, Mom, and I'm only going to say this once. Lloyd is what *you* wanted, not what *I* want."

"Of course an intelligent, gentlemanly, cultured, well-educated professional is what any mother would want for her child. Tell me how that's a sin?"

"The man disrespected your daughter," Karin said through her teeth.

Temporary silence.

"That's right," Karin pushed on.

"Perhaps there was a misunderstanding, baby. So, there's no need to be rash . . . and, uhm, men sometimes—"

"Mom, he thinks he's better than me, smarter than me, everything more than me. You should see how he flaunts his three-generations-of-doctors family in my face. Last night was my turn to do good on my job, and he almost blew it for me—now he has the gall to get on the phone with my mother and upset her? No. I'm done. His stuck-up sisters aren't even nice to me, they're all kiss-kiss-sugary-civil, but not nice, Mom. And his mother looks at me like I'm something the cat dragged in. So don't take his side without hearing mine, ever."

Hot moisture had formed in her eyes, and the thick emulsion of unspent tears slid down Karin's throat and closed it. Her mother was just like the very people she'd just lambasted—tall, light-skinned, flowing hair, highly educated, a school principal—and had married her father . . . a working Joe, an ordinary man that had loved the ground her mother walked on.

Problem was, Karin had come out looking like a Michaels—short, brown, curvy. Eloise Michaels' brains, Dad's heart and looks. Both women knew it, and it had been a thorn in her mother's side since the day she was born. Too many days spent at the hairdresser's trying to burn straight unruly kinks, and too many days in the bathroom trying to apply creams and cocoa butters to ashy, chubby brown legs, was this morning's testimony.

Her mother's temporary silence said it all; be thankful that a man of Lloyd Jacobs's stature had chosen her, despite her beauty flaws. Tears simply flowed down Karin's cheeks without restraint, and she sniffed hard, not caring that her mother heard. The heartbreak was real.

"Baby, I'm your mother," her mother whispered softly. "I'm always going to love you, no matter what. I just want to be sure you don't make a hasty decision that could limit your opportunities in life."

"Was what Dad gave you so terrible?" Karin said flatly. "Was his huge loving family that opened their arms for you so horrible a sentence? Was it so demeaning to not be a part of the social clubs that demanded he have a college degree, or such a loss that his child came out looking like him?"

"Karin . . . honey, I don't know where you're getting all that from, or how the conversation devolved into my marriage with your father while talking about Lloyd. I loved your father, and you know that."

She could almost hear the bite in her mother's tone, and knew without seeing her that she'd straightened her back and had lifted her chin. But it stabbed her soul that her mother never said a word about the part about her coming out looking like her dad.

"I have to get ready for work," Karin said, wiping her face hard. "I have to prepare a report, e-mail it to my boss, and get ready to go on a business trip—I'll be gone for a week, will call when I get back."

"I love you, Karin," her mother said quietly. "Maybe the business trip, and some time away, will give you a chance to think. It might also give Lloyd a chance to understand, too."

"Yeah. It will."

"Okay," her mother said with a sigh. "I wasn't trying to upset you, though."

"Yeah. I gotta go."

"I love you," her mother whispered, and hung up before Karin could answer.

Karin flung the phone across the comforter, sat down on the edge of the bed, and wept.

By eight A.M., she was able to push SEND on the interim report due to her boss and felt steady enough to call Kincaid at home. In truth, she hoped that he was puking his guts out, and several additional ugly thoughts swirled in her mind as she waited for him to pick up. His voice mail was her salvation, and she quickly rattled off the facts. She was going to St. Lucia, his first report was sent and in his Outlook inbox, and she'd be in the office once she'd packed—given that she'd followed firm edicts to schmooze the client at the concert last night.

She'd only made it halfway across the room when her phone rang, and she cringed. *What now?*

Betty's tentative voice filled the receiver.

"Uh, Karin. This is Betty."

"Hi, Betty," Karin said, and sat down heavily on the bed again. What a morning.

"We have a little problem."

Karin closed her eyes.

"Mr. Kincaid wants Jonathan Broderick to go on the trip, and is only willing to pay for one flight and one set of accommodations, so . . ." Betty let her voice out hard. "Girl, I tried."

"No problem," Karin said. "You did what you could."

Something so rash and so defiant flamed within her that for the second time in the same morning, Karin was off the bed as though something had burned her.

"Betty, do me a favor."

"You know I will, honey."

"Tell Kincaid that the client is flying me out this afternoon in his private jet and that I will be paying my own accommodations down in St. Lucia. Tell him I said that we are too close to contracting this very skittish client to do otherwise, since Mr. Dubois is not above taking a walk if we start changing players on him again suddenly and do not honor his in-flight meeting request, as we'll be going over details that I'll share with Broderick upon his arrival. Go ahead and give Broderick my tickets and room for tomorrow—the ones you'd made before I found out the band's flight was leaving today, and if you can just find me a cheap hotel, lady, I'd appreciate it."

Betty released a low chuckle. "Oh, without question, Ms. Michaels—and since Jonathan Broderick is booked for the day with corporate accounts, I'll be sure to let him know after your flight leaves."

Karin could feel all the tension seep out of her body as a slight smile crept across her face. "Thank you, Betty."

"Since you need to pack, and my personal suggestion would be to get your hair done and take care of a few feminine necessities while you're at it, I believe you have a morning meeting with Mr. Dubois's management or something, don't you?"

"Oh, yeah. Now that you mention it, I do," Karin said, sharing a conspiratorial chuckle with Betty.

"My girlfriend's daughter runs a salon down on Twenty-second, right off Walnut. I think she might be able to see you first thing, if I make the call. You tell Sharon that Aunt Momma said this is an emergency."

Karin closed her eyes and new tears squeezed out from beneath her lids. "Miss Betty . . ."

"Baby, I can hear the tremor in your voice. Now you go ahead, and you take that trip those old bastards are trying to rob you . . . and you go down there as sharp as a brass tack, you hear me? Spare no expense, and I'm not about to put you in a cheap, fleabag hotel. That's dangerous for a young lady. I'll get you into the Royal St. Lucian, *like them*. Okaaaay? All I gotta do is tell 'em the truth—it's tourist season, the other hotels were booked, this was an emergency, and for the sake of safety I couldn't put you out in no-woman's-land."

Karin nodded and sniffed. Her voice refused to push past her lips.

"We've got an office pool on you, doll."

Karin laughed, the only way her voice could be found. The cleansing breath that came with it allowed her to question Betty in earnest. "A pool?"

"Yes, honeychile. We're all banking on that recording company seeing who you are, and how good you are, and hiring you away from this insane place. So you have to go. My five dollars is at risk."

They both laughed, sharing a new bond, and knowing that it was about so much more than five bucks.

She was on a mission. Sharon had agreed to beat her hair lovely, and Karin wasted no time throwing on some jeans and a T-shirt and high-tailing it over to X-Pressions Beauty Spa on Twenty-second. She parked her car in the open lot and dashed across the street to the Sunoco gas station's mini-mart to grab a lemon-water so she could endure the process of getting her hair did all morning, and then made a beeline in a zigzag to avoid traffic back to the small salon.

Nearly breathless, she practically fell through the door of the clean, neat little shop that was painted a warm blend of bright yellows and orange hues. Three unoccupied hairdressers looked up, glanced at the clock, and then set their gazes back on Karin.

"Hi, I'm sorry I'm late—I'm here for an eight-thirty."

"Oh, chile—you *must* be Karin, because my Aunt Momma said your head was a mess, and she ain't lie."

"Now, Sharon, don't start," one round-faced, pretty stylist said, flopping into an abandoned chair. "I'm Erica. Don't let Sharon get on you too bad."

"I'm Michelle," the other said, her wide, inviting

smile adding to the cheery interior. "I'll be washing you, but Sharon is no-nonsense in the mornings."

Three women laughed, positively overwhelming Karin with their around-the-way brand of hospitality. She loved every minute of it as the shop owner came to her, shook her head and led her to a chair.

"Miss Betty told me you have this big-time client and have to be super sharp." Sharon put both hands on her narrow hips, leaning her petite frame back to look at Karin hard. "Now, are you gonna let me work and get some lift and bounce and life back into that rat's nest, put some color in there, and cut it right-eous, or are you gonna argue with me?"

"Sharon knows her stuff," Erica said, nodding. "You need to let her do you."

"Yup," Michelle added, "especially if you're rolling with high rollers, girlfriend."

Karin laughed. "I guess Miss Betty—"

"Told all," Sharon said, as the other two stylists flung a gown on Karin and began to talk at once as they shoved her into a chair.

"I say half off, honey-brown highlights, little wisps, a New York cut," Sharon muttered, cocking her head to the side as she felt the texture of Karin's hair.

"Yep," Michelle concurred. "Something that will go with her natural thickness of weight, the waves she's got, so if it's humid—"

"Yeah, so it looks good wet or dry, can go finger-combed just off the beach—loose the ponytail and whateva," Erica said.

"Uhmm-hmm," Sharon said, studying Karin's hair as though a doctor. "Call Linda in and see if she'll give her a French pedicure—nice sheer pink, like a sher-bet color, since she's doing the island thing; gotta get her nails done, too. Get her to wax those caterpillars off her eyebrows and do her legs smooth, while you're at it."

"You think Aya will open her shop this early?" Michelle asked brightly. "The chile needs some sarongs and what have you, can't be going down there raggedy, and Betty said she needed an entire overhaul."

"Call Aya," Sharon said, loosening the scrunchie from Karin's hair.

It was all happening so fast, so gloriously fast. Her business was in the streets and no one had consulted her as they descended upon her like mad fairies preparing Cinderella for the ball. Karin finally gave up, leaned back, let go, and let God.

Three hours later, Sharon spun her around and handed her a mirror. Karin accepted it with a freshly manicured hand, trying not to marvel at how her fingers looked with the sheer baby-pink polish and white French tips that matched her toes. The look was understated but elegant, and she gasped when she finally saw her hair. It was no longer near dark ebony like her skin. It was a warmer shade of brown, a bit lighter than her skin tone, with subtle honey-brown highlights that caught the overhead illumination and glistened. The finished product was like something out of a magazine—short, chic, silky, bouncing—no, her hair actually swung as she moved her head, and it had never done that.

"Oh . . . my . . . goodness," Karin breathed out.

"Rock his world," Sharon said, hands on hips, obviously pleased.

"What?" Karin giggled. "No, no, it's just a client meeting, er, a trip to a meeting and—"

"So?" Sharon scoffed. "A sister always has to be on

top of her game, and you never know who you might meet down there in the islands, girlfriend, so my suggestion is that you don't allow yourself to go back to the old way."

"Yeah, chile. Don't let all our hard work revert on you like a bad relaxer job and get all raggedy," Erica said, laughing.

"Maintenance is the key, baby," Michelle fussed.

"Now all you need to do is go see Aya out in West Philly—she's on Forty-fourth, hold your head up high, and let her hook you up with a few pieces so you have some nice business-island gear, and you'll be good to go," Sharon added with a wink.

She was going for broke, literally and figuratively, but didn't care. After the hair, manicure, pedicure, and wax jobs, she'd planned to go home and pack. But even if she was probably spending the rent, for some reason she felt like these sisters had her back and were dropping pearls of wisdom that she dared not discard. By the time she pulled up to the tiny little Ethiopian shop tucked away in West Philly, she was sure that she'd lost her mind.

A tall, exotic-looking African woman wearing an Afrocentric white gauze sheath approached her with a brilliant smile that showed off a pretty gap in her flawless white teeth. Her skin was of the smoothest dark walnut that Karin had ever seen, and for a moment she could only stare. Iman immediately came to mind, and with that near complete trust in the woman's fashion taste. The only problem was, she knew she wasn't a tall, exotic, willowy beauty. Karin sighed as her gaze raked the establishment that was well-stocked with expensive, one-of-a-kind pieces.

"Hi," Karin said quietly. "Sharon sent me, but you probably don't have my size in here—and I really have to get a move on to make it to the airport in about an hour."

The woman placed one delicate finger to her lips, studied Karin's frame for a moment, and moved toward her.

"Sister, I am Aya. Our forms are all beautiful and come in many shapes, sizes, and complexions, true?"

"I guess," Karin shrugged.

"If you trust Aya, I will find you things that will compliment what God has given you. Each woman is a masterpiece—art—to be draped in fabrics to show off that handiwork."

Karin liked her immediately, but still doubted that she could pull off the impossible within an hour.

"Sharon told me your hues and what you were traveling to accomplish. I've taken the liberty of pulling a few selected items from the shelves that you may want to consider."

"Okay," Karin said still unconvinced as she was led to the back of the small boutique. But her eyes nearly bugged out of her head as a full dressing room of clothing was presented in the back. "Girl, I'm on a real budget," she added in protest. "I can't—"

"We'll talk prices after you see the selections," Aya murmured with a soft smile, her voice like honey. "Let us begin at the top and work our way down."

The boutique owner pulled a soft, constructed, ivory-crêpe suit from the back of the door and laid it across a small Queen Anne chair.

"This is your foundation piece. Crêpe doesn't wrinkle while traveling, like linen—so we save the linen for after you arrive at your destination. The one-button jacket is cut to show off your best asset, your small waist, while it flares over your hips and is long enough to be professional and cover your posterior. The line gives the illusion of added height, and with a small mule heel in natural, you have comfort, but also a businesslike look."

She then unfurled a long mohair shawl of the same hue. "This is what you wear to the airport, and you take it off and you are in the right weight fabric for where you're going. It is dramatic, different, and you won't have to lug a coat along with you. Go with drapes and play with color on the accessories. With this, I suggest a nice ivory sleeveless shell to go under the suit."

Stunned silent, Karin ran her hand over the fabrics and nodded, beginning to understand and better appreciate Aya's craft.

"Now, we go orange, sherbet, yellow, lime for you. Your complexion can stand the bright contrasts— demands it, in fact. So I have a sarong wrap that can be tied at the neck to go under the jacket by day, or can drop down to a skirt to cover up a bathing suit—and I have several tankinis that I think will look fabulous on you, and will pick up the color swirls in the sarong fabric. That's three outfits," Aya exclaimed, clearly pleased.

"Add smashing earrings, take off the jacket, and you are in evening wear—even in the same shoes." She whipped out another sarong and displayed it with pride. "Tying it under your arms makes it strapless— but add the jacket, and it is a business sundress. You need white and black linen suits, so you can mix and match the bright colored tankini tops under each, with the matching skirts, or do a dress under each, and you, my dear sister, are good to go."

Karin calmly turned over the price tags, trying to seem casual. "This is rent," she squeaked.

"It is a business investment," Aya stated flatly with a

smile. "Two bathing suits, three sarongs, three suits, a pair of natural mules, low-heeled black straps, and white sandals . . . a Coach briefcase to match the mules, add a stunning collar necklace—say, one a confusion of pearls and crystals and ivory, another with stones the colors in your sarongs—and earrings, one ivory bangle—less is more—and voila. Oh, and don't forget a toe ring. A must."

"Okay, voila," Karin said, going into the dressing room unnerved. "Can I move in here when my landlord evicts me, though?"

Aya laughed hard, sending her melodic voice throughout the store. "Darling, some things are just a necessity."

Yeah, okay. Karin checked her purse, unnerved. The plastic she had on her might not stand the strain, not to mention, it was a debit card any ole way. But as she tried on each piece, and Aya made her come out and model the item and assisted her with how to make it work, the thoughts of her neat and tidy life began to evaporate. For the first time that she could recall, she felt pretty. And as Aya stood behind her, clucking her tongue in satisfaction, changing accessories until they both agreed, all resistance was futile.

"Sister . . . you are gorgeous," Aya finally said, staring into the mirror at Karin's reflection. Her tone held no hint of saleswoman fraud, but a genuine appreciation that Karin had never heard.

Karin peered at her, questioning. "You think so . . . I mean, you think I'll be okay in all this?"

Aya nodded. "Yes. I do. Kohl eyes, pressed powder, that's it. Honey blush. Sheer sherbets and coral on the lips—only. I have the natural makeup here. A few items are all your pretty skin needs; plus, so close to the equator, you'll sweat off anything else, and that is never pretty."

Karin just nodded and pulled out her credit card.

Her heart was still beating hard as she made her way through the airport security checkpoints. She'd gotten home, rounding the corner like a banshee, dragged out her suitcase on wheels, and practically dumped her load from the boutique into it.

Karin mentally chanted her packing list to be sure she'd brought everything. Laptop, cell phone, briefcase as carry-on, new matching shoulder bag, passport, toothpaste, and deodorant . . . Everything down to the drawers in her bag was new. Face beat by Aya, hair done, nails done, and a quick cool-water bath with head gently tied up to avoid any possible damage to Sharon's masterpiece. Toiletries and new makeup. Cocoa butter to chase away after-sea ash.

As she edged along through the security line and dumped her purse and shoes into the plastic X ray bins, she had to remember not to brush up against things that could soil the whole ivory-on-ivory ensemble. But her mind was a million miles away, and she followed the instructions given by the security personnel in a fog. Jacques had called, as promised, and had left a brief message about where to meet and how to get her e-ticket boarding passes while she was under the dryer!

She felt faint; the urge to call Lloyd and cuss him out had passed. He was a distant memory. The elegant shawl was a hazard while lugging suitcases and briefcases and half disrobing for security, but she managed to get to the other side of the X ray machines to find a ladies' room when she could reconstruct the drape as

Aya had shown her. Now the issue was tipping cutely to the right gate, and jogging shoes would have been her first choice. Much more practical. But since dawn, or at least after the unsettling call from her mother, every female she encountered had made this feel like an impractical, but exciting, adventure.

Karin froze when her cell phone sounded, and she was glad she was in the ladies' room when it did. If this was her boss telling her not to go, she could at least quit and keep going on this mission in semi-private— not all out in public. If it was her mom, she could say she had bad reception in the airport. If it was Lloyd, it was on.

Rustling through her purse, she found the offending electronic device and stared at the caller ID. Lloyd. She immediately clicked the button to take his call and faced the wall.

"What is it?" she said, not beginning the conversation with hello.

"I expected an apology and most certainly a call after—"

"You called my mother!" she said in a whispered hiss through her teeth.

"I was concerned."

"You had no right."

"I did have a right, Karin, given our relationship. The way you behaved—"

"You're right," she said, cutting him off.

"I'm glad to finally hear some contrition in your voice, and that—"

"You're right," she said coolly, not trusting her voice to hold the line of ice he deserved. She would not scream and act out in a public restroom while on the way to the biggest client meeting of her life. No. She glanced in the mirror and liked what she saw. "Given our relationship, I should have just told you it was over. Right then and there. I'm done."

"Karin, what are you saying!"

"You called my mother, you arrogant SOB, and I'm done. Have a nice life." She clicked off the phone and then turned it off and dropped it into her purse. She was about to use her fingers to blot away the slight sheen of perspiration that the conversation had risen in the oily T-zone areas of her face, but instead extracted the new pressed powder Aya had sold her. No. From this point forward, new attitude.

Steadying her nerves, she exited the ladies' room and picked her way to the right gate, trying to chase away the thoughts of bankruptcy that loomed in her head. Was she crazy? She'd spent more than rent on this whole escapade, and for what? To floss? Not to mention, if things didn't go down correctly, Kincaid might fire her, and then she'd be fly, but unemployed, with credit-card debt and no apartment, possibly no car—if she didn't make the note this month behind such foolishness . . . And she was an accountant? Crazy! But today, she wasn't going to allow an argument with Lloyd and a call from her misguided mother to steal her joy and to make her turn back to her old insecurities.

In her new apparel and with her new look, she felt like an entirely different person. No one could take that from her; she'd worked so hard for a moment like this to occur in her life . . . if just for once.

She began to walk a little taller, feeling a little lighter for having dropped some of the emotional baggage attached to her old boyfriend and her mom. Somehow the new items jammed into her suitcase seemed to temporarily replace all of that, gamble though it all was. But she'd rather be dragging the new feelings behind her on wheels than lugging what had been on her heart. She briefly thought of Brenda's belief in hopelessness and almost cringed. No. Today was a brand-new beginning. People were counting on her to prevail; she was counting on herself to do that, too.

The moment she opened the door to the VIP club and saw the weary band sprawled out on thick, blue chairs, she knew within her soul that this was indeed a one-time gamble she had to take. It was in their eyes, the way they glanced up and then peered over their sunglasses at her. Rockko removed his from his face, and Jacques stood up, hesitated, and allowed a slow smile of appreciation to cross his face as she waved hi.

"For a moment, wasn't sure if you were gonna make the flight," Jacques said with a grin, coming towards her. "Thought you might not trust my pilot and might decide to go commercial airliner on me?"

Karin smiled. "No, I had to get a report in," she said shyly. "Hi guys."

"Hey, Miss K," several band members said in unison, exchanging unreadable glances.

Rockko moved to help her with her bags and then hung back for a moment, unsure. It was a male thing, and they both understood. J.B. nodded to him.

"I got it, man," he said, causing more glances between his band members.

"Thanks," she said quietly. "I looked like a total klutz coming through security checkpoints with all of this."

"I doubt that," he murmured, truly meaning it. The transformation was mind-blowing.

He took her bags from her and set them aside for the crew to load on the jet, glad for the temporary distraction. Her hair was so alive; the shine from it against the winter white made him want to reach out and touch it, but he didn't, and instead just watched it naturally move with her as she chatted.

Her skin looked like dark porcelain, flawless . . . glowing, like it had an inner light of its own that set off her huge, brown eyes. Ivory, crystals, and pearls created a collar that kept her head held high like a queen—yes, definitely a queen. Maybe an angel in all white; at the moment, he wasn't sure. And the delicate scent she trailed as he bent in to take her bags, give her a brief hug, and then break away almost buckled his knees.

Karin Michaels was so much more than he'd realized. She was special. Today, it was settled—at least in his mind. She had to stay at his place, just like she had to be in his life. But he also knew that the offer had to be extended carefully, with all the home training his mother had ever bestowed. This was a true lady in his midst.

Chapter 6

Throughout the light banter, Karin kept her gaze intermittently fastened on the slurry of ominous gray clouds outside the windows and Jacques' brilliant smile. No matter how engaging the man was, the fact remained that she'd only flown in an airplane a couple of times in her life. Once was to Disney World when she was twelve. The second time was to Texas to a family funeral. Beyond that, her travel had been by car on long family junkets, by train along the Northeast Corridor, and by Greyhound bus. The jet that had been pointed out to her seemed waaaay too small, by comparison, to the jumbo-sized aircraft that were pulled up to various gates.

She kept telling herself that she could do this and not to act crazy. She had to. She wouldn't allow possible turbulence to incite a mental riot within her. Nope. She wasn't gonna think back on all the news accounts of stars and executives that had gone down in private jets. Uh-uh . . .

"Karin," a quiet male voice said. "Your eyes are closed. You tired, luv?"

"Just praying for a second," she admitted, and then

glanced at the window. "My policy when about to do something out of the norm."

Unsure of what she was referring to, Jacques cocked his head to the side. "Spontaneous prayer. Okay. I can go with that," he said, swallowing a smile as he watched her ball her hands in her lap and her lips begin to silently move.

He wondered what it was that had spooked her? Going off with him couldn't have been so bad that it had a sister about to kick the prayer benches over, could it? He watched her, mesmerized, his line of vision glued to her pretty mouth. Maybe her momma had told her she was off on an adventure with the devil, the way she was suddenly acting. He almost chuckled. Maybe she was. But if she would relax, she'd have a damned good time.

However, he knew that it was bad form to interrupt a prayer, so he just allowed the companionable silence to fall between them and waited her out. When she finally opened her eyes, he simply smiled.

"Feel better?" he asked, wanting to hear more of the sweet melody in her voice.

She nodded, but still had a look of semi-panic in her expression. When the pilot announced that the cargo had all been loaded and it was time to board, she shot up from the small sofa so quickly that he was sure he'd have to scrape her off the ceiling.

Her nervousness was doing crazy things to his mind. For some strange reason it was titillating to watch her so shook up just for him. On the one hand she was all business and dressed, accordingly, to the nines. Every hair was in place, and she was so professionally elegant in a casual sort of way that, her humorous behavior added an extra layer, another dimension that was simply disorienting.

A disgruntled, sleepy band filed through the door and down the small accordion connection hall to the jet. Jacques went behind Karin, always loving that position that allowed him to watch her curves work beneath whatever fabric she wore. As he spied her, he wondered why any man would want a woman to walk behind him. The view was so much better this way. But he let the errant thought go as they entered the plane.

She didn't know what to make of what she saw, and for a moment, she hesitated as the flight attendant and pilot greeted her with a big smile. Plush ivory leather upholstery and dark walnut wood was everywhere. Each huge seat looked like it belonged in first class, and there were little curtains around each grouping of two seats so that one could draw them closed and sleep while others carried on and made noise.

It made so much sense, given that the band probably traveled this way all the time or needed mental space to work on their music. Still, it was awesome for someone like her, who had only experienced the crowded coach sections on any conveyance. She tried not to gape.

Pausing in the aisle, she waited for the others to sit, and the band and other members of the Def Island group casually dispersed, dropped personal carry-on bags into overhead bins, and lounged wherever their bodies dropped from exhaustion.

She glanced over her shoulder at Jacques for a cue as to where to sit.

"Anywhere you want, luv," he said, as though reading her mind. "Window or aisle, or you can take up two seats by yourself to stretch out once we take off so

you can get some shut-eye. It's a long flight. Like five
to six hours."

She nodded and removed her wrap, and then carefully folded it over her arm, deciding. Aya had been so
right; the mohair shawl was versatile and could double
as a blanket. It was chilly on the plane, and she knew
she'd need it to cover her later. Karin nervously eyed
a window seat, drew a deep breath, and slid into it.

"Ma'am, do you want your purse and briefcase put
up into an overhead?" a flight attendant asked, "or do
you want to stow them under the seat in front of you?
They have to be tucked away during takeoff."

Karin tore her gaze away from the window and
looked at the stewardess, and then at Jacques, who was
still standing and waiting for her response.

"Oh, uh, no. I'll keep them under the seat. My laptop
is in there, and I might need it," Karin said quickly, shoving the items away.

Jacques slid into the seat next to her. "Then buckle
up, luv. Once they go through the safety routine, we
can talk. Cool?"

She just nodded and kept her gaze on the flight attendant in the aisle, listening intently to the directions
about where every exit and floatation device was lo-
cated. But the captain's mellow voice did not inspire
confidence as he rattled on about possible turbulence, thunderstorms over North Carolina, and a po-
tentially bumpy ride for a bit as they entered Miami
airspace. Her mental prayer became an incessant plea
to Jesus for safe delivery.

Engines engaged; the plane started moving. The
black asphalt beneath them began to look like a fast-
running conveyor belt. She heard something click
and the sound of what was like heavy metal objects
tumbling within a giant lock. Karin squeezed her eyes

shut tightly. Her hands gripped the armrests, as though holding on with fierce determination could keep her on the ground.

"If you don't look out the window," Jacques said, the smile implicit in his tone, "you'll miss the view. Takeoff and landing is a really cool thing you might not wanna miss from a window seat."

She nodded fervently, but didn't open her eyes or speak.

"You're afraid of flying?" he asked, sounding shocked.

Again, she only nodded, unable to fake it. Her body was pressed back into the seat from centrifugal force. Birds were supposed to be airborne, not people encased in tons of steel. Lawd have mercy.

"When the stewardess says it's clear to serve, how about a glass of wine?"

"Okay," Karin squeaked.

Jacques chuckled. "Or maybe a shot of bourbon?"

"No," Karin breathed out. "Wine is fine. I'll be all right. It's just this part that messes me up."

A warm hand covered hers and almost made her open her eyes. Almost. She tried to concentrate on the interesting texture of it. Strong, slightly calloused in spots, places where his instruments had claimed his palm and fingertips. Large enough to totally enfold hers, and for those few tense minutes, she was glad that it did. Glad that she'd given over to the exquisite feeling of comfort it provided, which was so much better than the armrest.

"You've got a good grip," he said, teasing her, once the plane leveled off.

She opened her eyes, stared at him for a moment, and then glanced down with an embarrassed smile. "Sorry I squeezed the blood out of your hand."

He chuckled softly. "Insured by Lloyd's of London, luv. That's my right—my guitar hand."

She snatched her palm away. "Oh, I'm so sorry!"

He laughed gently and retrieved her hand to enfold it in his again. "There are much worse ways to lose your playing hand. You hang onto me during the flight," he added, his smile fading to offer her a serious expression. "The plane is small, and I don't mind."

She held his hand tightly, but not in a death grip this time. "I don't fly much," she admitted.

"I remember my first time," he said in a quiet, private voice. "I was scared to death, but it wound up being a rush."

There was something about the way he'd turned the phrase, the look just beneath the surface of his eyes that made her face warm.

"I've flown a couple of times before, but it was never like this."

He stared at her for a moment, trying to read the expression that hid just behind her big brown eyes, trying not to read too much into her statement, or misinterpret what she'd said. But the comment had shot sudden warmth through him.

"I know what you mean," was all he could say. He glanced up as the seat belt signs went dark. "You can unbuckle now," he nearly whispered. Somehow he'd expected oxygen masks to drop—all the air felt like it had left the cabin.

He undid his seat belt with one hand, never taking his eyes off her. Unwilling to release her hand, he simply reached over and flipped open her buckle, then watched the belt slide to both sides of her lap.

Her breath hitched. His proximity, the sensual way he'd made the belt fall away was like he'd undressed her right on the plane. Others around her had their heads back, some with mouths open, sleeping behind sunglasses. A rush of wicked thoughts made her body tighten in places that were too inappropriate, but she was glad he was still holding her hand.

"How about that wine?" he murmured, still staring at her intently. "It's after four in the afternoon, and I won't tell the boss."

She had to force herself to smile. The ache he was producing within her was so out of order she didn't know what to do. "Thanks," was all she could manage.

Karin watched him hail the flight attendant, but then he placed that left hand over hers to gently stroke her knuckles.

"We have an infrequent flyer," he said with a casual tone. "I think she needs a nice chardonnay. Or some champagne?"

The flight attendant nodded. "No problem, sir." She turned to Karin. "Maybe a little bubbly?"

"Champagne?" Karin said, glancing at them both. "But . . ."

"It's a maiden flight. She's used to the big, clumsy planes. First time on a lean, mean jet. Hook a sister up wit some bubbly. Top shelf."

The flight attendant nodded with a wide smile and left them. Karin stared at Jacques, suddenly realizing she hadn't eaten at all today. The sum total of what was in her stomach was coffee and lemon water.

"I haven't eaten," she admitted.

"Then you'll really be relaxed," he said chuckling. "But we will feed you on the flight. You wanna eat now?"

"No," she said carefully, peering out of the window briefly, then sitting back and shutting her eyes tightly. "Not sure I'm ready to do that."

"The bubbly will make you feel better," he said, still

stroking her hand and sending shivers up her arm and down her spine. "Just sip it slow."

"Ma'am, your champagne," the attendant said, handing Karin a glass with a cut strawberry perched on the side of the flute. "Enjoy." She then handed Jacques a flute. "I'll be back to refill it, and should you need anything, just press the overhead button."

Karin accepted the glass, but watched Jacques seem to struggle with the decision to take one of his hands away from hers. He clicked his glass against hers and smiled. She took a slow sip, savoring the warmth of his palm beneath her fingers, but sorry that the top of his hand had abandoned her skin to the chill in the air. A slight dip in altitude turned what she'd planned as a slow sip into a gulp. Her eyes were closed again, and her palm was a death grip once more.

"It's going to take me a minute to get used to this," she said, not daring to open her eyes until the turbulence passed.

"I feel you," he said, his voice a hoarse whisper. "Especially when it's so unexpected and hits you right out of the blue."

She opened her eyes and stared at him. He tossed back the remainder of his champagne and pressed the overhead attendant call button. She drank hers down quickly, needing something to wet her throat. She could barely breathe sitting that close to him, his voice sounding the way it did, and his eyes quietly assessing her behind heavy lids. She had to be making things up in her own mind, just because of how she felt. It wasn't him, it was her, she firmly told herself—and she wasn't allowed to go there.

The flight attendant refilled their glasses, and this time he turned on his side in the seat and depressed the button so he could stretch out facing her.

"It's gonna be a long flight," he said, staring at her. "You might want to just try to chill and sip a little bubbly until they bring dinner. We'll have a chance to do business once everybody has gotten some real rest."

She nodded and snuggled into her seat, but didn't release his hand. He balanced the champagne flute and reached across her to press her seat button so her chair reclined like his. She took a small sip from her glass, feeling warmth creep over her entire body as she nestled in the seat looking at him, not knowing what to say. She wanted to take off her jacket, feeling a slight layer of perspiration beginning to add heat to her skin, but dared not pull out of the trance he'd created.

"Better?" he asked in a thick murmur.

"Yeah," she said quietly. "Thank you."

"You want your tray down so you can rest your glass?" he asked, his eyes searching her face.

She bit the strawberry off her glass and chewed it slowly. "Yeah . . . I think I'm beginning to relax enough to let go of it."

He nodded, took a deep swig from his flute, and lowered both trays, manipulating his fingers around the long stem of crystal while still holding his glass. She watched his hands intently, new heat spreading up her arms to her throat and cheeks as he worked at the small fixture. He hadn't let go of her hand, but simply set his glass aside on a tray, and then took hers to neatly place it beside his. Her belly was doing somersaults, and the heat had spread between her thighs to implode there. She fanned her face with her now free hand.

"The champagne packs a wallop," she said, chuckling self-consciously.

"I warned you to sip it slowly," he said, smiling.

"That was my plan, but the turbulence."

"You wanna take off your jacket?" He hesitated. "You wan' drape it over your shoulders, or put it over you, if the air conditioning gets to be too much."

"Good idea," she said, sitting up to unfasten the one crystal button at her waist. Oh, yeah, she definitely needed air and to cool down.

But she hadn't expected him to sit up, too, or to reach around her and help her off with the article of clothing. His forearms brushed hers, the fabric of his black linen suit teasing the skin at her shoulders, and the slow pull of fabric away from her arms raising gooseflesh on her arms. She settled back again, watching him neatly fold her jacket and then drape it across her legs. Without thinking, she reached for her champagne as he removed his jacket in kind and casually tossed it over his lap. She definitely needed something to wet her throat as she tried hard not to look at his muscular shoulders and chest working beneath French blue silk. The sinew that cabled his arms made her dizzy. No, no, no, no, no.

How was he gonna make it through a five-hour-plus flight lying next to this brown-skinned beauty who smelled like cocoa butter and something else divine? Her arms were pebbled with goose bumps, and the chill made the nipples of her petite breasts seem to stand at attention. His mouth went dry as he glimpsed her cleavage, and he could see her pulse beating hard in her throat. Hunger to pull them into his mouth tore at him. So close, but so far away, and so wrong to even be going there.

If he'd had his way, he would have simply untied the curtain to cloak them in private isolation, but he couldn't do that. Her breasts crested like small, chocolate half-moons beneath her silky shell, and he could glimpse a bit of lace push-up bra just at the very edges of it. *Mystery, thy name is Woman. Woman, thy name is most assuredly Karin.* Showing nothing, but a hint of delicate lingerie was making him crazy. When she'd put a strawberry into her mouth, he was done. But not half as blown away as he was right now.

Just looking at her had made him hard. Dropping her hand to help her off with her jacket had been the closest thing to painful he'd recently known. The break of skin contact wore on him, and he secretly prayed for more turbulence, just so he'd have a valid excuse to take up her soft, delicate hand again.

"If you want to block out some of the light, I can close the window and the drape so you can drift off?" he offered, wanting to kick himself after he'd said it.

She sipped her champagne quickly, and without even thinking about it he depressed the overhead button so she'd get an immediate refill.

"No," she said quietly, sending her gaze out the window. "I'm all right now. You don't have to go to all that trouble for me."

He drank down his champagne. "Cool. But it's no trouble. Whatever you want, whatever you need, you let me know, all right?"

"You have been wonderful, putting up with all my nonsense," she said, keeping her focus on the clouds. "Thank you."

"Wasn't nothin' to put up with," he said, accepting two more champagne refills and handing her a glass. He wished they'd put another strawberry on the side of it, just so he could watch her eat it away again. Instead, he settled for watching the translucent liquid wet her lush mouth and studied the small lipstick stain it left behind on the glass . . . wishing he were crystal for a moment. He then focused on the way the sun danced through her hair and over her shoulders, how it made her eyes sparkle as the sun went down in pink-orange hues. She would be gorgeous under the St. Lucian sun.

"So, did your people have a problem with you leaving them to go on this trip?" he asked, needing to know where her personal parameters lay. He'd wanted to ask about her man, but that was a too direct inquiry, so he settled for the vague—"people."

"My boss wants you to meet with one of the senior partners," she confessed, evading the ugliness that had gone down first thing that morning. "I'm afraid that Jonathan Broderick will be joining us tomorrow."

Jacques frowned and sat back, letting his breath out hard. "That's cool, as long as you're here and on top of things."

That was *not* what he'd meant to say. He needed to slow down on the champagne, but took another sip and stared at the seat back in front of him.

"Jonathan isn't so bad," she said with a slight giggle. "He's an ace, though. You want him on this, trust me."

"It's cool," Jacques said, trying to sound nonchalant. "What time's he coming?"

Karin sighed. "He took my old tickets, so he'll be touching down around five o'clock in the afternoon tomorrow."

"Good," Jacques said, perking up. "That gives me a day to give you the official tour of the island. Have you ever been to St. Lucia?"

"No, I haven't," she said with a wide smile. "I've never actually been to the Caribbean."

"Get out of here," he said, liberally sipping his champagne. "*Never?*"

"The only beach I've seen is the Jersey shore."

"Oh, gurl," he said, getting comfortable in his seat

again. "I'm gonna show you some tings dat'll blow your mind."

She didn't doubt that, but took a deep sip from her glass as she arched an eyebrow.

"First off," he said, emboldened enough to take up her hand again, "the beaches are white sand, and there is no water like what you'll see there. Rain forests make our island lush . . . luv, when I tell you the mangoes just get heavy and sweet and drop off the trees by the side of the road, it is no lie. It rains for five minutes, then the sun comes out—we call it liquid sunshine. Flowers so beautiful you'll think you were in the Garden of Eden; in fact, I am convinced that this is where it was."

She closed her eyes and squeezed his hand, the champagne edging away some of her business decorum. "It sounds like a dream."

For a moment, he didn't answer as his breathing hitched. It was the way she'd settled back; her expression had gone soft as her lids slowly lowered and she'd breathed out the words. The dull ache in his groin became an insistent thrum of unfulfilled anticipation.

"When we get there, Mrs. Orville will have probably left dinner, and the woman can cook," he added, trying to figure out a way to dissuade Karin from a hotel stay. "She makes this dish, salt fish and callaloo—it's like sautéed collard greens—and she pan-sears red snapper in butter that will make you smack yo' momma. We do this ting with mixed fresh fruit and mussels in spices, and shredded potatoes, fried plantains, grilled pineapple . . . gurl . . . I got sometin' for ya when we get home."

"You're making me so hungry right now, you need to stop."

He stared at her while her eyes were closed, loving

the expression on her face. "No, I'ma tease you for the whole flight so you'll really want it when we get there."

She opened her eyes and smiled. Did he say what she thought he said, or was she reading too much into the statement? Had to be the champagne.

"She makes this handmade ice cream," he said, setting down his champagne on the tray to get it away from him. Too close a call. But he couldn't resist stoking whatever inner fire within her that she'd allow to burn. If food was the ticket, then he'd nurse that for now.

"Oh, no . . ." Karin whispered, practically swooning. "Don't go there."

He felt his groin contract; it was the timbre of her voice that did it. "Coconut cashew—all fresh. We have the coconut trees, the cashew trees, nothing artificial, and from local, free-range cows. Lobsters as big as your foot drowning in fresh churned butter, prawns in spicy tomatoes, homemade breads, conch chowder—yeah, I'ma show you how we do the ting."

"Stop."

"No, luv. I'm on a roll now," he said chuckling, risking running a finger up her forearm, delighting that she released a little squeal. "How about fresh, creamy, mango ice cream . . . pineapple ice cream, all from the yard behind the house."

He watched her cover her heart with her hand and peer at him with what could easily be mistaken for outright lust.

"For real?"

He nodded. "You walk out my back door, and reach up and pick what you need for the kitchen."

"Whaaaat?"

"Yeah, baby," he said, becoming more relaxed as her sighs and breathy responses ate a hole in the rational part of his brain. "Like I said, I'm gonna take you there."

"I'll eat you out of house and home," she said, giggling as she sipped the rest of her champagne and set down the glass. "You've made me so hungry right now, I don't know what to do with myself."

He settled back, closed his eyes and let go of her hand, because that was prudent. "Yeah, luv, I hear you. I can barely wait either."

Nearly five hours of casual conversation with Jacques, his melodic voice pouring over every inch of her skin, had felt like almost five hours of pure foreplay. Every story he told about his family, every island fact, and every sonic boom of his laughter, felt like a sensual vibration that terminated between her legs.

When they'd hit turbulence in Miami, she was so loose she almost didn't notice the bumpy ride, but his constant holding of her hand and rubbing the back of it, the easy touch going up her forearm and back down again, nearly made her cry out. Watching his full mouth devour the meat from king crab legs was excruciating. The way his tongue and teeth worked, his mouth got moist, aw, Lawd . . .

She kept her knees firmly pressed together. She had to. She was so swollen and so wet that she feared she'd leave a visible spot for the world to see in her ivory crêpe pants.

"Okay," he finally said, leaning across her in a way that sent another wave of want right through her. "Look down, luv. Have you ever seen water so beautiful in your life?"

She did as he'd asked, fighting within herself to tear her gaze away from his face to peer out the window.

Her gasp was immediate. "Oh . . . my . . ." Jewel-green waters splashed with turquoise and sapphire greeted her. Lush, brilliant green mountains peeked through the parted plumes of clouds.

She turned back to him. "How did you ever leave Paradise?"

Her gasp had run through his skeleton to the marrow. He shook his head to chase away the sensation that was making him about to be foolish. "That's why I have to come back to it on the regular," he admitted quietly. "You like it?"

"It's breathtaking," she whispered.

He winced when she wasn't looking. No, she was wrong. Her voice was breathtaking . . . soul shaking . . . making him lose his mind. Had been for over five hours.

"Those are the twin Pitons," he said, opting for more neutral conversations. "There's an active volcano on the island, and those are what remained when the magma cooled. Tomorrow, I'll take you by there. We're flying into G.F.L.C. Airport, near the capital, Castries—as my home and your hotel is up in Rodney Heights on the north end, and the Pitons are down near the south end, in the town of Soufriere. If we'd flown into Hewanorra Airport at the south end, you could have seen it as we drove up, but I don't think the boys could have tolerated an hour and a half drive to get home after being on tour."

She kept her gaze glued out the window, suddenly remembering that she was indeed going to a hotel. "No problem," she said, still awed by the majestic beauty beyond the glass. "And you don't have to go to all that trouble to take me around. I appreciate what you've done already."

"No pressure," he said, not wanting to allow her to

slip away from his private company that easily. "You cannot come and not see tings up close and personal. There's one major road that loops the whole island. My boat is down in Rodney Bay, too, so we could go down the coast and even visit Martinique, if you want. It's French, and the shopping is good—it will give you more of the flava of the Caribbean. We've got an interesting mix of the people with French and British influence 'round here. I'll have to hip you to the patois, too."

He offered her a jaunty wink, and that made her laugh. He was glad.

"I'd love to see it," she hedged.

The uncertainty in her voice made him lean in closer as her gaze slid from the window to him, and then away again.

"But?"

"I can't go shopping."

He cocked his head to the side. "Why not?"

"I'm on a budget."

He chuckled. "I'm not."

She smiled. "No. And you will be soon."

He threw up his hands. "Tyrants, all accountants are tyrants."

She laughed. "It's our job."

He nodded and gave her a jaunty smile. "Okay, but I can show you the craft markets where you can haggle a deal down to ten dollars."

"Now that's what I'm talking about. Philly in da house."

She made him laugh so hard it was all he could do not to just gather her into his arms and kiss her. God must have also heard his prayers, because as the plane dipped, and the trees got larger, her hands grasped his. Were it not for a seat belt, she would have been practically sitting in his lap.

***

Somewhat shaken, she finally stood as the plane came to a rest. Everyone stood slowly, stretched, and yawned, and the exhausted band slowly collected themselves to debark.

"Don't forget your handbag and briefcase," Jacques said with a wry smile, retrieving the items for her.

"Oh, yeah!" She could have kicked herself. She'd gotten so comfortable that she'd nearly forgotten why she was even on this trip!

Hastily collecting her carry-on items and shawl, she tried her best to force the professional demeanor back into her tone. But as she exited the plane and the humid, equatorial weather enveloped her, she knew that would be the hardest part of her mission: to stay focused.

She'd expected a long customs process, but was pleased to note that there were some privileges afforded to local VIPs. All the authorities did was stamp passports and collect little forms they'd had to fill out, and then give Jacques and members of the band high fives and hugs.

"You gwan do de jazz festival dis year again, right, mon?" one official asked Jacques as they all passed.

"You know it. I'm always home in May for dat, mon."

"Cool!"

That was the extent of the customs process. She loved St. Lucia already. No pressures.

"You want me to drive you home, boss?" Rockko asked as they made their way through the small, one-story airport and waited by the curb for the redcaps to bring their bags.

"Naw, brother. I got dis. Go home to your lady."

The two men pounded fists and parted, like the rest had.

"Holla at you later."

Karin stood out in the Caribbean heat, amazed. They didn't have to wait with tourists at the carousel. Everybody was chilled out, and there was no media rush. Huge Mercedes sedans, Lincoln Navigators, and Jaguars were parked right in front of the strip of sidewalk at the airport entrance, something unheard of in the States. Each band member broke away from the group and went to a car that had an anxious-looking lady and eager children in the backseats.

Until this moment, she hadn't really considered what life on the road must be like. Each guy had a family. Children had to go to school. These guys were dads, not just some superstars. The women driving looked well cared for, but were still soccer moms. Deep.

She watched a gorgeous chocolate beauty burst from a car and run up to greet Rockko, her hand smoothing the back of his scalp as he swung her around. Wow. A combination of feminine instinct and curiosity made her glance up and down the street for whoever would run up and hug and kiss Jacques in homecoming. She was surprised when he simply motioned to a redcap and began walking.

"I'm in the lot, luv," he said quietly, a wistful tone seeming to make his voice weary. "It's not too far. Good to stretch my legs anyway."

She remained mute as Jacques came to a halt before a silver Jeep Grand Cherokee. She held her counsel as she watched him joke around with the redcaps, heavily tip them, and open the vehicle's cargo bay. But she studied his sad eyes and somber expression that had seemed to cloud over as though a mist had eclipsed his mirth. He said nothing as he opened the door for her, yet she did notice that he looked back and waved good-bye to his boys and their families.

He responded with forced laughter as they called out to him from opened windows, and oddly, she could tell that all his jokes about keeping the fellas straight while on the road was one of his best performances.

When he climbed into the car, she watched him lean his head back for a moment, close his eyes and rub his hands down his face with the motor running.

"The hardest part of coming home, sometimes, is coming home," he said quietly, and then cranked up the air conditioning. "Wonder what Mrs. Orville made for dinner?"

She didn't say a word as she watched him hit the button on the radio to send music blaring through the vehicle. He looked so tired and so alone all of a sudden. She knew exactly how he felt.

Chapter 7

Karin kept her gaze out of the window, watching the daylight wane and give way to evening. Jacques' silence was deafening as they careened along two-lane roads that seemed only wide enough for one car. Riding on the left side as a passenger felt completely wrong; it made her hold onto her purse to keep from jumping out of her skin each time they hit a curve and oncoming traffic appeared to be on the reverse side of the road. Each near miss told her that a collision was imminent. But she kept the mild hysteria to herself, sensing that it wouldn't be a good time to let him know how truly freaked out she was.

Maybe it was just her nerves, but the ride to the hotel seemed more harrowing than the flight. Pedestrians casually walked along the edges of open gullies that, to her mind, were deep, narrow ditches cavernous enough to break an axle. But the casual strollers never flinched as vehicles whirred by them. They seemed to have a death wish, just like the chickens, dogs, and bicyclers who seemed perfectly at home amid the wild drivers. She saw only one smashed chicken whose fate lay strewn in feathers at a crossing.

A cow casually chewed her cud along the roadside, swatting flies, and small goats never even looked up.

Enthralled, she watched teenagers gather at corners with loud rap music blaring, just like summertime back home. Her eyes took in the wondrous chaos of it all. Small lean-to houses of corrugated tin and wood were interspersed among businesses. Precarious wood planks led the brave over the open curbside ravines that caught and drained away rushing rainforest downpours and led to cinder-block front steps. Yet up in the cliffs over the bay, one could see wealth. Huge, palatial villas dotted the landscape like wildflowers in white, pink, and turquoise hues.

Jacques turned down what, to her, appeared to be another small street, which opened out to a more major thoroughfare, and sighed.

"The large pink building we're coming up on is the Royal St. Lucian," he said in a dejected voice.

She glanced at him, but his expression was unreadable. "Oh, okay. Thanks so much."

He said nothing as they pulled into the courtyard and she slid out of her seat without waiting for him to open her door. It was force of habit; moreover, she had to remember that he was the VIP, the client. Having him show her a little chivalry had been wonderful, but it was time to wake up from the dream.

However, he simply stared at her for the briefest of moments when she got out, as though disappointed, and then went to the back to get her bags. Awkwardness wrapped around her and commingled with the oppressive humidity. He loped forward with her bags, and a bellman took over from there with a bright, welcoming smile. Jacques barely grunted.

"You have reservations, madame?" the bellman asked as he motioned her toward the front desk.

"Oh, yes. Under Michaels. Karin Michaels," she replied, but turned to look at Jacques. "Should I call you in the morning?"

"Yeah . . . that's cool," he said quietly. "I'll just hang to be sure everything is all right with your hotel, then I guess I'll call it a night—unless you wanna grab something to eat back at the house?"

"I couldn't impose," she said, hesitating.

"There is a wonderful restaurant across the street," the bellman offered. "Buzz is quiet popular if you are partial to seafood. The concierge can make reservations for you, if they still have seating."

Jacques cut the uniformed brother a hot glare.

"See, the problem is he's already whetted my palate by telling me about Mrs. Orville's fare. Maybe tomorrow night."

For the first time since they'd left the airport, Jacques smiled.

"Very good, madame," the bellman said, and began walking them to the front desk.

Glad that Jacques' sunny disposition had begun to return, she wasted no time efficiently thrusting her passport and a credit card across the registration desk to the clerk.

"One for Michaels," she said, nervous anticipation wafting through her for no good reason.

"Welcome to the Royal St. Lucian," the clerk said, and began clicking the computer keyboard.

Karin noticed that Jacques had sent his gaze a million miles away. She wondered where he was mind-traveling to, he seemed so thoroughly gone from the hotel lobby. But when she glanced back to the clerk, he was wearing a serious frown.

"Madame, we have no reservation for you tonight. We can see where there had been one in your firm's name, and then it was changed to a Mr. Jonathan Broderick—but we have nothing for either of you for tonight."

Panic shot through her. "There must be some mistake?"

"Maybe you could call your office to see what has transpired."

"It's after nine o'clock, mon," Jacques said, becoming indignant. "There's only an hour differential, so she couldn't contact anyone tonight."

The clerk gave them both his most compassionate expression and mellowed his voice. "I would just book another room for her on the spot, but as you well know, Mr. Dubois, this is our high season and we are booked solid."

Karin closed her eyes and began to rub her temples. "Let me try to call my voice mail. Maybe something went wrong with Betty's reservation, or she has me booked elsewhere."

Both men peered at Karin intently as she fished out her cell phone and then turned it on. Her heart rate sped up the moment she realized that she'd disconnected herself from the electronic leash right after arguing with Lloyd. If Betty had needed to connect with her, she couldn't have. Stupid!

After several tries, Karin glanced at the two men, bewildered. "It doesn't work."

"Oh, man . . . If it's not on the Digicel network, AT&T Wireless, you have to make arrangements through Cable and Wireless down here," Jacques said, pulling his cell phone off his belt. "Use mine, call into the office, and see what could've happened, luv."

She felt like a complete nutcase, but took the man's phone anyway and dialed her voice mail. She bypassed several shrieking messages from Lloyd and tried to keep her facial expression placid as she heard herself being called a name that made her know she'd never go back to him under any circumstances. Then she heard Betty's fateful message explaining that the Royal St. Lucian was booked solid, but she was able to get Karin into the Hilton, near Soufriere.

"Oh, great," Karin muttered and terminated the call. She wasn't mad at Betty, she was simply travel weary, and her nerves were fried.

"What is it, luv?" Jacques accepted his phone back, but kept his eyes on Karin as he hooked it onto his belt.

"Sir, I'm sorry," she said to the desk clerk and then gave Jacques her full attention. "Betty wasn't able to get both me and Broderick here. She put me in the Hilton down in Soufriere, not realizing the distance, most likely."

"Oh, wow . . . That's an hour and a half away back the way we came."

"I know," Karin said quietly.

"That's bad driving at night through the mountains, even by cab," the hotel clerk interjected.

"I can catch a cab," she said, landing a hand on Jacques' arm. "You've done enough and been gentleman enough. You're tired, have been—"

"I won't hear of it. You come back with me, let Mrs. Orville feed you and make up a room, then tomorrow you can check in at the Hilton. All right?"

"That is truly the best bet, madame," the hotel clerk said, nodding hard. "Dis no place to be out and about roaming in the dead of night up in de hills. Lanes are narrow, dark. You're lucky to have good family here, and you can sort it out on the morrow."

Karin let her breath out hard, trying to dismiss the renewed energy Jacques seemed to possess. The merry twinkle in his eyes gave him away. "You *know* this was not supposed to go down like this."

"Like what?" he said, smiling wide. "This is God's hand on it, not mine—divine intervention, so no pressures." He calmly pulled out his cell phone again and notified Mrs. Orville to set the table for two, as well as asked her to make up an additional room for a female business guest.

Karin just looked at him as the bellman came to collect her bags and put them back into Jacques' car.

He was all lively chatter; she said nary a word. Oh, so now he had jokes and conversation, huh. She wasn't quite sure why her mood had gone foul, but it had. She felt testy and sweaty, and suddenly very, very tired. Maybe it was the calls she heard from Lloyd, maybe it was the need to be alone to process everything that had and was about to go down. She wasn't sure. All she was sure of was that it didn't look right, and didn't feel right; she needed space to keep her professional distance, and this man was too damned sexy to be spending the night with under the same roof!

However, the snit fit had to take a holiday, if only temporarily, when they pulled up to the ivory-toned, split-level villa built into the side of a cliff. Twelve-foot, recessed windows were framed by high arches that encircled the house. The deck seemed to begin somewhere around the back of the property, cliffside, and wrap around the entire structure. Ornate, lacquered, natural-oak French doors heralded the front of the house, while a turquoise, ocean-blue profusion of tiles gave the roof a bejeweled quality that nearly drew a gasp from her.

She swore she wouldn't gawk, but all that went by

the by as Jacques maneuvered into the driveway, which was lit by small halogen foot lamps. The landscaping alone was enough to steal her voice. Gorgeous hibiscus splashed vibrant colors against the night as palms in every variety swayed gently overhead. Huge fruit-bearing trees heavily laden with unpicked yields of mangoes, coconuts, and breadfruit littered the manicured lawn that terminated in a cutstone walkway. When Jacques depressed the garage door opener, four bays opened to a fleet that looked like a Center City valet port.

Before Karin could close her mouth, a short, round woman flung open the front door and quickly made her way down the path.

"Oh, you have come back just in time," she said, leaning in Jacques' window and kissing his cheeks hard, like an auntie. "You have been so missed."

He laughed and opened his driver's-side door to give the older woman a full hug. "Mrs. Orville doubles as mom," Jacques exclaimed, and motioned toward Karin. "This is Karin Michaels, from the States, and she's a businesswoman to set my records right. This is Mrs. Orville, the best cook and drill sergeant one could ever be blessed to have."

The older woman swatted Jacques' arm. "He teases me, but I keep him straight and feed him well. Pleased to meet you, Miss Michaels."

"Karin, please," she said, hopping out of the car to go over to extend her hand. "He told me all about your cooking for hours on the plane until my stomach growled."

Mrs. Orville shook Karin's hand hard and then folded her arms over her ample breasts and smiled wide. "I like her already." She immediately turned on her heels. "Come, come along. I always cook big when he's coming home, and you have been traveling. By the time you settle in and have your bath, you will have enough on your plate to make you pass out on de floor."

Jacques grabbed Karin's bags out of the vehicle and shouted down the walkway. "Follow her; she moves fast when her pots are on. I'll bring your bags—didn't I tell you she could burn!"

The moment Karin hit the foyer, Mrs. Orville was standing there with a package containing a pair of unopened flip flops.

"Oops, madame. Take off your shoes, and put these on. He's funny about vibes." She peered over Karin's shoulder and chuckled. "Someting New-Wave religion, I don' know what dat man worries over, but even I have to put on slippers, so I keep these in the basket by the door for visitors."

"My apologies," Karin said, quickly complying.

"Dat boy was raised Catholic, and gwan lost his mind out in the worl', but home does him good." Mrs. Orville waved her hand and gave Karin a jaunty pout that made her chuckle. "He tried to tell me one time he don't eat da lamb, don' eat da chicken, only certain seafood, and for a while was telling me no fish, no dairy, no shellfish, and I finally ask him, 'Den, man, whatchu wan' me to cook up? Fifteen flavors of mango?' Pishaw. He eats what I cook now, no pressures. But it's got to be all natural, right out the yard from local farmers, no preservatives and whatnot. So we compromise."

The down-home quality of this woman was so warm and inviting and her melodic laughter was so genuine that it threaded through Karin's bloodstream like a dose of balm for her soul. But she wondered how it came to be that Mrs. Orville was so much like a mother to Jacques, and yet neither his mother nor any of his siblings had been there to greet him when he came home. The question disturbed her, and she tried not to think about it as Mrs. Orville hustled her through the palatial house, chatting away. The pure hospitality of the woman made Karin feel like she was floating.

They passed a huge foyer with blond oak floors that were polished so meticulously they resembled glass. The open-air architecture gave the whole place the feeling that there were no walls. Everything was sand hued and ivory with splashes of color offered by exquisite African art. What appeared to be a living room and dining room were separated only by a double-sided fireplace. Arches separated rooms, not walls, and a sunken game room rec center flanked her as they made their way back toward private bedrooms.

She wasn't sure how many bedrooms they'd passed on the western side of the house, but she could see that each well-appointed, French Provincial room shared what seemed to be an enormous bathroom. Finally, when Mrs. Orville stopped, Karin caught her breath, only to have it ripped from her again when the kind older woman bade her enter what would be her room for the evening.

It was a suite. Blond-oak vanity, armoire, and rice bed draped in ivory satin upholstery and fine cotton linens. A thick-pile Turkish area rug made Karin want to slide off her flip-flops and just allow her feet to sink into the hand-loomed textures. Yellow hibiscus flowers had been carefully placed on each pillow swathed in a delicate ivory lace sham. An old-fashioned, white porcelain French rinsing bowl stood alone by a French screen made of delicate ivory and yellow ribbon fans, and a full-length, oak-framed stand mirror completed the set. French doors with slated blinds hid away a full walk-in cedar closet that Mrs. Orville opened with flourish.

"Hang your clothes up and just set out whatever you need pressed each morning, and I will collect it for you."

Karin just stared at the woman. "Oh, no ma'am, I couldn't ask you to do my clothes; I brought a travel iron and—"

"That's my job, sweetheart. What are you saying?"

Karin covered her face and laughed. "Ma'am, no offense. Oh, Lord, my own momma wouldn't iron a shirt for me, and I'm not used to the royal treatment."

"I knew I liked you from the moment I set eyes on you." Mrs. Orville smiled and relaxed. "Well, get used to it." She clucked her tongue and walked Karin into the adjoining bathroom. "I took the liberty to draw a cool bath when I received the call—traveling is hard on de body and nerves. I've set out some towels and a few chilled bottled waters by the tub, and once you are in your relaxed clothes, you will find me in the kitchen. Buzz line two for me on the intercom until I leave for the evening, and I'll be back bright and early at seven in the morning to fetch whatever you leave out for me in the small alcove to have readied for your new day."

Speechless, Karin simply nodded. The bathroom, which was bigger than her apartment's living room, was of the palest, most exquisite yellow she could have envisioned. Plush, thick, lemon-colored terry towels had been expertly folded into flower shapes with multi-hued hibiscus placed carefully in each fold. Flowers and expensive lotions, soaps, and bath salts dotted the back plane of the ivory porcelain and goldtone-fauceted double sink. Huge ferns lazily soaked up the steam.

Even the toilet-paper rolls next to the commode and bidet had a flower tucked into the new, unopened tissue. When she spied the gurgling tub with flowers tumbling in the rose scented water, she almost fell over.

"All right?" Mrs. Orville said.

"Beyond comprehension," Karin said, almost afraid to move.

"Good. Dinner in forty-five minutes, then."

Both women looked up at Jacques as he dropped Karin's bags in the bedroom entrance. He smiled and gave Mrs. Orville a wink.

"I'll be on the other side of the house—east wing. You holla when you're ready to eat. Most likely I'll jump in the shower and be out on the back deck."

"He's so fresh," Mrs. Orville fussed, walking across the room. "He doesn't like air conditioning; I can't cook like a fiend witout it. Humph!"

Karin laughed and shook her head, but noticed Jacques was still leaning against the bedroom's outer door frame.

"This room all right?" he asked, his eyes holding a quality of anticipation she hadn't expected.

"It's beyond all right," she said quietly. "It's out of a dream."

"Cool." He nodded, lifted his chin, and pushed away from the door, gently closing it behind him.

She stood in the middle of the bathroom, her gaze slowly raking the mirrors. Ever so timidly, she went up to the double-wide stall shower and almost screamed when she saw that it contained five different shower heads. She had to pinch herself. The gizmo seemed like one needed an engineering degree to simply turn it on. She backed away from it and gently closed the smoked glass doors.

Never again would she talk badly about people who

took cameras into the bathrooms of the stars, stole a roll of toilet paper, or carried off a sink fixture. She now understood the definition of overwhelmed.

Although it took a while for her to settle down, once she slid into the lukewarm tub water, her entire body became liquefied. Everything smelled good: the soap, the water, even down to the towels that had been spritzed with floral fragrance. She had to light the small vanilla candle tea lights that had been set around the edges of the water, just because. Sipping cool spring water kept her awake, and were it not for that and vanity, she would have slid beneath the suds, gotten her hair wet, and drowned from falling asleep.

But the awesome scents wafting through the house were what got her to part with the sensual diversion. Her stomach was growling, Mrs. Orville was da bomb, and refreshed, Kairn wanted to go exploring.

Swathed in a lush towel that was so long it hit her ankles, Karin made her way to her ragged little suit-case and pulled out a bright sarong skirt with green and gold swirls, and dug out her new, lime-green, matching tankini. She didn't bother with flip-flops. Bare feet just felt right as she added on layers of cocoa butter by rote and made sure no ash would invade her skin. Feeling light as a feather, she just added a bit of eyeliner and quickly applied one of her new lip-gloss colors—coral worked well—then stood back and gave herself the once-over, lightly finger combing her hair.

She almost skipped down the hall, following kitchen scents, and stopped briefly to admire the beautiful art along the way. But the dinner table laid for two held her for ransom. Mrs. Orville had set out a small globe vase filled with dramatic birds of paradise and calla lilies, and there was enough gold flat-ware and bone china rimmed in gold beside multiple crystal stemware to service the Queen of England.

Karin headed for the kitchen and paused in the doorway. It took her a moment to speak. Stainless steel appliances rimmed the walls; a butcher-block main island with grill accessories and overhead hanging copper pans presented a formidable environment. It looked like a mini restaurateur's universe. One wall was devoted to an eat-in nook; another was an awe-inspiring wall of glass and screens that seemed to extend to a deck that overlooked the cliffs. Karin covered her heart.

"Is there anything I can do to help you, Mrs. Orville?" She knew it was a foolish question, but some things were just home training, where she was from.

"Oh, no chile. Thank you for asking. He's outside on the deck. I'll be ready shortly with your dinner. Just go have a nice glass of wine, and I'll call you."

Karin glanced around, not even sure of how to properly access the deck. Seeming to sense her uncertainty, Mrs. Orville turned, walked over to the sliding doors, and slid one back for Karin.

"He may be in the pool, knowing him. He'll come to my table all wet and not properly washed up, but what shall we do with him, eh?"

Karin smiled and followed Mrs. Orville's lead, knowing that she had been nicely dismissed. But a *pool*? She shut the doors behind her with care to be sure not to leak out any of the precious cool air needed in the kitchen.

"Hey!" Jacques exclaimed, pushing away from the deck rail. He turned and took a sip of his chardonnay and came up to her with a wide grin. "Feeling more relaxed?"

Any relaxation she'd achieved immediately vanished.

He was standing there with no shirt on, barefoot, and wearing only white gauze drawstring pants that left little to the imagination. She kept her eyes on his face, willed herself to do so.

"The bath was awesome."

"Wine?"

"You bet," she said, laughing as he spied her bare feet.

"You have definitely relaxed," he said, going over to the ice bucket to pour her a glass.

"It is *gorgeous* out here," she said, honestly marveling at the midnight-blue sky. She had to look at anything but him, and the sky was up and therefore a solid choice. "The stars are so . . . I don't know," she said quietly, accepting the glass from him as he led her to the rail.

"Not a lot of city lights to compete with them," he said, clinking his glass against hers. "This is where I come to get my head right. The pace is slower; Mrs. O takes care of me. It's all good."

There was a quiet wistfulness in his tone when he made the statement, and the slight melancholy in his voice made her look at his handsome face.

"Yeah, it is all good," she said quietly, sipping her wine and returning her gaze to the stars. Then she glanced over the railing to the bay and beach further below. Small white yachts dotted the harbor. Her gaze swept over to the east side of the house, where a small waterfall seemed to run off the pool in the room and into an Olympic-sized pool. She couldn't immediately figure out the design, and wrinkled her nose trying to better see.

"Master bedroom," he said, swallowing s sip of wine with his smile. "Half the pool is in the room; the rest of it spills out to the grounds next to the deck. Hot tub's on that side of the deck, too."

"Oh . . ." Her mouth remained in the O shape longer than she'd wanted, so she took a sip of wine to close it.

"The studio is on that side, too," he added. "Sometimes I just get up in the middle of the night—gotta get the sounds out of my head so I can sleep—then I stumble back to bed. It's easier that way."

"Oh . . ." This time, she sipped her wine more quickly.

This time, he laughed.

"You think I'm extravagant, don't you?"

"I think you've worked hard for what you have, and deserve to have what you want—we just have to make sure you can keep all of this."

He sighed and nodded. "Karin, you ain't said a mumblin' word."

"Jacques, I know it has to be scary, but we'll figure something out. After seeing this, I can only imagine what's keeping you up at night."

He folded one of her hands in his. "Tomorrow, I'm gonna take you on the south side of the country, all right?"

"All right," she said softly, staring into his eyes.

"Then I will show you what keeps me up at night, before we go around and see the good-life tings."

She knew enough about men to simply squeeze his hand at this juncture and not inquire more. Tonight, he was obviously showing her his best. Tomorrow, if his trust in her held up, he'd show her his fears, perhaps even where he'd come from. Both, she inherently accepted as a gift.

The air was getting thick around him. This all-natural woman had squeezed his hand like she'd read his mind, and was cool enough not to dig for an immediate explanation. She'd floated out of his house like a breeze: green, the color of healing, barefoot like she was Mother Nature herself, her voice low and warm and filled with care, her eyes . . . beyond compare as they drank him in.

If she only understood how barren this house had been—how it echoed when not filled up, how little life, save Mrs. Orville and his music, resided here. Parties were a mirage that lasted until his grasping siblings left, his band went home with their families, or VIPs from the industry finally caught a flight back to what they called civilization. It didn't last, didn't provide warmth, solace, a real heartbeat to the home.

But tonight, Karin's giggles had ricocheted off the walls, along with her warm, breathy gasps, and her stunned questions . . . the tone of caring in her voice was stirring new music within him. He could feel it coming alive, needing to surface and roil over him into lyrics. And he wanted to make love to her so badly now, to hear that sacred melody spill forth from her, that his hands were almost shaking.

"I think Mrs. Orville is going to spoil us tonight— and I have you to thank. She's only particularly nice to me if I have company."

He watched Karin's face become somber and saw her force a smile.

"No, no, no . . . That didn't come out right," he said, trying to correct himself as quickly as possible. "I don't always have company; it's been years, okay?"

"I'm not making any judgments about what—"

He grabbed her hand and held it tightly. "Karin, stop. Listen to me. I know this is a business arrangement, but it's also important that you understand me."

He watched her gaze soften and let out a quiet breath.

"The company I have here is normally my family scrambling for whatever they can get, and they come in and boss that poor woman around like she's their slave. It always gets ugly, because I defend her. She is like family to me, and how my people suddenly got all high and mighty with no money in their pockets is something I can't even begin to figure out. My mom, because she suffers badly from diabetes, stays with my sister, Annette, the nurse, and her husband and children. When I come back into town, I need a day or two before they come over and start with what I should be doing for them next. My other sister, who is a professor, always reminds me of how much more education she has than me, and we will not discuss how my brother behaves. That's my company, here at home. My boyz, they come over with their wives and children and they fill up my life here. If I was to go dating someone from here, drama—like you would not believe. You know how many times I've brought someone here?"

Embarrassed by her irrational jolt of jealousy, she simply shook her head and studied the deck planks.

"Three times. Once a very long time ago when I began building, and I wound up with a paternity suit—God was on my side and so was DNA testing."

Her eyes went wide. He nodded.

"Drama," he said, raking his hair. "The second time, it was a chick from South America that became a stalker, and I almost got my ass blown away because her family was crazy and wanted me to use my plane to transport their product. That's why I don't play the drug ting, luv. Then I was dating this Brit, and I come to find out she had a heroin problem. When she died of AIDS, I freaked, got tested every two days, and finally believed the doctors when they said I was clean. After that, I was done. I went all natural, cleaned up my act, and became a monk, practically—scared to death I might wind up in some suit or whatever behind some gold digger—so I don't have that kind of company in my house. This is the only sanctuary I've been able to claim, and Mrs. Orville is the only person in service that has consistently had my back. Even the landscapers my brother recommended were robbing me blind and giving him a kickback."

He pushed away from the rail and turned to walk toward the house. Her hand on his arm stopped him.

"I'm sorry," she said quietly.

"No pressures," he snapped.

"No, hear me out," she said calmly, making his eyes meet hers. "I am sorry that I heard you wrong, took what you said the wrong way—but more than anything, I'm so sorry that a man like you who is trying very hard to do the right thing has had to deal with so much treachery. For real," she said, shaking her head. "I am sorry for all of that."

"Don't pity me, Karin. That's crazy."

"I'm not, and I don't," she said, her voice firm but gentle. "I'm sorry that a lot of stuff in the world sucks. I'm glad you take all that pain and put some beauty back into this black hole with your music."

He stared at her for a moment and then looked away. "I never thought of it like that."

"That's how I see it. You're a catalytic converter."

He chuckled and sipped his wine, his former calm returning by degrees. "A what?"

"You take negative energy and convert it to positive energy through your music, and people run like fuel off of that."

"Okay, now you've gone deep and metaphysical on me. Accountants aren't supposed to do that."

They both chuckled.

"No, they're not," she said. "But I don't often get a chance to stretch out, let my hair down, and be who I am, or get philosophical. The stars out here help."

He nodded and glimpsed her from the corner of his eye, now leaning on the rail with his glass loosely balanced between his palms. "I have to say this, and you can tell me it's none of my business. But how did you convince your man to let you run away with me? I for one, wouldn't have let that go without a fight."

She smiled. "What man? He's history."

He pushed away from the rail. "Get out. Seriously? What happened?"

"You're in my business, now, brother."

Jacques laughed hard. "You're way into mine, so?"

She laughed hard and sipped her wine. "He accused me of spending the night with you, gold digging, and a bunch of mess . . . called my mother, told on me, and, six o'clock in the morning, my phone was blowing up with my mom coming down on me—and believe me, she isn't the warm and motherly type like Mrs. Orville. Then, in the airport, I get a dozen voice mails calling out my name. That's why I didn't get Betty's message. I turned my phone off. Drama."

He blew out a long breath until it whistled. "Drama."

"Precisely." She clinked her glass against his and took a full swig. "I've got a boss that thinks I haven't earned the right to be here, a mother who thinks I've lost my mind, and an ex that can kiss my butt."

He smiled. "No brothers or sisters?"

"No," she said softly.

His smile became sad and tender. "You're lucky then."

"One brother died stillborn after me, and then Mom wouldn't try again. My dad died hauling U.S.

mail on the streets, and she blames me for looking
like him and acting like him. What can I say?"

"Then he must have been a helluva man, to produce such a wonderful daughter."

She couldn't look at him. "I miss my dad. He loved
life and would laugh. Odd, but he was the philosophical one, even though my mother had the degrees.
Weird how that works."

"You got the best of both of them, then."

She stared at him and marveled at how the stars
framed him. "Thank you for saying that."

"It's the truth, and either this is some very good
wine doubling as truth serum, or we've both just had
some much-needed therapy on my deck."

"Either way works for me," she said laughing, and
loving how he always seemed to take the most morose
situation and find the diamond within it. "But I've gotta
be real honest. The bugs are eating me alive, brother."

"We've got rain-forest mosquitoes out here the size
of dimes, sis, and you're new to the island, all sweet
meat—let's go back into the house."

"I was trying to be polite," she said, scurrying
toward the deck door.

"Stop!" he hollered. "Don't move, and don't freak.
I know this is gonna seem fresh but—"

He whacked her behind so hard that she almost
dropped her glass.

"Are you crazy?" she said, half offended—and half
delighted, but she couldn't allow that part to show.

"Lizard was riding your—"

"What!?" Her voice hit a decibel that brought Mrs.
Orville out from the kitchen.

By the time Mrs. Orville opened the sliding doors,
Karin was doing an on-tiptoes, run-around-in-a-circle
dance, swatting herself, spilling wine, and screaming.

"Lizards," Jacques announced, doubled over laughing.

"Oh, they're nuisance little buggers and you're all in green so they will slide up on—"

"Get 'em off, get 'em off, get 'em off!" Karin squealed, halting Mrs. Orville's nature lecture, shedding her skirt, and brushing down her legs.

"Chile, they're just like the tree frogs on the deck at night, they don't hurt—"

"Frogs?" Karin, shot into the house and set down her wine on the counter hard.

Laughter echoed from the deck behind her.

"I guess you gwan hafta keep dis chile in de house day and night," Mrs. Orville said, doubled over, slapping her leg. "Whoowee! Good ting I cooked plenty!"

Chapter 8

It took a few minutes for Karin to settle down in the kitchen and get her sarong back, and for Jacques and Mrs. Orville to come into the house and stop laughing, but eventually order was restored.

"Well, at least it wasn't a snake or something," Jacques said, mischief totally consuming him as Karin fidgeted with her sarong and tried to get it back on. Truth was, he loved the view. Thick thighs flashing beneath the cute little bathing-suit skirt bottom—he hadn't realized it was under the wrap until she'd whipped it off. Then that thing she did jumping up and down . . .

"You need to stop teasing that po' chile, or she'll never get out from underfoot in my kitchen, Jacques," Mrs. Orville said, wagging a finger at him and still chuckling.

"Stop lying, J.B. There's snakes, too?"

He laughed hard and leaned against the refrigerator in Mrs. Orville's way. She'd *finally* called him J.B.

"Only about a hundred different kinds up in the rain forest that can kill you, but the boas don't bite. They're just about six to eight feet long when babies, and can crush the bones in your arm, but hey, they ain't as bad as the spitting vipers that can send paralyzing venom—"

"Jacques Bernard Dubois!" Mrs. Orville fussed, shaking her head as Karin blanched. "Behave yourself."

"Is he playing?" Karin said, sidling up to Mrs. Orville for comfort.

"No, sweet pea," she said, trying hard not to smile and losing the battle. "All is true, but unnecessary information." Mrs. Orville cut a glare at her young boss. "He's just being fresh."

"I'm trying to give da girl the realio dealio, ma'am. See, this is stuff they don't tell you in the brochures. All you see is the pretty landscape and they say, 'Oh, come on an exotic safari through the rain forest,' but neglect to add that you might want to go with an experienced guide, Agent Orange–level bug spray, and knee-high combat boots, not flip flops and a towel. Miss Karin don' strike me as the type to like not-in-the-brochure-surprises, and I'm just tryin' ta school her for when she leaves here and books in the Hilton tomorrow."

Karin laughed. "A'ight. I hear you. . . . Sorta like when the brochures to visit Philly tell you to experience the Liberty Bell, but neglect to add that if you turn down the wrong street in the wrong section of town, you might want to have S.W.A.T. as backup."

"See, girlfriend knows what I'm talkin' 'bout, Mrs. O."

"Really?" Mrs. Orville asked, craning her neck closer to Karin. "That bad?"

"Mrs. Orville, we've got some badlands that no tourist wants any part of, too."

The older woman nodded. "Ah. Well, I guess every place has dat."

"Yup," Karin said, all formality gone. How could

one go back to being proper after doing the Watusi and stripping off one's skirt? "Can I help you get some of this great-smelling food on the table? We should all just eat and laugh and forget about serving dinner according to protocol. After a lizard jumps on your behind, what more real can one be?"

They all laughed.

Karin edged to the simmering concoctions on the stove. "Besides, my question is, how in the world did you just whip up all this fantastic stuff in less than an hour?"

The smile on Mrs. Orville's face was worth the question. The query had been an earnest one, but Karin watched the older woman stand up taller as she took off lids and waved her hand before her creations.

"My dear," Mrs. Orville said with definite pride, "I always start early in the day when I know he's coming home. I make enough to last him a few days, that's my little secret that I'll share—only because you're a sweetheart to me. So it isn't like I made all this from scratch forty-five minutes ago. But you visit long enough and I'll show you how to make some favorite dishes."

"Hold up," Jacques said, pushing off the wall to peer into a pot and try to dip in a finger. Receiving a whack from Mrs. Orville, he drew his hand back and chuckled. "How you gwan allow her to get in me stash? If dat's supposed to last me days—"

"I'll come back and cook again during the week, only because *she's* here."

"Oh, so it's like dat now, huh?" He shook his head and laughed harder. "You upsettin' me household, woman."

"Yes, it's like dat," Mrs. Orville teased, dishing out a bowl of mussels and mixed fruit for Karin to take to the dining-room table. "She holds check. You, sir, do not."

"That's what you get for the frogs-and-snakes com- ments," Karin said, gladly accepting the bowl and sashaying into the dining room with it.

Mrs. Orville's eyes followed behind her and then fell upon Jacques's face. "I like her," she said quietly, and then nodded with a grunt.

He nodded. "So do I."

"Do tell. I was completely oblivious," Mrs. Orville said, handing him two soup bowls on a small silver tray.

"For real," he said, his tone serious as he accepted the conch chowder.

"I know."

"You gwan eat wit us?" He waited and stared at the woman who'd become his second mother.

"Nope. It was just nice that she asked, though. Real class."

"Yeah . . ."

He found Karin in the next room setting down the mussels, and slid the soup on the table.

"This looks fabulous," she said, breathing in the aroma and briefly closing her eyes.

The way she'd done that made him pause to breathe her in. "Yeah. Mrs. O can burn, like I said. I don' know what she puts in it, spicewise, but she cooks the mussels in pineapple juice and somethin' else, then cools it, and dices up mangoes, pineapples, and honeydew, and has this sort of lime-ginger ting going on as a dressing served over greens for the salad. I can make a meal on that alone."

"I hear you," Karin said, heading back toward the kitchen.

"Where you going?"

He followed behind her only to find Mrs. Orville re- moving her apron. "All right. It seems my services are no longer needed for the night, so I'll just walk on home and will call in the morning before I come." She glanced at Jacques who looked away toward the counter.

"You're not eating with us?" Karin said, bewildered. "After you made all this?"

"Chile," Mrs. Orville scoffed. "I pick and taste-test as I cook. Me belly is long full. I've put everyting under covered dishes, so you two eat your fill, and den just put what's left in the fridge. Leave the dishes, and I'll clean up later. This old bird is sleepy and needs to go to bed."

"But it's pitch-black outside," Karin protested, alarmed that Jacques didn't intervene.

"I live across the street in a small cottage," Mrs. Orville soothed. "Dat's the only way I can keep an eye on his rusty behind and can make sure he eats."

"I'll walk you across," Jacques said, smiling. "Don' want no frogs or land crabs and lizards to eat you up in the night."

Mrs. Orville laughed. "Don' listen to him. If you go in the pool tonight, make sure he dips a screen in it to get any wayward frogs out, or he'll have you dancing in the water."

Karin had to laugh. "I will most assuredly do that."

"Good. Now you two eat. Your soup is getting col', and I don' worked too hard on it to have it left cooling." Mrs. Orville waved her hand. "He don' need to walk me, just stand in the doorway for me, hon."

"I'll walk you," he said, offering the older woman his elbow. "We have this argument every night, Karin. Pay her no mind."

But rather than immediately accept his arm, Mrs. Orville first came up to Karin and held her away from her for a moment, looked her over, and then hugged her hard. "So pleased to have made your acquaintance." She dabbed her eyes, nodded with a soft click of her tongue, and sighed as though content. "I can go home, now."

Karin watched Jacques escort Mrs. Orville through the house as though on a promenade. He held the door open, and then argued with her some more, their lively voices filling the walkway as he guided her to the small home across the street. When he returned, he gently shut the door and stared behind it for a moment, and then crossed the room toward Karin. There was a tenderness in his expression that made her sit down slowly. For some strange reason, even with all the wonderful food before them, she wasn't hungry.

"Where did you ever find that angel? She's like the mom I wish I had."

He sat across from her and began picking at his salad. "God sent her, that's all I know."

An easy, natural, companionable silence surrounded them as they ate the fruit and mussel salad and quietly devoured the chowder.

"It's so quiet in here," she whispered, closing her eyes and tilting her head. "You can even hear the crickets from outside through the walls."

"Those are the tree frogs," he said, just above a murmur. "They make music. The night is awesome to listen to, and they don't bother you. They belong here, owned the land before we." He stood, took their plates, and nodded toward a buffet. "Why don' you put on some music. I'll go dish up the rest of dinner."

Karin glimpsed the remote control and leaned forward to stare at the sophisticated sound system in the adjacent room. "I've never worked for NASA," she said with a sheepish grin. "I'm not an engineer, so how about if I go get the plates and you put on the music?"

"All right. This time. But I'll show you how it works."

He walked into the living room, she headed for the kitchen. There was something so natural about the way they flowed in each other's company that she took her time familiarizing herself with the varied dishes in the solitude of the kitchen. A sudden peace had claimed her, and she hadn't known that feeling in years. Soon, soft jazz wafted through the house to combine with the smells. Wynton Marsalis? She would have never guessed he'd pick that.

"I'm not sure how much of each thing you want," she said as he entered the room and leaned against the door frame.

"What's she got under lid?" he said, smiling as he pushed away and came to inspect the larder.

"Rice and beans—"

"Pigeon peas and rice cooked in coconut milk," he corrected. "A lot of those."

She smiled. "Ahh . . . Okay."

"Greens."

"Nope. Callaloo."

"Oh. All right. Then, wow . . ."

He laughed. "I see she went all out. Broiled kingfish with mango chutney. Shrimp and scallops in sauce Creole—dat's the tomato red sauce with lime juice, onions, pimientos, chilies, and whatever else she dumps in from the spice rack."

"Lawd, have mercy . . ." Karin shook her head and simply held the empty plates midair. "What's the orange-colored pudding?"

"Yam soufflé. I see she also put up coconut bread, made some plantains, and if I know her," he said, going towards the refrigerator, "she's got some key lime pie—yes!" He flung open the freezer and shook his head. "An angel, I tell you. Coconut, pineapple, rum-cashew ice cream—from scratch, girl." He winked at Karin. "Special house blend. Tastes like a piña colada with nuts added."

"Okay. Stick me with a fork, I'm done."

They laughed as they raided the dishes Mrs. Orville had left and raced back to the table to savor the meal.

"Do you always eat like this?" she asked, digging into her plate with complete abandon and wondering how he kept fit.

"First day I'm back, I eat like a dawg," he said, shoveling food into his mouth. "Then, the next day, I've got to get real again. Go running five miles; work out before the sun gets too hot. Purge with a fruit-only regime, drink gallons of water, and refuse to eat garbage while on tour. It's de only way around her. Otherwise, you'd have to roll me onto the stage and my cardiovascular wouldn't be crap. Two songs, a few dance moves, and I'd need oxygen."

Karin nodded, mumbled sounds of pure satisfaction while chewing, and finally sat back in her chair with one hand on her belly. "I need oxygen now."

"We go for a swim, let the food find a wooden leg, then raid the fridge for some key lime and ice cream later."

"I'll sink," she said, laughing. "Aren't you supposed to wait an hour after you eat before going in the water, man?" She fanned her face with both hands.

"Superstition. I won't take you further than waist-high, and it's relaxing out there at night."

"Hmm . . . but there's frogs."

"Itty, bitty little guys who are more afraid of you than you're afraid of them."

His infectious smile was hard to resist. Just as his hospitality and charisma were impossible to decline.

"Maybe," she said, closing her eyes as she sank deeper against the comfortable, overstuffed satin upholstery. "If I can waddle away from the table."

"I'll take that as a yes. After grubbing like this, I've broken a sweat."

They both laughed.

Although she could barely move, he coaxed her back out onto the deck to take a stroll to the poolside of the house. A large Adirondack lounge chair was calling her name.

"Don't do it," he said, stripping off his drawstring pants. "Go to sleep and the bugs will fillet you alive. In the chlorine pool water, they'll back up."

"Point made," she said, slowly taking off her sarong. It wasn't an attempt to be alluring, just the fact that she was so sated she could barely move. Black Speedos? With a body like his? *Oh no he didn't.*

"Tell me lizards don't swim, though," she said, trying to sound casual while attempting to ignore his physique. Black Speedos, wet. Packed like . . . she couldn't even think it.

"They don't," he said, walking down the wide tile steps to knee-deep. "C'mon, girl. It feels like bathwater in here, it's so warm."

Black Speedos, on a tall, fine brother almost the same hue, with pool lights shimmering against the fabric and his thighs, about to get for real wet. Hair all free on his shoulders. *Talk to me Jesus. I must be strong.*

"All right, all right, don't rush a sister after eating." *That's right, go for Philly attitude as a shield. Oh, baby, you are so fine that you gonna make me lose my mind up in this piece!* "I'm moving as fast as I can."

"You moving like a turtle, woman," he said, laughing hard, and then plunged into the water.

She almost had tears in her eyes. This didn't make no sense.

Creeping by degrees, she edged into the water from the shallow end and finally submerged her body to the shoulders.

"Oh, this is nice . . . just like bathwater. You have it heated?"

"No, luv. The sun heats it all day. Everything you need is provided for here by the Almighty."

"No lie," she said with unmasked appreciation, and then caught herself and looked away.

Rivulets of water cascaded from his hair, over his sinewy shoulders, down his broad chest, over his nipples, down his six-packed abs, and she had to fight not to visually latch onto the trail of dark curly hair that began just beneath his sunken belly button and disappeared in his swim trunks. Just watching him glide beneath the blue, underwater-lit surface toward her and then stand inches from her, wet, that megawatt smile set in his dark face, lights dancing in his eyes, skin slicked . . . her palms ached to touch him. But she didn't.

"I see you're gonna do the black-woman ting and not get your hair wet," he teased.

She stood on tiptoes. "Correct. I paid for this hair and it needs to last twenty-four hours." He had a look in his eyes that made her back away and squeal. "Don't even try it!"

"Naw, naw, I was just messing with you," he said, plunging his body down to the neck while laughing. "But I did think about it."

"Don't even go there," she said, moving further away from a possible pool splash attack.

"I like what you did with it. I wouldn't wet it up," he said with a mischievous grin. "Unless you want me to?"

She folded her arms over her chest and tried for a glare, but to his mind she looked pleased by the honest compliment. Truth was, he'd wet her up, wet her down, sweat out her new hairdo, whatever she wanted . . . if she'd let him. He needed to be in the pool just to cool off and derail his thoughts, but the water, and seeing her all shiny and wet, bathing suit clinging to her, was messing him around worse than he could have imagined. He dunked his head again and wiped his palms down his face.

She lowered her body in the water. "You'll behave?"

He didn't immediately answer. "Yeah . . ."

Whoa. Maybe she did need to let her hair get wet. Her face was suddenly hot, even in the pool. It was the low tone of his voice that reverberated through her as though it were ripples sent across the water. Her skin was on fire, small tingles nagging at her breast, every inch of her feeling the touch of the coolness around her and yearning for the heat of his hands at the same time.

"Coconut, rum, cashew, pineapple, huh?" she said as a diversion.

"Want some ice cream?"

"If you gonna do it," she said laughing, and stealing a line from the Nelly song they both knew well.

He hesitated, hope stroking a brushfire within him. "I'll bring a bowl and two spoons," he said, and pulled himself out of the water in one lithe move.

She held onto the edge of the pool to keep from floating away, and couldn't deny herself the eye candy as he strode across the deck, dripping. The dip of his spine simply called out to her senses for a thorough evaluation as it sensually bent and gave rise to the most phenomenal male buns she'd ever seen up close and personal. Frogs, mosquitoes, lizards be damned—if she had to endure the nature tour to see this, it was worth it.

But as he hurried back with a sinful mound of creamy confection in a bowl, she couldn't even play it off. Her eyes briefly locked with his, then slowly followed the line of his regal nose, paused at his lush mouth, and then traced his shoulders, his chest, his arms and hands, landed on the ice cream, and then carefully slid down his torso.

"I think you might have too much," she said, trying to focus on the ice cream.

"Don' worry, luv," he said in a low tone, "if we take our time, we'll finish it all."

She swallowed hard, and was glad that he had, too. It was the slightest hint of his Adam's apple bobbing in his throat that finally clued her in. He was feeling it, too. Big problem. But she hoped that as long as she didn't lose her mind, he'd stay within the correct boundaries. She could get through this night. Mrs. Orville was just across the street. She could have dessert without really having dessert, and all would be professionally correct. Tomorrow she'd make a beeline for the Hilton, her senior boss would be in town, and she could get herself together. But the man had lowered himself into the pool and was wading toward her, bowl in hand, and eyes burning fire. *Okay, breathe, girl. Breathe and act like you know.*

"Now, lemme explain something to you about the whole art of what Mrs. Orville does," he said, putting a bit of ice cream on a spoon and offering it to her.

Karin leaned forward and opened her mouth. The man was talking all low and sexy and feeding her half naked in a pool, oh Lawd! She closed her mouth over the spoon and allowed the cold sweetness to fill her mouth. A moan escaped of its own accord. And her hand went to her chest in reflex. "Oh, my God. This is so good. I've never had anything like it."

She watched his eyes go to half-mast as he took a dip of the ice cream and allowed it to roll around on his palate before closing his eyes.

"What she does is take fresh coconut," he said in a gravelly voice. "Shred it by hand. Get pineapple from the yard, and let it soak in rum for a day. All fresh cream and fresh butter, with raw sugar. Here, the cashew trees drop fruit in the yard, too. Then she blends it in an old-fashioned rock-salt hand-crank—doesn't trust technology, you feel me?"

He opened his eyes.

She moved closer and took a spoonful. "I feel you," she said in a very quiet voice before putting another glob of ice cream in her mouth. "This oughta be against the law."

"It should be when something is this good, but luckily it's not."

She watched him eat another spoonful and close his eyes with a sigh.

The heat of his hand against the bowl and the steamy humidity above the surface of the pool was quickly turning the dessert to sweet soup. She dipped in another spoonful and accidentally dribbled some down her chin.

She laughed and began to pat away the spill. "I'm sorry, this was just *so good.*"

He didn't even smile, but reached out a thumb and wiped her chin, and then licked it slowly. "No apology necessary."

She didn't move.

"You also missed a spot," he whispered, and gently swiped the rise of her breast with the pad of his thumb where a small splatter had landed. "But you're right. It's so good."

She watched him put the finger in his mouth and slowly extract it. Every place his thumb had briefly landed left tiny needles of want etched across her skin.

"You want some more?" he asked in a barely audible voice.

She nodded, rendered practically mute. "Yes."

He dipped his spoon in and scooped up a small heap. She opened her mouth and slowly closed her eyes.

"You have to tell me how much," he said quietly, moving closer to her. "A little bit or a lot?"

She let the ice cream melt slowly in her mouth before answering or opening her eyes to stare at him. "I'm not sure," she murmured. "All I know is I like it very, very much."

He nodded and took a large glob and swallowed it quickly. "I can dig it. Then I'd better eat this before it melts in my hands."

"Yeah, no sense in wasting it."

"Now that would be a true crime." He stared at her for a moment and then looked down at the bowl. "To let the heat get to it . . . make it all runny, and then not eat it."

"Don't do that," she whispered. "Don't waste it."

"You want some more before I kill it?"

She shook her head no. She'd already melted down.

He removed both spoons, turned the bowl up to his mouth, slurped hard, and then set the dish on the edge of the pool. He looked at her and turned up his palms. "Now I'm all sticky and truly a mess." He dabbed his mouth with the back of his forearm and plunged under the water with a very wicked smile. For a second she'd jumped; her nerves were so bad.

He did a lap and returned to her, shook his hair like a hunting dog coming out of a lake, and raked back his locks. It was the most majestic spectacle she'd ever seen.

"I should probably go get you a towel and let you get some rest. Tomorrow, we've got sightseeing to do, your hotel room to get organized, business to handle, and if you let me, I'd keep you out here all night for company."

"Yeah, that makes sense," she said, wrapping her arms around herself beneath the water and willing her legs to help her stand. "I'll help you put the food away and whatnot."

"Naw, it's cool. I can navigate around the kitchen pretty good. Besides, if I chip a china plate, then Mrs. Orville can fuss at me for breaking up the dishes and being clumsy."

"I can't imagine you clumsy," she said. It was the truth.

He stopped moving in the water and came very close to her. "Luv, for real, right now, my nerves are pretty bad. I don't tink I could hold a dish steady, right through here."

They just looked at each other.

"I can help you put 'em away," she offered, staring down at the water.

He didn't say a word, just got out of the pool, leaving her slowly. The way he did it was as though one foot was cemented to the bottom of the pool, while the other foot was the rational one, making him tear himself away from sure professional disaster. The erotic charge that he left in the water behind him felt like two hundred and twenty volts had passed through it. There was no mistake that he wanted her; the Speedos told on him. But he moved away from her like a true gentleman and had gone to fetch a towel.

She got out of the water, teeth chattering in the heat of his wake. She rubbed her arms in an unsuccessful attempt to chase away the gooseflesh that had risen to her skin. Watching him saunter back in her direction, towel wrapped around his waist, slowly opening another towel for her to step into—which would include an embrace—made her shiver more.

"Turn around and lemme dry you off," he said in a tone so low that it sounded like a command. "Can't have you tracking water across the kitchen tile and accidentally slipping on the floor."

She didn't argue, just turned and allowed those fantastic arms to enfold her in warmth and terry. She bit her lip as his forearm grazed her nipples ever so slightly while he tucked in her towel to make it a strapless dress, but she did notice that his body lingered in a slight press against her back. "How about if I wash the china so that wonderful woman doesn't walk into a mess when she comes in the morning, and you stash away the food in the fridge?"

"All right. Teamwork," he said in a low rumble of hot breath against her neck, and then released her.

She almost fell when he walked away.

They moved in the kitchen like choreographed robots—never in each other's way, not saying a word, focused on the task at hand while trying to remember not to touch each other. The music had long stopped playing and there were only the sounds of dishes being set down and the silent padding of bare feet moving back and forth across the floor.

She scavenged her mind for trite, easy conversation, but every brain cell she'd owned had definitely been melted down in the pool. So she washed the fine china by hand, taking her time, trying not to glimpse him as he carried food from the table and put covered dishes into the refrigerator. Then she made a process of drying each piece and setting it on a clean dish towel in a way that would have done her mother proud.

"Oh, don't forget the bowl by the pool," she finally said, forcing her voice to sound light.

"How could I ever forget it?" he said, leaving her rendered mute again.

He came up behind her; she went still. He reached around her, barely brushing his arm against hers, and set the bowl with two spoons in the sink. She didn't move for a second. He lingered in the body heat discovered within the inches between them. She turned on the water. He stepped back and leaned against the center island, his intense gaze boring into her back as she worked.

"You know," she said, searching for acceptable conversation, "I've been listening to your choices of music this evening."

He didn't answer; she prattled on, her nerves making her talk quickly and lather the dirty dishes with jerky motions.

"I wouldn't have thought you'd put on smooth jazz. I don't know why, but that puzzled me. Like, what's your inspiration? How do you come up with stuff out here all by yourself?"

"Sound," he said quietly. "It's all around us, in everythin', luv."

"Yeah, I know, but . . ."

"The stuff that's being sampled today is taken from artists who actually played the instruments you hear, and they got that in their heads from the natural sounds around them—that's why they're always the foundation of what gets layered on top. I listen to the classic oldies, jazz, R&B, rock, all the originals, and then layer upon what's been built."

She turned to face him, having stalled at the task of washing out one bowl and two spoons long enough. The kitchen was clean, all countertops wiped, and the food was put away. She had to keep the conversation on some professional topic, or say good night—but there was no way she could endure another erotic encounter with him and not give in.

"That's what I like about your style, though," she said, nodding and meaning every word. "You can actually play several instruments, and it's like your songs are built—no, designed—with the instrument in mind, and the samples beneath them are always those songs that make you go, 'Oh, yeah . . . I remember that cut!' But the ones you choose actually compliment the instruments and lyrics you've selected—it's so deep to me. You understand what I'm saying? Then you add this extra funky, natural beat that just blows me away, you know what I'm saying?"

She was talking with her hands now, excited to have come up with an engaging topic that she was truly passionate about, that they could groove on without things getting too crazy again. But for some reason, his eyes had nearly slid shut. He seemed to be taking shallow inhales through his nose, as though he could barely breathe.

"I know, I sound like a fool, right?" she said, making herself chuckle. "I probably sound like some crazed fan. I am, but I'm not; I just appreciate what you do . . . and I'm no musician, so I find the whole creative process really fascinating, is all I'm saying. Like . . . as a kid, did you just wake up one day and know you could play, or had to play? You know what I'm saying?"

He held up his hand, grimaced, and closed his eyes.

"I know, I know. It's late and I'm asking you ridiculous questions. I wouldn't answer me, either, you've probably been asked this mess a thousand times and it's old. You don't have to answer me." She wrapped her arms around herself and found a tile on the floor to stare at.

"I'm not answering you right now because I can't," he said quietly.

She looked up at him and met what seemed like pain in his eyes.

"I'm sorry," she whispered.

"You're taking me wrong," he said on a thick swallow. "I didn't know you liked my work like that, had really felt it, heard what was in it." He paused and let out a heavy breath. "I never thought a sister like you might be able to hear the respect for the classics in it. . . . I just . . . never had my work deconstructed like that."

Instantly, she understood. It made her lean back against the sink and hold onto it to keep from falling down, much in the same way he was gripping the butcher block island. Never in her wildest dreams would she have imagined that what to her was innocuous banter would so flatter and turn him on that he could barely stand.

She could only stare at him; he couldn't even play it off. It was all in the way his chest rose and fell in stuttered breaths and his eyes sought the sliding glass doors, as though trying to fight a losing internal battle. His lips had parted and he was breathing through his mouth. Oh . . . Lord . . . no man had looked like that for her, *ever*.

Maybe it was her own body talking, mischief, curiosity,

or all of the above, but while she had him on the ropes, open and vulnerable and something so much more, she decided to take a risk and push the envelope.

"J.B." she murmured. "How do you compose?"

He closed his eyes and wiped both palms down his face. "Come 'ere. I'll show you."

She froze.

"It's nothing sexual, but it is a very sensuous process."

She pushed away from the sink. The word had been said, at least, and he was holding the line better than she at the moment. "Okay."

He stepped away from the center island and stood her before him, and then turned her around. He extended his arms out to the sides. "Follow me. Extend your arms to take in energy and spread your legs in a solid stance to ground it. I'm gonna show you something metaphysical and very deep."

"All right," she whispered in a reverent tone, doing as he'd requested. A master musician had taken her as a pupil, and anticipation to learn bubbled within her.

"Close your eyes."

She did what he'd asked, and could feel the body heat wafting from him to her as her arms hovered millimeters above his flesh.

He slowly rotated his palms upward to graze hers. "In a few moments, if you remain very still, you should begin to feel electricity, almost like static charge between our palms."

She waited, and was rewarded with the sensation. "Yeah."

"Uh-huh," he murmured. "Now let me guide one palm to your solar plexus and the other to your lower belly. Breathe in and out and draw in air down to your diaphragm."

"Okay," she whispered, feeling tingly and light-headed and so aroused that pulling in air was a challenge.

His broad palms covered hers, almost fusing to them and adding a layer of heat that she never knew a touch could generate through cloth. Yet he remained immobile, calmly taking in and releasing air into his body, his pelvis only a millimeter away from her back-side, so close that a very deep breath would have made her brush against him. It almost hurt to stand that close, that still, in such an intimate embrace with him. But he was teaching her some deep Zen whatever, and she was down to learn what this whole thing that he did was about.

Fascination congealed with want and, oddly, also felt like a very comforting, natural position for them . . . which didn't make sense, because they'd only just met. But it felt like forever, standing there like that. She could feel her heartbeat pulsing between her legs and the urge to lean back and hold his hips almost made her ball her hands into fists. But she didn't. She kept breathing, more deeply, harder, with more force each time.

"Take it in slowly through your nose and let it out through your mouth," he whispered, standing as still as stone behind her.

"All right," she said breathlessly. "It's just hard to . . ."

"I know," he conceded. "We're going to move in a minute, once the energy has found you."

She kept her eyes tightly shut, her focus on everything and nothing, searching for a release. The slight drip of faucet. The hum of the refrigerator. The air conditioning in the background. The slightly loping

whoosh of the overhead fan. A wall clock. The pool
motor pumping. Tree frogs outside. Distant surf. His
breaths, slow, steady, deep. Hers. Anything to capture
and pull into herself the way she wanted him inside
her right now.

"Tell me what you hear?"

"Everything," she gasped.

"What do you feel?"

"Everything," she whispered. "My skin's on fire."

He nodded and pulled her into a real hug from
behind and rested his chin on her shoulder. "I know.
So's mine."

"Is that how you do it?"

He nodded his breath hot against her ear. "Yeah . . .
you've gotta take it all in, get still, and hear the universe speaking to you."

He rubbed the back of her hands, allowing his fingers to splay against her stomach, beyond it. Her
breath hitched. She wanted the towel gone.

"I'm composing right now. Keep breathing."

"I can't," she admitted.

She felt him stop breathing.

"You have to, or I won't be able to," he whispered
between his teeth.

She slid her palms from beneath his and then covered them so they'd press against her belly. She had to
feel his touch, needed it like the breath she could
barely draw in. Immediate heat shook her. The low
noise he released deep within his chest made her lean
back on him, and it ripped a gasp past her vocal cords.
She could feel his hard length pushing against her
backside, almost parting the halves of it through the
towel, and the sensation sent a shiver through her that
seemed to connect to a shudder that ran through him
and back into her again.

"Oh, God . . ." he whispered harshly, kissing her shoulder, her neck and her cheek in a quick, frantic pattern as his hands played over the surface of her torso.

Swallowed in a wash of heat, she reached back and held his hips against her, making the seal between their bodies almost impossible to break. The sound of his breathing was her undoing; it made her move, creating more sound, wet fabric friction that made her yank at the terry barrier and hear it thud at her feet. His towel followed, but the gasp he released when his wet suit hit hers made her dig her nails into the flesh beneath them.

His hands parted in a smooth hot sweep, up and down her torso, finding the edge of her tankini top, burning her stomach until they reached her breasts, and made the ache that had been there for too long worsen. Her response was an immediate arch. She couldn't have censored the moan he caused if she'd wanted to. She'd always been the lover, not the loved, not the touched to exquisite fire. Parts of her anatomy had been groped but never caressed like this, never cared over or fondled until her entire body shrieked for more.

Half crazed, she writhed beneath his palms, her skin soaking up the sensations he wrought, inhibitions peeling away with each gently delivered brush of skin against skin. Every facet of his member she could feel sliding between her buttocks in long, determined strokes, the ridge of the head making her die where she stood, shaft pulsing. His face hot against the side of hers, his fingers rolling against the hardened pebbles of her breasts; her legs parted, legs widening without her consent.

He'd heard her without words, sending long graceful fingers to the edge of her bathing suit to pet away the fire. The sound, wet, squishing, her bud a key that he played with tender authority, her ear a place for a capella vocals, her name: *Karin. Sweet Karin.* Then she remembered that this wasn't supposed to happen about two seconds before she convulsed in a stuttering wail. Her voice rent the kitchen, bounced off tile and stainless-steel appliances. He hugged her hard until she stopped quaking and then turned her around to face him, his kiss hard, breaking away for air, and his eyes brimming with tears of want.

She heard him without words, and found his mouth and her hands scrabbled at his trunks. Her tongue slid against his in a fervent dance, his lips warm and moist, a perfect fit against hers. She swallowed his moan, took it into her lungs, and breathed it out with a gasp. Slick, wet skin so hot it was hard to hold burned against her palm and demanded that she not break the rhythm. She understood; he'd just taken her there himself.

He answered in shudders, a hard torrid shiver, his hands in her hair, which had been sweated out in the kitchen, standing against butcher block, the unchanged rhythm making his head hang back and eyes roll in ecstasy beneath his lids—then it was all over with his sudden, aching, agonized gasp. Silence. The tick of the clock returned to the kitchen with the refrigerator hum. His breathing, hers—impossible to separate. Damp foreheads touched. A salty emulsion of life covered her hands and had splattered her stomach.

"I'm sorry," he whispered.

"Don't be," she whispered back.

He kept his eyes closed and took in several huge breaths. "This was really messed up. This wasn't supposed to . . . oh, Karin."

She kissed him softly. "The only problem is, we just

cleaned up the kitchen and Mrs. Orville *cannot* find this in the morning."

He enfolded her in his arms and laughed softly between deep breaths. "Wanna come to my room?"

"I think maybe we should quit while we're ahead."

He grudgingly nodded. "Maybe you're right, I suppose."

"If we keep going," she said, still stroking him, allowing her hands to revel in the slick wetness, amazed that he was still hard, "we might not be able to stop." It was next to impossible to part with him; no man had ever made her experience what he just had like this. As she continued to touch him, need and curiosity battled for dominance within her, chasing away the tiny voice of reason.

He pulled in a deep inhale that hissed through his teeth. The sound made her crazy and increased her tempo. Watching his passion spread across his face made her feel so alive, so beautiful, so wanted, that she knew right then she couldn't go back to feeling anything less.

"Then you've gotta stop, baby. It's been way too long since—all right?"

She stopped stroking him but couldn't immediately let him go. "I hear you."

He laid his cheek on the crown of her head, wincing. "No, you don't," he whispered, beginning to pump against the small orifice her fingers had created. His hands covered her hips and then swept over her behind, searching for the edge of the swimsuit to pull it away. "You are so lush, dear Gawd, woman, every curve is just right."

She let him go and hugged him

"You sure you don't want to?" he said, breathing hard against her neck.

"I do, but how can I look people in the eye and tell them I haven't slept with you? They'll know I—"

"You won't be asleep, I promise."

She chuckled, but the way his hands repeatedly circled her butt and ran over the mound of it had made her hot again. "I know, and you know what I mean. At least let's try to . . ."

"Baby, I'm down to try whatever you want. Just say it."

"We have to try to chill until at least my boss goes home—"

"Then let's get it all out of our systems tonight— hard down, go for broke, then tomorrow we can chill until he leaves. I'll come up with a reason, somethin' for you to stay. Baby, please."

Panic claimed her as reality slowly reentered her mind. "We've gotta clean up the kitchen."

He closed his eyes and let out a long breath, slowly, removing his palms hand by hand from her backside, and then made fists with them so he wouldn't touch her again. She gently hoisted his trunks back into place.

"I'll clean up the kitchen," she whispered, an apology resonant in her tone.

"That's how this got started," he said, offering her a lopsided smile.

"Not really," she murmured, her tone still gentle and apologetic. "You broke out some metaphysical mess on me."

"I was composing," he argued with a quiet chuckle. "Shit . . . still am . . . in my head."

"Hand me some paper towels," she said, trying her best to ignore him, without success.

He grabbed down a handful and thrust them towards her. "Lock your door tonight. I'm irrational, luv."

"I will," she promised, giving him her back to consider as she began cleaning up. "'Cause me too."

He remained very still, watching her wash her hands and bend to get the disinfectant under the sink. "I didn't need to know that," he whispered, his eyes glued to her every move.

She stopped but didn't set down the items she grasped. "Yes, you did. It was like that from the moment I saw you. I've lost every professional bone in my body—I'm liquefied for you and I'm supposed to be your accountant. Not good."

He nodded. "I was dying on the plane."

"Me too," she whispered and began aggressively cleaning what she'd already cleaned.

He briefly closed his eyes, pushed away from the wall, and headed for the door. "Good night, Karin. I gotta go work this off in the studio. If I go to bed, I'll lose my mind."

"I hear you. That's why I'm cleaning so hard."

Chapter 9

Either her mind had turned to mango chutney or it had accidentally gotten washed down the kitchen sink when she'd done the dishes. Probably both. All she was quite sure of as she stood before the formidable shower in the guest suite was that she didn't know how to work the danged contraption. However, the last thing she was going to do was reopen Pandora's box by going down the hall toward Jacques's bedroom or studio to ask him to show her how to use it. Now how would that seem?

After a full five minutes of fidgeting with dials and brass levers and getting surprise bursts of pulsing sprays of either freezing or steaming-hot water, she finally was able to figure out how to get the multiple shower heads to all spew the same temperature, even if each one ejected water in its own rhythm.

Karin stripped off her soiled bathing suit, carefully sudsing and rinsing it before wringing it out and hanging it across the shower door to dry. She meticulously inspected the damp towel, giving it the sniff test, and then hurriedly placed it in the hamper where she'd been shown dirty laundry for that room should go. All evidence of any impropriety had to vanish before Mrs. Orville came back in the morning. She stepped into the spray, feeling oddly like a teenager who had been sneaking around with a boyfriend while her mother was at work. Why that visceral impression leapt into her brain was silly, but it felt real.

Pummeled by a thousand beads of water in different beats per second, she leaned into the spray and closed her eyes. Her hair had to get wet. Damn. Jacques had lost his mind, run his fingers through it after touching her, and all she could imagine was hugging Mrs. Orville in the morning, or shaking hands with her boss later that afternoon, with the heat of St. Lucia bringing the scent of raw sex to her new coif. Now how would that seem?

Karin squeezed her eyes more tightly shut and pumped shower gel from the brass rack into her hand. New day, new scents; this never happened, no. This wonderful, fantastic, sexy man was not her boyfriend, he was her client. *Get over it, girlfriend,* she firmly told herself as she lathered her hair and body. It was situational. They were both under duress. He'd been celibate a while, strangely enough . . . wow. Okay. But, in a way, so had she.

Memories of being with Lloyd scampered through her mind, and she made a face like she'd tasted something sour. It *was* sour. Most of it. In the beginning, she'd been thrilled that someone like him had chosen someone like her. Their first encounter had been . . . well . . . basic. He'd taken her to dinner and talked about himself the entire evening. They'd come back to her place to sit on her sofa, where he'd talked about his plans for his career some more, and she'd made coffee that he didn't care for. It wasn't the right strength, wasn't the right brand, didn't have cinnamon in it. She should have known right then that he was a jerk . . . if her self-esteem had allowed her to.

Karin sighed and rinsed the soap out of her hair. Eventually, Lloyd had kissed her that night. But now, thinking back on it, the kiss had contained a certain entitlement, as though the dinner and his time deserved no less. It wasn't like the kiss she'd just shared, which was ardent, breathless; something a man was grateful to have bestowed upon him, as though it were a gift.

The more she thought about it, the more outraged she became at her own lack of self-worth, then. Had she known then what she was aware of now, she would have flat-palmed Lloyd in the center of his chest and asked him to leave. He hadn't been entitled to her body in exchange for a dinner or his so-called precious time—not when a superstar with mega millions didn't appear to behave as though he were the least bit entitled to anything.

In fact, Jacques Bernard Dubois seemed as unsure as she, as hopeful—unless she was reading what she'd seen in his eyes wrong. Lloyd had only been her second real boyfriend, the first being a six-month flame in college. All those before that fool and Lloyd had been serial dates, casual hookups that never materialized into anything more, and wanna-be booty callers. High school, college, and then the hectic workaday world didn't really provide a good training ground for any of this. None of her girlfriends had had a clue either, and she sure wasn't asking her mother intimate things like that. The truth was, she really hadn't had enough relationship experiences to figure it all out, and all of it was confusing as hell.

But what was markedly clear was that Jacques had been gentleman enough to see her intrinsic value as a human being, and had calmly said good night when she'd said no, even with his dick still hard. On the other hand, when she'd hesitated that first time with Lloyd, not sure if she was ready, he'd almost become surly, and she'd given in, not wanting him to leave and never come back. Screw Lloyd Jacobs. He wasn't entitled to squat. She wanted to punch a wall, suddenly becoming angrier with herself than with Lloyd.

She kept her eyes closed as she let the water beat against her body. The signs had all been there from the beginning. With an admirable comparison to any man she'd ever known, it was crystal clear. Jacques had shared his life in conversation, not bludgeoned her with it, and the conversation had flowed both ways. Lloyd had touched her a little bit once lovemaking was imminent, and then the deed was swiftly done. He'd rolled over satisfied; she'd basked in the glow of just being made love to by a guy like him. She didn't expect the big O, didn't really know how to achieve it or ask him to take her there, and figured, until now, that's what it felt like. None the wiser; that was the way it had always been. There was no music, she noted. Never was, not even with her first love . . . especially not with him. It was all about a quickie in the dorms.

Yeah. Every time was sorta like that, as she recalled. Always about Lloyd, when he wanted it, her going to lengths to please him, and him accepting whatever she would do—that was their foreplay, her offering, him accepting, but he'd never made her actually reach a peak . . . and this man down the hall had done that without even entering her. And Lloyd Jacobs was a freaking doctor! A doctor?

The realization made her angry, and she soaped her body harder, watching the spray hit her legs and stomach and shoulders and chest. The water hit every part of her, just like Jacques' hands had—comprehensive, gentle, a different stroke and rhythm for the different textures of her skin. His probes against her soft flesh were gentle. The touch exacted pleasure, sharing his body heat in delicious increments with caring hands concerned about her. He had caring eyes that waited until her body language said it was all right to proceed. He was a man who listened very hard and acutely to everything around them, heard her breaths and measured his tempo by that, not just his own needs. Whew . . .

Karin placed one hand against the tile to hold herself upright in the spray. Rivulets of water streamed over her breasts, making them ache for his touch there again. Every other part of her had returned to life as she'd clutched the recent sweet memory within the secret compartment of her heart. The way his hand slid down her belly and slipped beneath her bathing-suit bottom; just the thought made her swell and moisten again for him.

She had to get out of the shower. The water reminded her too much of his caress. This was a client, not a boyfriend, and this had all gotten out of hand because of time, circumstances and stress. She had to get it straight and keep it straight in her own mind. Therefore, she needed to get out of the gentle spray that lit her skin on fire, put a towel on her head, find her nightgown and robe, jump into bed, go to sleep, leave this alone, shake off the new heat created by just thinking about Jacques Dubois. What a man.

The cold spray that hit his body almost made him holler, and he made quick work of soaping up and washing off fast and getting out of the damnable shower. He hadn't had to do anything like this since he'd been in high school, for chrissake!

Karin Michaels had stolen his peace of mind. The woman was a gorgeous sanity thief. A robber baroness. A mental interloper. If he ever told any of his boyz about this, and he never would—this went to the grave—they'd tell him he'd lost his mind. Was crazy. Yeah, he was. Because how in the hell did a man just flip out in his own kitchen, having only met a woman forty-eight hours ago?

He'd been a playa. A global force of nature. No. Uh-uh. Any fool knew you didn't mix business with booty. It wasn't done, if you wanted to keep your mind on your money. Not to mention the girl was stubborn. Was all rules and regulations. What sister didn't want to go shopping? Unheard of! Wouldn't even let Mrs. Orville bring out the food. Bossy!

And had the nerve to sashay her fine behind all around his kitchen and pool, making him want her more than whatever Mrs. Orville had cooked. Crazy. Acted like his room was the last place on earth she wanted to be, when he had women all over the world throwing their thongs on the stage and begging to come with him to any room he occupied. Hallways, backstage, in a car, they didn't care. But, noooo . . . Miss Karin wasn't having any of that. Cool.

Jacques toweled his body off hard and flung the offending texture across the room. It didn't feel like her, and he wanted no part of it touching him right now. No comparison. A towel had blocked him access to her wonderful, satiny brown skin—*he hated towels!*

He angrily snatched up a pair of green scrubs that his sister had given him from the hospital. Comfort. The raggedy, worn drawstring pants were the most comfortable thing he could think of to put on, especially since the erection wouldn't go down. Green. Damn, Karin looked so good in green . . . bright lime that set off her fantastic brown skin.

No. He wasn't going there. She was right. This had gotten out of hand; this was about business. He needed to handle his, and she needed to handle hers . . . but damn, she had such soft hands. Stop. Reset the brain. Scratch that. He rubbed his hips. Whew . . . she'd scratched him, too. Just clutched him tightly and dug her nails in when she came. No, he was not going there! Tomorrow his sanity-stealer would be out of his house and safely deposited at the Hilton, an hour and a half away. Good riddance.

He peered at his bed. "Go to the studio, mon," he told himself out loud. "Be productive."

He had to get out of the bedroom. Too many thoughts were jumbling around in his brain. As he exited the room, he willed himself not to even glance down the hall toward the direction of her room. *Keep walking. You can make it. Shake it off. Think music. That's what funds this joint. Always the music first. Everything else is secondary. Stop tripping. She made it perfectly clear that she wasn't going beyond third base. Accept the fact. No means no. Walk. The studio. One foot in front of the other, brother.*

Jacques pushed the studio door open and flipped on the light. He stood inside the expansive room and briefly closed his eyes, steadying himself for a moment with a deep, cleansing breath. The quiet was surreal within the soundproofed space. Good.

She'd invaded his sanctuary, had allowed her voice to soak into his walls and imprint itself on his brain. It was good not to hear anything but the sound of his own breath and heartbeat thudding in his ears. Now maybe he could think. Normal house noise would just be a reminder of her short pants, which had been indelibly linked to the sound of a kitchen clock, the drip of a faucet, and the hum of the refrigerator. The woman was welded to all of it, just like she had threaded her hands around him, and was fused to the heavy ache that wouldn't go away.

His groin contracted with the thought, and it made him open his eyes and go over to the baby grand piano and sit down. He needed to play. Something, anything, to put a new sound in his head. Her gasp had filled it up. Her laughter and soft sighs, her sassy responses when he was teasing her were all up in his head. That's what he needed to do; chase her out of his mind. She was renting space in his brain, and he allowed no one to do that—especially while he was working. No.

Before any of this had gone as far as it had, he should have made the big head think wiser, rather than allowing the little head to temporarily take control. Problem was, she'd entered the big head first and now practically owned the smaller one. Jacques shook his head, flinging water from his locks everywhere.

Water. When she'd stepped into the pool water, it was all he could do to stay away from her. When she'd gotten wet just for him, he thought he'd lose his mind. He'd never dreamed she'd be so passionate in his arms, at least not so soon. Then she'd seemed to realize that she shouldn't have and had backed away.

But as frustrating as it was, he couldn't really be angry at her. If he was honest with himself, it wasn't even like she was playing some female game. He'd seen every game out there, and this was raw truth she'd shown him. Pure, unadulterated battle against what one *should* do and what one *wanted* to do.

It was written all over her face: the desire, the struggle, the shock that she'd gone there, the repressed need that followed as she viciously cleaned the already sparkling countertops. *That's* what was messing him up. It was genuine; he knew where she was coming from. There was no fraud in how badly she wanted to be with him, too. It was just that her brain and social mores were working way better than his had been. He sighed. He liked her brand of honesty, no matter how inconvenient the backhanded blessing was. Not many people in his life, save his boyz and Mrs. Orville, had been honest with him.

And all Karin Michaels wanted from him was his respect, and maybe his friendship. Not money, not fame, not presents, not a relationship, not anything more than what any good person deserved. Deep. She definitely had that from him, if she'd only trust him.

But then again, how could she really trust him after he'd stepped to her sexually when he'd said he wouldn't, and then made her feel things that she obviously hadn't felt in a while? He'd said it wasn't going to go there, and when he'd told her that, he'd meant it . . . things, admittedly, just ran hot all of a sudden. It wasn't intentional, or some game he was trying to play on her. . . . It just happened, ignited; her standing so close, being all of who and what she was.

Guilt stabbed him. He should have been more in control. The sister deserved better. Yet it boggled his mind that her body had responded to him the way that it had, given that up until twenty-four hours ago, she'd had a man. It was unconscionable to think that that Lloyd's ass hadn't thoroughly and completely kept a woman like Karin Michaels totally satisfied. And the man called himself a doctor? Pitiful. What were they teaching in medical schools? he wondered.

Jacques stared at the droplets that had hit the ivory keys and then made the mistake of touching an errant drop. His finger slid along the smooth surface and the sensation produced a mild shudder that made him close his eyes again. Admittedly, he had it bad for her, but he refused to be ruled by something as foolish as an urge. But his fingers kept sliding against the keys, reminding him of her . . . the minute separation between each, like her slit, the small rise in black sharp keys, her bud. Damn, she'd even taken over his baby, his piano.

He covered his mouth and nose with his hands and breathed in deeply . . . and then remembered what she smelled like on his hands before he'd showered. Sweet, good Lord.

Okay. Stop, mon, he told himself, nearly shouting the internal command. *Yeah, before you truly humiliate yourself and go to her bedroom door, begging.* No. So what if this woman was the complete package—gorgeous, round, curvaceous, smart, nice, funny, caring, professional, sexy, conservative, and wild. *Focus.* He wasn't in the market for a relationship, and obviously, neither was she. After a few days, she'd be back in the States anyway, and would probably hook back up with her man after the spat they'd had. She had a life; so did he. Two separate and nonintersecting paths to follow. He had to remember that.

Jacques depressed the keys, filling the room with a new sound that chased his thoughts away. Words began to form in his head as the rich, melodic timbre of the instrument echoed throughout the studio and vibrated against his bones. *I know we've both got things to do, and I only have serious respect for you—but baby, don't you hear me dying out loud?*

"Cut that shit out, man. Too syrupy!" he hollered at himself, and repositioned his hands on the keys.

Jacques cocked his head to the side, closed his eyes and began again. "'Dying out loud.'" He nodded. "That works." A hook leapt into his consciousness. It had a long, soulful, ballad melody to it that made his hands race across the keys in classic flourish. A combination Michael MacDonald/John Lucien sound began to evolve as he tinkered, stomping pedals with his bare foot.

> While I'm trying to hold on
> I'm ready to figure out a way . . .
> While I promise to be strong
> I'm searching, can't stand another day . . .

"Get the hell up from the piano, mon, and stop trippin'." He laughed and leaned his head against the instrument. "Woman got you talking to yourself and composing like you're some lovesick kid."

But the music in his head just wouldn't stop. Drawn back to the keys of their own volition, his fingers arched and pressed down hard, just like everything in his mind did, until it filled up his soul and poured out against the ivory.

Head thrown back, eyes closed, he belted it all out, telling himself the whole while it was just an exercise to purge his system so he could then really work.

> Don't you hear me dying out loud?
> Every time I'm near you,
> the pain just slips away.
> Don't you hear me crying out loud?
> Baby, know I hear you, feel what words won't let you
>   say. . . .

He stood up and stepped over the piano bench, and then walked in a circle, raking his locks. He owed her an apology.

A light tap at the bedroom door made her sit bolt upright and stare at the knob. She hadn't been asleep, couldn't get her mind or body to stop racing, and she knew she looked a fright. Her hair had to be standing on top of her head since her dryer and curling iron wouldn't fit into the foreign sockets. Another light tap almost put her heart in her mouth.

"Yes?" she said as casually as she could the moment she could breathe again.

"Uh, Karin. It's me. Jacques."

She just stared at the door. Like, who else would it be at almost three in the morning? "Yes?" she said, as nonchalant as possible.

"Can I apologize to you?"

The gentle tone in his voice ran all through her like pristine rain-forest water. The bass line in it was so low that she could swear she'd felt it through her skin. She stood up too fast and almost fell from the tangle of sheets that had somehow wound through her legs while she'd been tossing and turning. "Uh, just a minute. Lemme find my robe."

Quickly flipping on the nightstand light, she glanced across the room at the full-length mirror and nearly shrieked, and then began hacking at her hair with her fingers, forcing it to at least lie down in a wavy, blunt-edged bob. She raced around the side of the bed like a nut, and snatched on the baby-blue silk robe that thankfully matched her teddy.

But as she neared the door, she glanced at herself again. Dang! No makeup, looking crazy, bed a heap, and the man comes to the bedroom door. Plus, once she opened it, what was she gonna do? Did she just go ahead and sleep with him, or gently rebuff him—that is, if he was even thinking like she'd been—but of course he had been. The way they'd parted in the kitchen left little room for doubt. *Oh, maaaan . . . what to do, what to do, what to do?*

She opened the door and pasted on the most serene expression she could. He was standing there with no shirt on, in just a pair of green hospital scrubs, his majestic locks tousled about his fine black shoulders. Jesus . . .

"Karin, listen," he said quietly, taking up her hands. "I'm sorry I sorta pressured you in the kitchen, and I don' want you ta think I don't respect you or know your job and public image with your firm are important. I just wanted you to know that, and have a chance to say it before Mrs. Orville comes over to make breakfast, and so you don' feel all weird tomorrow when your boss finally arrives. Needed to get that off my chest, 'cause I like you, girl. You're good people, and I sorta fell back on my word in da kitchen."

She could only nod and look down. His gaze was too serious, too intense, and it was releasing the butterflies again after they'd just settled down for the night.

"It's all good," she murmured. "We both sorta got carried away and caught up in the moment."

"Yeah," he said, letting his breath out hard. "But I'd said it wasn't gonna go there, and it did. Which was my fault, because you were just making conversation, talking, asking questions, and I . . ." He paused and looked away. "I should have said good night earlier. That's all I'm trying to say. I'm sorry."

"Apology accepted, but not necessary," she said quietly. "I could have excused myself earlier, too."

He smiled a half smile. "No bad vibes? You still wanna work with me?"

She smiled a half smile. "No bad vibes. You still want me as your accountant?"

"Yeah."

His eyes searched hers, and a gentle understanding passed between them.

"Good," she whispered. "I'd hate for what happened to ruin things."

"Me too," he said in a near whisper. "Couldn't stop thinking about how crazy it got . . . how maybe it happened too fast."

She nodded. "Friends again?"

He smiled wider. "Yeah, Miss Karin. Friends is good. I like that . . . 'cause, if you haven't noticed, I also really like you."

"Same here. I do really like you, too." She released a small sigh. "No matter what happens, I really want to keep liking you."

"Me too."

She smiled wider and looked away again. "Then it's settled. No pressures, mon," she teased.

He laughed. "Noooo pressures."

Silence engulfed them in awkwardness.

"You sleepy?"

She nervously glanced over her shoulder at the bed. "Not really. Weird, isn't it? I should be dog tired."

He glimpsed her gnarled sheets. "I hear you."

She swallowed a shy smile, but noticed that he hadn't let go of her hands.

"I should be knocked out, right about now. But couldn't sleep. Started working on some new music."

"Yeah?" She perked up and couldn't keep the smile away from her mouth.

Anticipation shot through him. Her eyes had ignited it, the spark within them just enough to threaten reason.

"You wanna hear what I was working on?"

"You would let *me* come into your *studio* while you *work?*"

Why had she said it like that . . . all breathy and excited, with the low lights sparkling in her big brown eyes? Why had he put the bait out there, knowing it was the wrong thing to do, a bad move, when the only reason he was at her door was to offer her a legitimate apology?

"Yeah," he heard his voice say without sanction from his brain. "I got inspired. . . . And since we're friends, I'll let you hear it, even though it's really raw and not finished."

"Really!"

If she didn't lower the enthusiasm wattage, he was gonna burn.

"Cool," he said, as casually as he could. "Studio's right down the hall." He let go of her hands. Had to. Turned his back to her bed. Had to. Lifted his chin and focused on the long hallway ahead. Needed to. Could hear her bare footfalls following him in the direction of his bedroom, and banished the concept. *Studio, studio, head for the studio, do not stop, do not make a left turn, keep walking.*

He opened the door for her with unnecessary flourish, unable to help himself, and then stood back to allow her to enter the room. She turned around in a slow circle with her hand covering her mouth, giving him glimpses of her nude form beneath the thin fabric of powder-blue satin that washed over her sheen of brown skin, her body making it flow like a gentle surf. He was done. But her voice was his complete undoing as she gasped at the surroundings.

"Oh . . . Jacques."

He nearly closed his eyes.

"This is me," he said, struggling to sound nonchalant.

"Oh, my God . . ."

He needed to sit down before he fell down. "Yeah, this is where I work out stuff in my head," he said offhandedly, moving to the piano.

"This is fabulous. . . ."

Mic check? Shit, he needed a pulse check or an ambulance.

"It's a'ight. Just space."

"Are you crazy?" she said sweeping around the room and peering at everything. "Look at all this equipment. I don't know what half of this stuff does! The wood floors look like glass! Is that the sound booth back there?"

"Uh-huh." He'd been reduced to monosyllables.

He watched her find the very center of the room, close her eyes, open her arms the way he'd shown her in the kitchen, and then begin to twirl in a slow circle, as though she were a human antenna trying to pick up a signal. Mesmerized, his hands automatically depressed keys out of reflex.

The ballad that he'd been working on just came off the ends of his fingertips out of the blue. Her head dropped back, she stopped twirling around, and it made him play that much harder for her, made him find his voice. The congested words that had been trapped in his diaphragm erupted and demanded that he belt them out. She wrapped her arms around herself; it brought new lyrics to his mind, made him work even harder against the instrument, abuse it.

He was sweating, she was swaying. The room was

suffocating, no air. When he stopped, she opened her eyes. All he could do was stare at her for a moment, breathing hard.

"That's what was keeping me up tonight. Had to get it out." He couldn't pull his eyes away from her. "You like it?"

She didn't immediately answer, just simply closed her eyes. "I have to go back to my room."

Neither of them moved.

"You didn't like it. . . . Like I said, it was raw, not commercial. I was—"

"I have to go back to my room before I'll have to apologize to you for crossing the line."

She opened her eyes. He wiped his brow with the back of his forearm.

"You liked it?"

She nodded. "It's a masterpiece."

He looked away, couldn't take the strain.

"You came up with that, *just like that*? In a few hours . . . out of the blue?"

He still couldn't look at her. "I was inspired."

"That was genius," she whispered.

"You should go back to your room, before I have to apologize again."

"You wrote that for me?"

"Yeah."

"No apology necessary."

He swallowed hard and returned a gaze to her. "If I get up from this bench, there will be. I ain't that much a gentleman."

He watched her hesitate. His breathing still hadn't evened out. Nor had hers, and that battle, that struggle, was in her eyes again. She wrapped her arms around herself in a tight, personal hug.

"No man has ever written me a love letter, or a poem,

or even given me a corny holiday-greeting card . . .
much less even flowers," she said, so softly that he
almost couldn't hear her. "For any special occasion, I've
only received excuses, or a gift that the man giving it to
me hadn't really thought about. I'm not talking price;
I mean, there was no feeling, nothing special to it that
said he'd picked it out just for me. And here some guy
who I really don't even know, who's supposed to just be
a client, goes down into his soul, touches a spark in the
universe, and gives me a piece of something God gave
him—a little bit of his talent sectioned off and created
just for me? And he's just a friend, I haven't even slept
with him, and he doesn't expect that?"

She shook her head as her voice became shaky. "No
apology necessary. I owe you one for getting all
simple-acting and whatnot while standing in the
middle of your studio."

He watched huge tears quickly well in her eyes and
then fall. She turned away wiping her face, seeming
embarrassed by the naked emotion. It put him on his
feet, pulled him across the room, and somehow made
his arms enfold her. Yet she wouldn't turn around
when he initially tried to get her to look at him. A repressed sob shook her petite form, and then gave way
to a good, hard cry.

Finally she allowed him to turn her and hold her
and rock her. But she still wouldn't look at him. He so
wanted her to do that in order for her to see the truth
in his eyes; she needed to witness no evidence of fraud
as he spoke.

What she had told him was a travesty that made
moisture form beneath his shut lids as he gently
kissed the top of her hair. How in the world could this
gorgeous woman have been treated so badly by his
kind, he wondered? The injustice stabbed him,

turned like a blade right behind his ribs as he rubbed her back, felt her shaky breaths enter and exit her body. It made him softly press her head to his chest, stroke her velvety damp hair, and repeatedly murmur her name to soothe her.

When she'd calmed, he lifted her face and kissed the tears off her cheeks, then chased away the streaming runnels with his thumbs. No woman had ever so honestly wept from simply hearing his work, or had so appreciated that it had been composed just for her. He'd never been so quietly, privately moved in all his life.

"Karin . . . luv . . . I can't profess to understand what's on another man's mind—why he might have done what he did or didn't do. All I can say is this, they were stupid. If they threw away the gem that I have in my arms right now, I'll gladly take it as the gift it is. Their loss; my gain. I don't care what people think. I just know what I'm feeling right now, and what inspired me . . . what captured me from the moment I saw you . . . your honest heart, your beautiful, friendly eyes, the way you see the world with dignity and gentleness of spirit. . . . But I will respect however you want this to go down, because I always want to have you think well of me."

Her voice was lodged in her throat behind a new torrent of tears threatening to break free. If this man only knew what his words and his impassioned song had meant to her. He'd called her beautiful; not just said it, but conveyed it in his eyes in a way she'd never seen it reflected. The level of respect that he'd demonstrated left her speechless. His gentle embrace was so tender, not forced or sexual, but an easy, caring hold . . . the way his eyes searched her face, as though he were trying to look past skin and bone to see what was inside her, staring down to her soul, while opening his so she could also glimpse it. Sharing. His voice was mellow, honest, even though his body was eager for more . . . his touch, tender, so light against her back that it was sensual and awakening.

"I will always think well of you, Jacques Dubois," she whispered.

Then her body responded in a way she couldn't have imagined. It lifted her up on her tiptoes, made her head tilt to find his mouth, needing the warm nourishment it offered. She watched him close his eyes slowly as her own lids eclipsed the room around them. His hold tightened as his tongue found hers, salty tears mingling with the dinner they'd shared. Thoughts of tomorrow fled her, taking fear with it as his hands slid down her shoulders and hers found a path up his back, tracing warm, bare skin.

One long, gentle, probing kiss; no sound but his breath, her breath, in a sound-proofed room. Echoes in her mind, his voice, his music. His body against hers; tall, hard, not moving, as though waiting, almost seeming afraid. Her choice. Her decision. His patience unparalleled. His gentle caresses unraveling her sanity and all stress with it, yet adding new layers to that released tension, peeling away pressures, concurrently building blood volume between her thighs . . . swelling her, wetting her, spilling her until she almost cried out in pain.

He broke from the kiss, needing to fill his lungs up with air, needing to move against her, but he dared not offend, needing a moment to listen, perceive, to see if it was all right with her. Because God only knew he needed it to be.

Not sure, he cradled her face, hands trembling. "Karin, I'm not playing games with you, or just trying to get you—"

She placed a finger against his lips. "I know."

What did that mean? His mind tore at her statement. Was that an *I know, but we still can't go beyond this?* Or an, *I know, I'm ready, too?* Or an *I know, once there's been more time between us?* Never in his life had a woman made him feel like this. Confused. Caring more about the way she'd react than how his body felt.

"Baby—"

Her kiss ended all confusion. It was more aggressive than he'd expected, her body began the dance of subtle movement—dear . . . God . . . the answer was yes.

He found her robe sash, untied it, then made the silk lingerie fall away, and still she didn't stop him or pull out of the kiss. His mind was on fire as his hands came in contact with her overheated skin, and he savored the slow stroke down her shoulders and arms—oh, Jesus, she was a gift. The thin spaghetti straps on her teddy came down with the next caress, and she pulled her arms from under them on her own accord. She did it so subtly, so naturally, that it had buckled his knees, because then he knew for sure.

Her nipples grazed his as she pulled the drawstring of his scrubs loose, which forced him to deepen the kiss, made his hands seek her hair, his tongue twining against hers. Gentle hands slid cotton away from his hips, freed him, creating a pool of cloth at his feet. Cocoa-buttered satin skin against his, tore a moan out of him, gave his hands license to touch her smooth back, tiny waist, full, thick hips, and luscious behind. She was sliding against him, almost like she was a waterfall . . . going down his body in a slow wave of agony that lowered him to meet her until they both wound up on the floor.

Baby-blue silk and green cotton scrubs surrounded

them like they were a single piece of driftwood set afloat on the Caribbean Sea. Their motion a steady, continuous ebb and flow of natural rhythm; her thighs parted, thick and fleshy, wet like the ocean, demanding that he enter to cool off under the heat.

Her mouth, plundered by his tongue, her sea inviting, calling to him a quiet siren's whisper, awaiting his *petite morte*. There was no tomorrow. He slid into the deep ocean, eliciting her cry of pleasure that sent shudders throughout his system, riptides hard and fast, no safety vest—hold up. He was going under. Yet she moved like the surf, unrelenting, undulating, crashing against him in hard returns that he knew no way to avoid, couldn't.

Her hands raced down his back, found the valley in it and then flowed over his ass. Smooth legs had his in a lock, oh, God, she felt so good. Tiny, dark brown pebbles bit into his chest, he just wanted to see them bounce beneath him, and he pushed up to taste her mouth, free her breasts, witness the expression of sheer ecstasy on her face until he could look no more.

Head back, sweat dripping, not enough air in the room, sound forever in his head, of this . . . her name a part of his exhale as he sank deeper, "Oh, Karin."

He wasn't wearing a condom; she had never felt a man without one. The sensation was unspeakable; she was crying it was so good. Her mind had shut down ten minutes ago. Sanity lost; she had to get up before it was too late. It was already too late, but at least she could try. But how did one stop thunder and lightning? How did one stop the rain? That was the Father's province; she didn't have it in her. She was already in heaven, was dying, weeping, hollering like a fool. Didn't care, didn't want to.

Male sweat, earthy and humid, splattered her chest

as it rolled down from a rain-forest-born mountain of pure, solid magma. Black, majestic, strong, and it had come to her, patient. Moving in long hard strokes, now unstoppable. Sending pleasure so vast and wide through her that her toes curled and her hands went to fists at his back . . . she couldn't even hold on. A voice like Thor throwing a hammer tore through her brain. Her name in low, island-male timbre, said correctly, long and slow and oh . . . my . . . God . . .

Fast frantic kisses pelted her face, her neck, his exit so sudden she almost sat up. His head dropped against her stomach made that impossible. Burning hands covered her breasts, and then an even hotter kiss pulled both nipples into his mouth, a tongue suckling the ache until her hands slapped the floor.

His mouth retreated, his sweat-streaked cheek suddenly found her belly. Hands were under her hips, holding her bottom tight, kneading the flesh and putting new tears in her eyes.

"Karin, baby, I've gotta put somethin' on, and fast, okay, you understand what I'm sayin', luv, I almost messed up, oh, my God, woman, don't go nowhere—no, come to my room, a'ight, oh, damn, I can't breathe."

She understood completely. The rapid-fire sentence uttered in near patois made all the sense in the world. But she couldn't speak, could only nod. Had no idea how she would get up off the floor, or if that was even possible. He moved back, and she thought she might have a chance, but his slow lick down her stomach made her close her eyes, arch, and give up with a gasp.

Hot stone hands parted her thighs. . . . Whatever he wanted to do, she couldn't argue. Protest was moot—his mouth had captured her, his tongue had opened her, and her manicure was in jeopardy against polished wood. Sobs of pleasure didn't stop the man, calling his name only drew his hands up her torso to cover her breasts and add more agony. He'd found a spot that she didn't know existed. He was doing something to her that she'd only heard of by many names. He was exploring the natural part of her that had rarely been even touched by human hands, much less by an exquisite mouth, devastating tongue, and the slightest grazing of perfect, white teeth.

But the sound, oh, God . . . the sound of what he was doing to her would live with her forever, if this glorious rapture never happened to her again in life! *Just don't let him stop* . . . right there, he was right there, had found what she never had, oh, baby . . . pulling her hips up off the floor, her breath catching in short bursts of disbelieving ecstasy, dred-locks tickling her thighs as they tried to close against the excruciating pleasure, shoulders like granite holding them open until the first frenzied spasm hit, and slid into another, and another.

She didn't even have time to catch her breath or try to recover. A mad Sagittarian musician had grabbed her around her waist, somehow lifted them both off the floor, and she was over his shoulder caveman style. The wildest thing about it was, she didn't even care. Mrs. Orville could have been standing in the hallway with her arms folded, and she would have simply told the woman: *Stand aside—fire, coming through hot.*

Karin bounced twice on the bed when Jacques dropped her. She watched him intently, couldn't even make out the room nor cared what was in it. Her eyes simply followed him around the room while he tore through dresser drawers, leaving them hanging open. A small part of her was glad that he had to go searching for what he needed—that it wasn't readily available, like a planned, smooth thing he did all the time. The man was visibly panicked. She liked that. It endeared her to him even more. The few moments it took him to destroy his room made her feel like this had never been done for anyone other than her . . . and that was a gift of the subtlest kind.

When he found the box he actually kissed it and made the sign of the cross over his chest. She turned away briefly as not to ruin the moment by laughing, but she could dig it. Where in the world at this time of night in St. Lucia would a man go, stranded on an island of need to score latex? God was good.

She watched him sit on the edge of the bed, breathing like he'd just run a marathon, hands shaking, opening the foil like he was about to disable an explosive. She anxiously watched him. No words. Just temporary insanity. When he finally got the barrier on, something in his eyes made her nervous. He was taking in air through his mouth, blowing it out through his nose like a racehorse, almost snorting. There was not much else to do but ease back against the pillows and prepare to hold on for the ride of her life, that much was clear.

As good as he felt, she couldn't help watching him. The stalk towards her on all fours was swift, his entry immediate, but the look on his face as he sank deep within her was paralyzing.

The expression of agony spread across his face so slowly that it was like watching dawn break. For an interminable moment, he didn't move, just remained lodged within her, holding his breath it seemed, his locks down his back, arms trembling as they held his weight.

Her legs just naturally followed the curve of his butt and found the right niche to lock around that perfect dip in his spine; that's when he released the gasp he'd been holding . . . that's when it became a deep, thunderous moan combined with movement. That's when her hands found his shoulders, and suddenly he dropped to hold her tightly against him, one hand beneath her behind, the other flattened at her back. That's when she really understood how much strength five miles a day in an uphill run could produce. That's when she clenched her jaw so tightly that she almost chipped a tooth and didn't care. *Dental work notwithstanding, just give it all you've got.*

He'd thrust her halfway up the mattress, pushed hard against it to give her head room, but never broke stride—expression so intense that the muscle in his jaw pulsed. She touched his face; he leaned into her palm and nuzzled it, but kept riding. The way he did that finally made her close her eyes.

Every muscle in his body seemed to tighten, strain against skin, became one interlocking band of steel beneath flesh, bringing the sensations within her to a single throbbing point that his thrusts repeatedly stroked. Then he stopped breathing. It was a fraction of a second, the same time she'd stopped breathing, too, and the seizure that followed slammed her as his body convulsed, making her weep, it was so damned good.

For a long time they lay there, entwined, bodies intermittently twitching like they'd been shot. Ever so slowly, he rolled over, pulling her with him without breaking their seal. Her head remained on his chest, listening to his heart thud. He lay there, eyes closed, locks flung every which way across the pillows, petting her back.

Finally she lifted her head.

"Don't move, luv," he whispered, his fingers trembling as they trailed down her spine. "I'm still composing."

Chapter 10

"We have to cut this out before Mrs. Orville comes back!"

Karin squealed and tried to get out of his reach before he pinned her to the bed again.

"She's cool," he murmured against her hair.

"Noooo," Karin giggled, warming under his attention. "I will die if she walks in here and sees me coming out of your bedroom. Please Jacques, don't make that nice lady think bad about me."

He sighed, but didn't immediately let her up. "Mrs. Orville is really cool, Karin. She probably already knows what time it is."

"What!" She pushed him off her while he rolled over with a thud and chuckled. Her line of vision ripped around the expansive room, looking for a clock. "What time is it? She said she'd be back by seven in the morning. My hair is a wreck, I have to take a shower, and how could she possibly suspect . . . ohmigod, you don't think she thinks that's why I really came here, do you?"

"No, but she isn't blind."

Karin folded her arms over her breasts, suddenly

feeling her nakedness, and then grabbed a section of the sheet. "What's that supposed to mean?"

"It means that she's old and wise and probably saw how you'd messed me up real bad when that lizard got on your behind and I tapped that—"

"Don't say it," she squealed and covered her face, dropping the sheet.

"Yeah, girl, when you started jumping up and down, whipped off your skirt, the woman would have to be blind not to know a brother was jacked."

"Oh, Jesus . . ."

"But dat's no slam on your character, luv. Only mine. Now, it could be dat she only saw that hungry dawg look in my eye or the slobber runnin' down my face. Not to cast aspersions on you—since you were cool." He pushed himself up on one elbow, his eyes raking her body. "But I could sure use another meal this morning before Mrs. Orville comes 'cross da road . . . since I know once she's here, I'll be cut off until she goes back home tonight."

Karin held up one hand. "Jacques, I'm not playing. While that nice woman is here, no mess, okay?"

"Then hook a brother up one more time so I can behave myself." He laughed and began coming toward her.

"What time is it?" she asked, backing away.

"I don't know . . . really can't say that I care, right through here."

"But what if she comes in!"

"She won't do that."

Karin folded her arms over her chest. He stopped moving toward her.

"How do you know?"

"If my car hasn't moved, and, uh . . ."

"She doesn't come when you have female company in the house till you call her, right?"

He rubbed his palms down his face. "Luv, you are worse than the feds."

She began walking in circles, looking on the floor for her robe.

"It's in the studio."

She looked up and glared at him, but when he saw tears in her eyes, he got up off the bed and walked toward her.

"Hey, hey, hey, it's—"

"No. That's fine. I understand. She's in your employ. Would necessarily have to have a signal when you're entertaining. Does this all the time, so there's no embarrassment for your guests."

"Not true."

"Yeah, right."

He held up both hands, becoming annoyed. "Last night I was a prince, a sensitive, caring lover; now this morning, what happened?" He snatched up the spread and wrapped it around his waist.

"Nothing!" she said, yanking a damp sheet off the bed and swathing it around herself like a toga. "Ab-so-lute-ly nothing."

She stormed out of the bedroom, down the hallway, and barged into the studio, snatching her robe and teddy off the floor. He stood in the doorway, totally stupefied.

"I have to check into the Hilton. I'll have breakfast there." She spun on him. "You can give Mrs. Orville the secret code that the new girl just left and it's safe for her to come across the street to do your dirty laundry," she said, flinging the sheet at him, "now that you have finished."

"Whoa!" he shouted, body blocking her like a

linebacker as she shifted from side to side, trying to get around him. "I'm offended, Mrs. O doesn't have any secret code, and I tol' you that I don't bring women to my house, Karin!"

"Yeah? Well then how would she know not to come until you called for her, then!" she shouted, her voice bouncing around the studio. "She's done this before, or—"

"She's sixty-five years old, has nine children and twelve grandchildren, and ain't crazy!" he hollered, his voice booming. "She knows young, hot, and falling in love when she sees it, and the woman don' need no special code, glasses, or a psychic to tell her! It's basic math, no rocket scientis' required—you and me, both single, in da same house, vibe so thick between us we could barely eat dinner. She's too ol' and long in the tooth not to recognize what time it is, and she don' need to walk in here and have a heart attack—so she wouldn't just barge in here witout sending up flares, making a racket, to be sure she ain't walk in on nuthin' too risqué! The woman is practical—that's what I love about her. Diplomatic. Didn't you hear her tell *you* she'd call in the morning before she came? Respectful of you as a lady, and if she didn't tink you was a lady, she would have stayed all night and made privacy really impossible, knowing Mrs. O! She's old-school, Karin."

He snatched up the sheet, indignant.

"Oh." Karin swallowed a smile, remembering. "My bad."

"What!" He was so outdone that he walked back and forth for a moment and then folded his arms, his gaze unable to focus on any point in the room.

And did the man say "young, hot, and falling in *love*"? "Jacques, I'm sorry," she said quietly.

"Well you should be," he said, still puffed up. He

raked his locks, feelings hurt. She had no right, after he'd told her the truth. "Secret code . . . like Mrs. Orville would stand for such nonsense, if I even wanted to try it."

Now she really felt bad. Of course a woman like Mrs. Orville wouldn't be party to no booty-call mess. The matriarch was plainly the type to walk off the job over a matter of principle rather than be a coconspirator. Karin's shoulders slumped. Not only had she thought wrong about him, but had offended a lady who was like his mom. Karin closed her eyes and let out a hard sigh.

"Jacques . . . I'm really sorry. I went there because maybe it's still hard for me to believe that you feel . . . well . . . I'm sorry."

When she opened her eyes, the look on his face made her want to run to him, but it also froze her where she stood.

"You are finding it hard to believe that I can feel? Why is that, Karin? Because I'm a man? Because I'm successful? Which is it? Both!"

"No," she said, moving to him before he bolted out of the room.

"Well, that's what you said: Quote 'It's still hard for me to believe that you feel.' Period."

"Oh, my God. No. That was half a sentence."

"Then what's the other half?" He folded his arms and stared at her, hard.

"It's still hard for me to believe that you could feel this way about me—not because of what you aren't, but because of what I'm not. There. Okay?" She turned and gathered up the soiled sheet so that Mrs. Orville wouldn't have to.

"Wait a minute," he said quietly, stopping her with a touch at her elbow. "Is that what this is all about?

You don't think I would want you?" Incredulous, he came closer and lifted her chin with one finger. "Did you hear anything what I said to you last night?"

She looked away, pulling her chin off his finger.

"So, now I'm a liar?"

She glanced at him, relieved that his dashing smile had returned. "No."

"Then what is it? I can't coax you into the shower with me, so you're putting up all this fuss to derail my dishonorable intent?"

She chuckled. "No."

"No I can't coax you, or no you don't believe me?" His arms found their way around her, just as his mouth brushed hers.

She gently broke the kiss and leaned her head against his chest. "You have all this stuff going for you and—"

"And I'm still a man. Flesh and blood. And a woman has never inspired me to come up with anything just for her." He made her look at him, lifting her chin again. "I won't lie; I've composed for women, plural, as in the species itself—the whole. I've written about them, talked good and bad about them in lyrics, but nobody dragged me from my room at no o'clock in the morning, jonesing, half out my skull, to write some bleeding-heart, wailing, hollering, 'oh baby' kinda song."

She chuckled softly, and his laughter wound deep around hers. "For real?"

"You've heard my CDs, right?"

"Yeah."

"You hear no mess like dat?"

"No."

He laughed deeper and kissed her forehead. "You will now."

"I'm sorry . . . and I'll take that shower with you this morning."

"I don't know," he hedged, teasing her. "Hurt me feelin's. Sorta blew the groove, making me think too hard . . . making me check me—"

Her hand slid down his chest, stopping his words.

"I can be coaxed, though," he murmured as she began to unwrap the spread from him.

"I know," she whispered. "Let's go get wet."

He was dressed and humming in the kitchen, making herbal tea, by the time she came out of her room. How men were able to just jump through water, snag any ole thing out of the closet and be good to go was still one of the great cosmic secrets. She'd found another sarong and a tank top, and sandals were no issue, nor was a brief application of makeup, but to her mind, her hair was a wet fright.

"You ready for some breakfast?" he asked in a mood so bright that the island didn't need sunshine.

"I have to get a blow-dryer before you call Mrs. Orville over. My plugs don't work in your outlets."

He glanced at her over his shoulder and chuckled. "But mine sure work in yours," he said under his breath.

She only caught half of what he'd said, but didn't need to hear the full statement to guess. "Fresh!" she said, swatting his arm.

"Ow, that's domestic abuse and my music arm, baby. All I said was I have adapters to fit."

"Yeah, right."

"Well I do," he argued, laughing, and then opened a drawer. "Pick a nation, I have adapters—and don' go all weird on me again. No, there's not a woman attached to each plug. Okay? I travel. Here."

She smiled hard and bit her lip, feeling foolish. "Thank you." She snatched the adapter and walked away.

"Looks good as is."

She peeped back in the door way. "As is?"

"Your hair. I like it the way it is—wild."

"I look crazy."

"You are crazy, but you don't look that way."

"Go 'head, man," she said, about to leave again.

"But I'm serious," he said, setting down the kettle and staring at her. "I like it curly, all over, funky, natural. Come 'ere," he said quietly, his eyes on hers.

Slowly she went to him.

"You're beautiful in hot pink . . . just like hibiscus," he murmured, digging his fingers in her hair, lifting it as he spread his fingers through it. "Soft, like velvet. Should be natural. The humidity here won't allow bone-straight to last . . . and I swear to you, I'll sweat it out every chance I get—so leave it, and come out into the yard and have breakfast with me."

What could a woman say to that? The brother was incredible, and had just made her feel so sexy and attractive that she didn't even dash to the bathroom to see what his crazy finger-comb had done. At the moment, for all she cared, her hair could have been sticking up like a banshee's. If he liked it, she loved it.

"All right," she whispered. The adapter slid across the counter. "What do you want to eat?"

"Loaded question," he said, hesitating for a moment before he moved away from her. "Ask me that again like that, and you'll never check into the Hilton so your boss is none the wiser."

"Oh, yeah," she said, coming out of the daze and patting her face.

"Damn . . . if I had known I had that affect this morning, I would have kept my big mouth shut."

She laughed. His chuckle was less enthusiastic than hers, and she knew he'd meant what he said. "Later."

"Promise me."

"Definitely."

"I feel better." He pushed off the butcher block. "Wanna eat on the deck?"

"Don't start."

He laughed, and opened his mouth and then closed it. "You stop. Your mind is in the trash, woman."

"I know you didn't cook," she said, ignoring his charge.

"God cooked. He does every day. C'mon. I'll show you. Bring your tea."

Curious, she watched him gather up two small china plates, a paring knife, and his tea. She brought hers, allowing the fresh mint to filter into her nose as she walked. Everything in St. Lucia smelled so alive, was so bright. She followed behind him, mimicking his moves as he set down his tea and made a show of arranging the plates.

"Let's cook," he said, and then walked away from her.

She had to jog to keep pace with him, and when she caught up with him he was standing in a grove of trees in the yard. He opened his arms and pointed with the knife.

"Madame, should you take lemon with your tea— we got it."

"Oh, snap!"

"Oranges—right there."

"Wow!" she hurried over to the tree and looked up.

"But be careful of that one, cashew. The nut has a small shell on it that leaves acid burns on the skin. The fruit is sweet and makes for good jelly, but the nut has to be roasted correctly; even the oil from it can burn if not handled properly. Don' want dat beautiful skin of yours burned." He glanced up. "Mangoes. Pineapples." Then he waved toward what looked like a tall elephant fern. "Bananas."

"You have *got* to be kidding me . . ." She ran over to the plant and marveled. "Just growing up in a yard, just like that?"

"Yup. When I take you around, you'll see. They're everywhere. We have huge banana plantations for export, but they grow wherever they feel like it, just like the mangoes."

"How about fresh mangoes, oranges, and bananas, then?"

"Comin' up."

She watched him go off a bit, find a long stick, put the knife between his teeth while he poked at the fruit laden branches, and then gracefully catch what fell before it hit the ground. Once he'd acquired an armload, he sauntered up to her, removed the knife, and pointed to her sarong.

"If madame would be so kind as to lift her skirt for me," he said with a droll wink.

She laughed and knew what he meant, making a fabric basket to hold his yield.

"Now bananas, and we're done."

He hacked a few ripe ones off the bunch and headed back up the slight incline to the deck. The air smelled thick and sweet. The bees were hard at work. Small blackbirds were fussing and fighting amid the branches, and the grass covering the dark, rich, volcanic soil felt too good between her toes. Oh, yes, this was heaven on earth.

She carefully took out the fruit and set it down for

him to cut. He spied her from the corner of his eyes, seeming pleased.

"You look like a pro, carrying fruit in your skirt. Brings back memories."

"Old girlfriend?"

He laughed. "Yes. Josella. She was a much older woman, fifteen. I was twelve. She never let me get next to her, so the most I could do was watch her gather fruit, and I would wait for the moment she'd lift her skirt to show her legs off. The fantasies she fueled."

"Aw, she never even gave you a kiss?"

"Nooo . . . you had to know her brothers. Five deep. Eighteen, nineteen. And so forth. I was twelve, horny, and a dreamer, but not stupid. So I let her be, and another man married her. She's got four boys, three girls, I think, and gained forty pounds, so God evened the score on my behalf."

"You are a mess!" she said, laughing as he expertly peeled the fruit. She watched his hands work, the succulent nectars dribbling between each digit, and she had to pinch herself to keep from jumping him in the yard.

Once he was finished arranging each plate, he stood back from the table and flung his hands down so that most of the juice ran off, and then began sucking each digit.

"You are really going to have to go into the kitchen and wash your hands," she said, not completely trusting her voice.

He looked up at her, stopped, one finger still lodged in his mouth. "My bad. I know that was too ignorant, but I was home and comfort—"

"No," she said, laughing, "I just can't watch you do that and ever hope to get to the Hilton."

He smiled and stood up, going toward the sliding screen door, "Oh . . . that's a different matter, then."

"Wash your hands, man."

"You don't *have* to check in, ya know. You can stay."

"Been over this a hundred times. I do. Even if I go AWOL, I have to at least make it look like I was there."

"All right, all right," he said, defeated, and slipped into the kitchen.

She leaned her head back and let the sun warm her face. If this could only last forever, she wouldn't ask God for another thing. A small whir of motion in her peripheral vision caught her eye, and what initially looked like a bug the size of a quarter almost made her jump up from the chair. Then, as she stared at it to see which direction the monster insect was headed, she realized that it was a beautifully delicate, black and iridescent blue-bodied hummingbird. It zoomed up toward the nectars on the table. She squealed, and it darted away.

Jacques was back on the deck in seconds. "Lizards?"

"No—he was so pretty, though!"

"Aw . . . and I thought I was going to see you strip and bounce for me again."

They both laughed.

"It was a hummingbird—he was so cute and little and he moved so fast."

"The fruit, the sweet juices; they love it."

"Wow . . . and so do I," she said, picking at her plate, then she stopped, mouth filled with mango. "Oh, my God," she mumbled, closed her eyes, and held onto the side of the table.

The expression of ecstasy on her face and the timbre of her voice held him for ransom for a moment. His tea was suspended in midair, and he had to force the thought to either bring it to his mouth or set the cup down before he spilled it.

"Karin, for real. The vocal highs and lows have got

to stop if, A, you want to get out of here without needing another shower, and, B, if you want me to drive
you for an hour and a half to check into the Hilton
without pulling over into the bushes and jumping
your bones in the wild."

She covered her mouth, laughing, jaws still packed
with fruit, chewing. "I'm sorry, I'm sorry," she mumbled, trying not to choke.

"Certain registers of sound in the morning are my
weakness—know that."

She just waved her hand, still laughing, grabbed a
piece of pineapple, shoved it in her mouth, and
closed her eyes.

Upon her insistence, Jacques walked across the
street to fetch Mrs. Orville before they left. He was
trying to keep a cool, slow stroll going, but his legs
wouldn't cooperate. That extra bounce in his step just
wouldn't go away, and he knew the moment he hit the
porch, she'd tease him.

"Well, good afternoon," Mrs. Orville said, all smiles,
looking at her watch.

"Don't start," he said, laughing. "It is only eleven,
and good morning, therefore. Plus, I got some fruit,
so you have one less meal to worry about—and by the
way, dinner was *excellent.*"

She gave him a smiling scowl. "No breakfast,
hmmm. But I bet plenty of laundry."

He let out his breath, smiling way too hard, and
sent his gaze across the street. "Please, please, I'm begging you this morning. She insisted that she wanted
to say good-bye to you properly and thank you for all
you did to make her stay nice. Don't make jokes
around Karin or she'll die."

"That's because *she's* a nice young woman and I know *you* took advantage of her morality last night. But I would never blame her, only the scoundrel that romanced her pants off. But that's not my business."

"C'mon, Ma."

"Oh, so now I'm Ma, not Mrs. O . . . whoo wee, you must really be sweet on her. You only call me 'Ma' when you really want something from me."

"You like her?" he asked, smiling wide but watching her expression closely.

"Does it matter?"

He nodded, his smile fading as his mood sobered. "You know it does."

She nodded and kissed his cheek. "Would I have been here, sitting across the street sipping my coffee with nothing to do till eleven if I didn't?"

He hugged her. "Good vibes?"

She nodded and hugged him back. "I've only seen you bring a couple around before her. Have I ever stayed away till eleven?"

He laughed and let her go. "No. One you refused to leave when she came, and the other had you banging pots at five A.M."

"Then this is the one I like best," she said laughing. "Now take me across before the poor girl tinks we've been talking about her."

"Well, we have."

"Shush," she said, peeping through the porch shade. "I don't want her not to like me—you, she sleeps with, so she'll like you automatic. Me, well, she might not, and I like her, so don't mess it up."

It was crazy, old-woman logic, but he nodded and opened the door. Yet it also confirmed all he needed to know. If Mrs. Orville was acting extra nutty around Karin Michaels, then she was definitely the one.

* * *

Broad daylight revealed what dusk had mercifully kept from her view: the real size of the road, the real depth of the gullies beside it, and the real hazards whirring by. She promised herself that she would not stomp her foot on the floor in an attempt to hit non-existent, phantom brakes, but the oil truck did it.

It was lumbering down the mountainous incline and headed in their direction, with the road the width of a single-lane highway—steep, jagged rock on one side, a two-thousand-foot drop to the rain-forest floor on the other, and night-rain-slicked roads were just too much reality for her to cope with. The truck slammed on its breaks; Jacques downshifted. Karin's forearms covered her face and both feet stomped invisible brakes.

"What?" Jacques said, accelerating once the truck passed. "He saw me, I saw him. No pressures."

A thin sheen of perspiration covered her body. She bit her lip to avoid commentary. She kept her eyes fastened to the small Toyota vans that were actually pedestrian buses, but didn't fully relax until she saw schoolchildren in uniforms walking about for lunch.

"Did you go to one of those schools?" she asked, marveling as the children navigated the no-sidewalk terrain, didn't get hit, and then raced up steep hills to small homes without even breathing hard.

"Yep. My uniform was gray and white. I always wanted somethin' flashier, like the maroon and gold ones," he said, smiling and pointing at another group of children passing by.

"I think you would have looked quite handsome in either," she said, her fascination growing as they moved away from the more metropolitan area to the residential, mountainous zone.

"I was tall and skinny, pants always too high, arms too long. The girls liked my brother better. He was the cute one."

"Oh, pullease. I find that hard to believe."

He chuckled. "All right, what he had in looks, I made up for in personality. I was the one who got in trouble, but could fish my way out of it."

"Now that, I believe," she said, laughing harder as she watched houses become less opulent and begin to resemble poor Southern clapboard lean-tos. Gone were the villas and whitewashed stucco. Corrugated tin replaced Spanish tile. Rotting wood railings replaced wrought-iron gates. Driveways were mud flats for chickens and goats; gone were the expensive stone and nicely paved asphalt. There were no lawns, just houses that seemed to spring up amid junglelike vegetation, and clothes hung outside on lines, across porch banisters, and from windowsills. Outdoor plumbing said it all. She kept talking as he grew quiet, understanding.

"So, what did you do to get in trouble?" she said, keeping her voice and the conversation light.

"Oh, me, well . . . hmmm . . . should I tell all? You might change you mind about hooking up wit me."

"Yes, tell all—give up the tapes," she exclaimed, shaking her head, laughing. "I know you were a bad little knucklehead boy." She was too giddy to even backtrack and mentally address his comment about hooking up.

"I would tease my sisters with bugs and garden snakes. I got a real bad whipping, once, for letting a boa go in their rooms, but they would torment me— so that was my way of getting back at them: find a tree frog and stash it in their sock drawer so it would leap out."

"Oh no, I would have died!"

"When me da got hol' of me, dat's what I thought would happen." He laughed and gazed out the window. "Finally, after they realized that I couldn't be much help around de house, since I was a kid dat needed outdoors—but if you sent me on an errand, I was liable to get lost on an adventure—they gave me a guitar. Then when I started getting really good, people in the family and neighborhood would listen, and I liked that. So I wanted to learn more, but my parents didn't have the money for that—the guitar was a big deal. But at church—and we *had* to go to church—after services, I was allowed to tinker on the piano there. Mom harassed the rector until he gave in, as long as the lady who cleaned the brass and who taught Sunday school would stay to monitor my behavior—since she had a key and I was known for tricks."

He sighed and fell quiet for a bit. She let him drive without a word, but noticed his sad expression as the towns they passed got poorer and poorer.

"Then I got so good," he said suddenly, as though he'd never taken a break in conversation. "I was asked to play one song, once a month, for the youth choir. But that service would be the most attended one ever, 'cause you *know* I wouldn't play it by the book—hell, I couldn't read the music, went by ear. I jazzed it up so much that people came."

"If I know you, you jazzed it up," she said, smiling, suddenly no longer worried about the road.

"But there was intrigue," he said, suddenly laughing hard and wiping his eyes. "The organist didn't appreciate some young buck taking his audience. So for a while, he gave me stress."

"But you were just a kid! That ain't right—in the church, too?"

Jacques wagged a finger. "By then, I was a young teen, he was a man—you know how ladies like music, right? You've been to concerts. Well, out here, the man with an instrument is the man who gets to play, feel me? Otherwise, hmmm . . . it can be very, very conservative for a looong time. Especially in the old Catholic parishes. You kissed, you got married. He was in his early twenties, and did not appreciate me *at all.*"

She covered her face and laughed hard behind her palms. "Oh, my goodness."

"Yes, luv. Drama. The young ladies back here operate under some very strict guidelines."

"My mother would be right at home."

The both chuckled and slipped into very private thoughts. But he'd told her a lot, and she better understood why he could deal with her mores and hesitancy. It all made so much sense.

"You still play by ear?" she asked out of the blue.

"No . . . an angel saved me and taught me."

"Really," she said, and turned towards him in her seat.

He nodded. "Sunday-school teacher who also cleaned the brass and did the Rector's laundry for extra money to make ends meet. She could read music. Had learned because her mother did laundry for rich folks and my teacher, when she was young, would keep their little girl company while she had to do all her music lessons. When the child wouldn't want to practice, she would make it fun by doing duets—so those rich people put both children into lessons to ensure their little monster would stick to it. Then she taught me."

"Wow . . . Jacques, that is deep."

"Yeah. That's why I believe in divine intervention."

"Me, too," she said quietly, thinking of how she'd met him. "You ever see your old teacher when you come home?"

"Every day," he said.

His voice had become so gentle that she wanted to reach out and touch his face.

"That is so nice. . . . Every day you drive all the way out here to see her?"

"No," he said with a knowing smile. "She lives across the street."

"Mrs. Orville!" she said, touching his arm. "She taught you the instruments and how to read music?"

"The one and only. I love dat lady like me ma. She gave me a life, now I give her whatever she wants, whenever she wants, no questions."

He glanced at her and then sent his gaze back to the road. "Mrs. O believed in me more den family, K. Family even got jealous, thought she was taking up too much of my time, then even suggested that she was liking a young man's company too much—cut dat woman to the bone, my family did. Actually accused her! But we pressed on, working, me learning, her teaching. When I hit it big, she was the one I took care of first, and people said I'd shamed my mother. Mom gave me life, and I did right by her, but Mrs. O gave me *a life*—so I do right by her as well."

Pieces of the giant jigsaw puzzle of this man instantly fell into place. He'd stopped speaking, and his eyes were on the road but also looking out to some far away place of pain and family bitterness and struggle.

Her hand fell gently on his bicep, just to let him know she'd heard him.

"She sat with me, Karin," he said in a much less impassioned voice. His tone was quiet, distant, as though he was trying to explain this all to someone far, far away who still didn't understand. "She was encouraging, made the piano fun, made the guitar understandable beyond the few songs I could mimic off the radio. She brought comprehension, respect, discipline. Her mother washed clothes for the wealthy, just so her child could one day, maybe, get what I got. She had intellect for music; I had passion . . . so dat woman, her spirit free and unselfish, didn't hold knowledge away from me jus' because I might be better at the craft. No. She labored, corrected, studied me down until I knew it cold, and den made me apply to music schools until I got in. I dropped out of Julliard. But I went," he added proudly. "That's just it. I went on scholarship all from her labor."

Chapter 11

She stroked his arm as he drove. Silence was their companion. For this particular ride, he hadn't even turned on the music, as though he preferred to intermittently exit and enter a conversation in sharps and flats when needed, where needed, offloading things from his mind at will. She flowed with his rhythm, accepting what he would reveal or not along the way, her eyes fastened to the spectacular scenery that millions of years of volcanic evolution had created.

"I could have shown you the banana plantations and Bounty rum distillery, or where sugar cane was once cut," he said in a flat tone after a while. "But to me, that would be like taking an African American through a Dixieland tour, you feel me?"

She nodded and squeezed his arm, sensing that he was about to either shut down any further revelations or become very philosophical. But she knew how he felt, could only imagine as she watched the homes become more rural. He pulled off on the side of the road into a little parking lot, and to her delight there was a small, white, open-air refreshment stand.

This time, she waited for him to set the pace of the discovery and allowed him to open the door.

"Bottled water. I should have grabbed some from the house, but I like to spread it around, you know?"

She nodded, understanding him better by and by. At every opportunity, she watched him devise reasons to buy things, thus recycling U.S. dollars at home, and smiled when he vastly overpaid a very happy vendor for several bottled waters and a small black beaded bracelet.

"Polished lava," he said, offhandedly, giving her the five-dollar trinket with a spring water. "C'mon. Stretch your legs for a moment and let me show you something."

She accepted the gift and slipped it on her wrist, marveling at the glistening black stones, but more at his seemingly carefree manner that belied so many deeper, more complex thoughts.

"This is beautiful. Thank you," she said, moving beside him to lean on a rail overlooking an impressive bay miles below.

"Marigot Bay," he announced. "It's a hurricane hole, and one of the safest harbors in the world, most beautiful, too. Lots of movies were shot here, like *Doctor Doolittle*—Disney liked the location a lot. Over there," he added, pointing, "George Foreman has a house; married a woman from St. Lucia. Up in the rain forest, a lot of Hollywood stars have hideaways. They call St. Lucia 'The Helen of the West Indies.' Beautiful, so much undeveloped virgin land, pristine natural environment—and only one major export, bananas, when anything grows if you just spit on the ground. Not enough jobs outside of tourism, working for the major resorts."

He pushed away from the rail and raked his fingers through his locks. "We started up in Gros Islet in the

north, passed Castries, the capital; in a while, we'll
be passing fishing villages on the western side of the
island: Anse La Raye, Cannaries, then Soufriere, then
you'll understand my dilemma."

Again she touched his arm, feeling the roiling agi-
tation beneath his skin. "Jacques, talk to me."

"The poverty makes me crazy," he said quietly, staring at her. "I want to do something to make some
change. Up in the north, all people generally see are
the resorts. When they hit the fishing villages, all they
care about is the great Friday fish markets where they
can eat home-grilled fish on the beach, and party, and
haggle over their cut of fish by weight, and drink,
then go back to their hotel. Or when they come to the
natural mineral baths down in Soufriere, tourists see
the volcano or the craft marts where they can bargain
and go home. They see the natural beauty. They see
the ecology. But they don't see the young boys on the
corners with nothing to do but become a busboy.
They don't see the HIV. They don't see how Soufriere
is like a tiny Rio, with an undercurrent. I'm from
here, and I see it all. Hear it all, spoken in patois that
the outsiders cannot understand."

"I hear you, and I see it," she said quietly. "When we
go back to the States, I'll show you my side of Philly. I
didn't grow up on the Parkway. It isn't all Art Museum
and Constitution Center and Liberty Bell, that I assure
you. My job, right now, as I see it, is to get you into a
position where you can invest here in a lasting way, without jeopardizing what you've worked so hard to obtain."

He nodded and moved away from the rail, clasping
her hand as he led her back to the car. "That's what I
love so much about you, Karin. You hear me."

* * *

They rode in relative silence for another half hour.
The quiet that befell them was like a comfortable
blanket that they shared—warm, covering, complete.
What he'd said about Soufriere was so true. The
artists had a colony there where they sold works of art
for a song, but the quiet desperation could be seen in
the people's eyes.

A young boy walked along the road selling what Karin
at first glance thought to be balloons, only to see upon
further inspection that his fist clutched half-inflated
condoms—which meant working girls were nearby. A
tiny Rio de Janeiro was exactly what it was. May jazz fes-
tivals in the north, cricket tournaments, Carnival—the
Caribbean's version of Mardi Gras—in July but still,
there was the reality of economics, pure and simple.

Jacques pulled their vehicle to a dusty gray roadside
hut and paid for two passes to the volcano tour: four
dollars in Eastern Caribbean currency, with an exchange rate of two dollars and seventy cents to an
American dollar. Karin watched him just leave a U.S.
twenty without waiting for his change.

Now she completely understood where his money was
going. It was being left on the streets of St. Lucia along
the way, in very small but meaningful increments—
no receipts, no paper trail, but with intent that was so
honorable she knew that some of her recommendations
would be impossible for him to follow. The infrastruc-
ture of his life, what he wanted to do, needed to do, just
didn't fit into the neat world of Uncle Sam.

Yet the thing that was so ironic was that his reality
was truthfully no different than that of the young rap-
pers Stateside. There was an underground economy
that they all initially tried to reach back and support,
one necessary for the poor to live. It was illegal, but
not necessarily unethical.

Colonialism had forced people into very narrow margins of survival. Those that broke free came home, gave out what they could, shared. It wasn't always the drug economy they were fueling, even though that was popular opinion. It was the salon that couldn't afford to pay taxes, the lady who had a restaurant that wasn't Licenses and Inspections–approved, the bootleg vendor that sold on the streets because he or she couldn't get the small-business loan to open a Center City store. It was keeping a vast and unnecessary entourage, not due to ego, but because how could one not hook their boys and family up, once hitting the proverbial lottery?

These young men had to be able to sleep at night, and after experiencing Jacques's villa, and then looking at the corrugated-tin roofed homes amid the mud and outdoor plumbing, she understood why there was no way he could just live up on the hill eating lobster and not have it turn in his gut if he didn't take care of practically everybody he knew. Her biggest problem was not in coming to that understanding, but how to convey this to her bosses . . . or even the IRS. If they shut him down in the U.S. and took his most profitable business venture there, then the tap would turn off here.

And after looking into this man's eyes and feeling his heart, she knew that his greatest fear was not losing his house in Rodney Bay Village. Even busted by the feds, he'd have enough assets to keep that. What was rubbing his nerves raw was the potential of not being able to carry all the people he had on his shoulders. All she had to do was think of Mrs. Orville to understand.

"Not much to see but a smoking sulfur hole," he said, smiling. "But we tip the tour guide, let her take you down the steps and show you the smoking crater where the water pours down with minerals to the baths; we can hit the botanical gardens—"

"Jacques," she said quietly. "Tip the lady, and tell her you're anxious to get me to the hotel so she's not offended and just thinks we're lovers . . . but I've seen enough, baby. I understand."

"I can do that," he said, his expression serious. "Since we are definitely lovers."

"Okay," she said softly, and waited for him to hop out of the car, communicate apologies, and return.

"Your boss comes in when?"

She smiled and looked at her watch. "Around five."

"I'm so sorry, Ms. Michaels," the desk clerk at the Hilton said. "When you did not arrive last night, or call, we assumed you'd canceled, and we gave your room away to another guest."

Karin closed her eyes and counted to ten.

"It is our high season, and we're usually booked solid this time of the year. However, we'd had a last-minute cancellation, which is the only reason why we were able to squeeze you in, but—"

"Fate," Jacques said, seeming amused. "Go wit da flow, Karin."

"I have to pull messages, need to explain—"

He gently tugged her arm so that she would step away from the desk to allow a private conversation, far enough from the clerk's prying ears.

"Look. We'll go have drinks at Buzz across from this hotel when he arrives, then I can have Mrs. Orville prepare a nice dinner for you, me, and your boss. I'll take him on a house tour and explain that our flight got delayed, it was dark and raining when we got here, and my villa is always open to business guests—so you and I stayed up very late discussing my business goals, or somethin'."

"This is so shaky, it'll never work," she whispered, peering around him at the curious clerk. "Plus, I must have fifty messages in voice mail that I should check, not to mention—"

"He's flying into Hewanorra Airport in the extreme south, and once he takes the hour-and-a-half, poorly air-conditioned jitney shuttle bus all way up to the north, loaded with passengers and luggage, with drivers who are on a mission to dump their passengers, he will need a drink and will understand why you didn't trek all the way down from G.F.L.C. Airport in the north to the Hilton in the dark. Plus, once he sees the house where you are situated with the housekeeper, et cetera, he won't tink nothing about it."

"All right, but we have to really be cool," she warned. There was no other choice. It was either go back with him, or risk being alone in some foreign land in a very inferior fleabag hotel too far from her boss and client to make any sense. That was not an option. "But I have to get my cell phone working. Once Broderick gets here, I'll be on an electronic leash, so to speak."

Jacques frowned. "We could do that, but you know how tings work in so-called third-world countries, mon. Unreliable. Need ta come back tomorrow. Might have to just give him my home-office line, if he needs you, and dat way Mrs. Orville can screen."

Karin raked her fingers through her hair. "Jacques, I have to handle your business while I'm here."

"I know, luv," he said with a wink and picked up her suitcase. "Dat's what I'm arguing about wit you to preserve."

* * *

He'd made a complete loop around the island, seeming more relaxed as they made their way north on the east side. He was back to humming, and had turned on the car stereo as though he didn't own a care in the world. She, on the other hand, used his cell phone to gather up her lost tension, redefine it, and wade through sixteen frantic voice mails from work and home.

"You haven't seen the beaches here yet, luv," he finally said, glimpsing her as he drove.

"I haven't prepared a report for my boss yet," she said, pressing the cell phone to her ear. "Shush, I'm getting yelled at for no contact."

He chuckled. "Tell the old bastard you've had plenty of contact."

"Be quiet," she said, giggling and oddly unconcerned about Kincaid's threats. "I have to leave him a message."

"Thunderstorms knock out power and transmissions all the time, delay planes—natural acts of God. Tell him dat so he'll get off your back. Internet is shaky until you get connected downtown in Castries."

"Shush," she said, turning down his stereo. "Calypso in the background will send the wrong message."

"I guess I should reserve any heavy breathing till you're off the phone, too—unless you're talking to me?"

She slapped his arm and gave him the eye. "Mr. Kincaid, sir, the weather here has been just unbelievable. Thunderstorms make power sporadic at best, and I am using Mr. Dubois's cell connection right now, because the people down at Cable and Wireless had a very long story for me—you know how it goes in foreign countries; not the way it is in the States, things take more time. But I'll be looking forward to filling Jonathan Broderick in as soon as he arrives and gets settled into his hotel room at the Royal. Once I get reliable Internet, I'll send the reports. I need to go, as not to run up the client's cell-phone bill. I hope you're feeling better, sir. Bye."

Karin clicked the phone off and slumped back in the seat. "Satisfied now that I have lied three ways from Sunday to my boss?"

"Lied?" He laughed. "I see no lie, actually."

"Oh, *actually*, huh."

"It did rain really, really hard last night," he said with a sexy wink. "Roads were slick and wet, while we were in the studio."

"Man, quit it," she said, laughing and looking out the window.

"You know what?" he said, his voice brightening. "We should put your bags back in your room and head off to Martinique for the afternoon."

"What?" She shook her head and folded her arms over her chest.

"Girl, put on your bathing suit; it's an hour run by boat. We can get somethin' good to eat, you can see the French quarter, and—"

"No."

"C'mon, K."

"Stop calling me 'K' and using your voice to work on me."

"Karin," he said, dropping his voice an octave.

She laughed.

He chuckled, sucked in a deep breath and cut off the radio and began singing the song he'd written for her, a capella.

"Not fair, secret weapon." She closed her eyes and settled back in the seat.

"Not trying to be fair, trying to get you to Martinique alone with me for an hour."

"You win."

"When's your birthday?" he asked, smiling.

"February, and you ain't right." The man was incorrigible.

"What? I missed it?" He said, seeming genuinely shocked. "But you're an Aquarius, which makes all the sense in the world why you hear me as a Sag."

"Now you're trying to run zodiac club lines on a sister," she said, laughing. "Old. And I already said yes."

He laughed harder. "Trying to lock in my position, dat's all."

She smiled. "Already locked."

He lifted an eyebrow. "Really?"

She nodded and pecked his cheek with a kiss.

"Musta thrown down righteous last night, then."

"Yeah . . ." she sighed. "This morning, too."

If there was ever a reason to possibly lose one's job, this was it. Karin closed her eyes and held onto the stern rail, letting the Caribbean breeze and surf splash her face. Witnessing the man pilot his own vessel was a sight too sexy to behold, so intermittently she just closed her eyes and flowed with the dream.

He'd pulled the double-deck, power catamaran out of the small bay, leaving behind the picturesque moored yachts, and then opened up the throttle like he was driving a speedboat, his locks and white linen shirt and slacks billowing in the wind. Have mercy. Music blasting like he was driving a car in the 'hood, vessel all crazy-plush. Liquor on board. She opened a Piton beer and sipped it. Oh, yeah, she was gonna lose her job.

But she loved how they could just be in each other's space, sometimes talking so fast that they'd finish each other's sentences, and other times, like now, where they'd share space and quiet solitude where they each could think and reflect with no pressure for conversation.

He'd also been right. This was just what the doctor ordered to get her to calm down about the arrival of one of the firm's partners. How could one be stressed with jewel-water all around and a view inspired by God?

"Luv, you should go below deck and put on some sunblock out here," he hollered over the motor.

"I'm cool," she said, enjoying the breeze.

"Naw," he argued and cut the motor back. "This ain't Philly sun. You're real close to the equator, and not used to it, even being a sister. Go down there, put on a baseball cap or something, and some 45 strength, or you'll be burned by dinnertime and in no mood for me touching you later."

She smiled and made her way along the deck and down the short flight of stairs, trying not to gawk at the fantastic woods and furnishings in the cabin below. It had everything, even a small kitchen. But she loved the fact that he just sent her on an exploration mission alone, seeming unconcerned about anything to hide. Big points.

As she hunted through the bathroom medicine cabinet, it suddenly dawned on her that even after dating Lloyd for as long as she had, he wouldn't allow her the free reign to simply go through his apartment unescorted. There were always boundaries and rules. His nightstand and closet were off-limits, like his office and dresser. Yet in Jacques ridiculous bedroom, he left everything out, hanging wherever it fell. A new awareness of trust entered her as she found the sunblock, but noticed there was no evidence of any other female on the boat. If ever there was a bachelor playground, this should have been it . . . but there wasn't anything that gave her pause.

She returned to the deck and sat near him, slathering her arms and legs. She noticed him watching her from the corner of his eye.

"Let me do your shoulders and the part of your back your tank top isn't covering."

She stood and handed him the bottle as he adjusted the motor again to slow the craft down. Putting a dab on his finger, he slid it down her nose and across her forehead.

"What are you doing?" she said, giggling.

"Keeping you from burning," he said, smiling, but there was also a quiet, serious undertone to his voice. "If you're going to be down here a lot, you have to protect yourself from the sun."

He didn't say more as he filled his hands with the lotion and smeared her shoulders slowly, making her straps come down, and then turned her around to let his hands gently trace her back.

"Want me to do you?" she whispered, the heat from his touch having severely affected her.

"I'm already covered up," he murmured, smiling, and pulling her into a backward embrace. "Got on a shirt . . . but, yeah, later, you can do me."

He easily turned her so that she was facing the wheel and simply nuzzled her neck while he operated the gears. By the time they'd pulled into the harbor, she was ready to ask him to find a hotel room, but didn't. If she'd thought to bring a change of clothes, she might have.

"All right, luv. We're in Forte-de-France, the capital. There's this great little restaurant, not far," he said, bringing the vessel to a mooring, and jumping down. He gave her his hand and helped her hop off the boat to the pier. "You like French cuisine?"

"Stop playing," she said, still feeling the heat of his hands on her skin. "I like anything you wanna show me, right through here."

He chuckled, and drew her near with his arm around her waist. "Then French it is."

As much as he'd turned her on, she couldn't help but be distracted by the quaintness of the town around them. The picturesque landscape looked like a snapshot right out of the seventeenth century, with small sidewalk cafés, flower vendors, baguette shops plying fresh French breads and cheeses, and enough upscale jewelry stores and boutiques to make Rodeo Drive in Beverly Hills envious.

"Wait," he said, tugging her by the waist into a jewelry store. "Pop in here with me for a minute, luv."

Instant frigid air-conditioning chilled her body, as did the outrageously expensive items behind the glass cases. Instinctively she knew this man was about to do something very impromptu and crazy, but she kept her mouth sealed, just hoping he was there to window-shop.

He brought her to a counter filled with emeralds, and then glanced at her. "You look good in green."

She shook her head no, but he seemed oblivious as he tilted his head and waved over a salesman. It was all she could do not to go slack-jawed as Jacques burst into a flurry of fluent French, to which the salesman simply nodded and kept enthusiastically repeating, "Oui, oui, monsieur."

"I didn't know you spoke French, and what did you tell the man?"

Jacques just smiled as the salesman came back and opened the case, then began setting jewelry in front of her with flourish. The salesman held out a diamond and emerald tennis bracelet and then began talking a mile a minute, ending in an uplift that told her a question had been asked.

"Mademoiselle?"

She blinked twice and gave Jacques the eye. It dawned upon her that if he'd spoken in fluent French, and she knew enough from her old high school days that, *mademoiselle* meant unmarried, *madame* meant married—Jacques had referred to her as "madame" earlier in the day.

"Can I talk to you for a moment?" she said, holding Jacques by the arm.

"Yeah, but you don't like it?"

The salesman looked dejected but not dissuaded, and then brought out another series of offerings that she knew, just by looking at the jewel weight alone, would have a price tag that would make her eyes cross.

"Jacques," she said quietly. "Just a moment alone, me and you."

He sighed, said something to the man, who eloquently bowed and moved back, but was courteous enough not to remove the jewelry from the counter, as though they would steal it. This was definitely not the States, she noted, as she pulled Jacques away to speak quietly for only him to hear.

"I can't accept anything like that from you, honey."

He toyed with the lava bracelet on her wrist. "Why not? You look good in green and said that no one had ever picked out anything for you, just for you . . . not for any special occasion."

She sighed. "This lava bracelet is more than enough," she said as gently as possible.

He smiled. "Karin, it was five bucks."

"So?"

He just looked at her, appearing stunned silent for a second. "The first one he showed you was only four grand, and truthfully, I was offended. But he—"

"Four thousand dollars, U.S.? Are you crazy? On a bracelet?"

He leaned closer. "Like I said, my bad. He should have pulled out the one he has out now worth forty, because you really deserve—"

"Jacques, Jacques, listen," she said, placing a hand against his chest. "This is what's been getting you into trouble. First off, something that expensive, I can *never* wear as long as you're my client. Gifts over twenty-five dollars aren't even allowed in the federal guidelines of my profession. Second—"

"You mean I have to fire you in order to give you a rock?" he asked, joking.

Exasperated, she grabbed her hair. "Will you stop! Now, listen . . . I appreciate the wonderful gesture, but you don't have to do this. In fact, I won't allow you to do this." She dropped her hands away from her hair and held out her wrist. "This meant more to me because it was from the heart; you were thinking, feeling some type of way about home when you picked it up, and it's literally a part of the St. Lucia earth where you're from—plus it gave some poor folks in the hills an American five-spot, whereas money for one of those bracelets will probably go back to African diamond exploitation mines. Besides, what you've given me is worth more than all the ice in here. You gave me your trust, and I'll take that to the bank any day."

She expected him to be salty about the rebuff, but instead his gaze burned hot for a moment and the next thing she knew, he'd pulled her against him and had his tongue down her throat—a complete public display, as though there was no one else in the store. It was so ridiculous that the other tourists started clapping. When she came out of the kiss, breathless, the several salesmen and even a manager behind the counter were scurrying and opening ring cases with huge solitaires.

She closed her eyes and groaned; he almost dragged her to the counter.

"All right," he said, his hand rubbing her back much lower than appropriate for public viewing. "Even if you won't take it now, show me what you like."

"No," she whispered. "Let's get out of here and go eat lunch before you do something totally rash and totally crazy."

"All right, all right," he whispered, brushing her shoulder with a lingering kiss. "But I still say you look fabulous in green."

Between the Creole crawfish and lobster, and somewhere after the banana flambé, she knew getting through a dinner with Jonathan Broderick was going to be a challenge. Jacques hadn't taken his hands off of her the entire afternoon. One palm had gently stroked her thigh under the table, the other rubbed the back of her hand until the man had to make a decision to use one of his hands to eat. Walking, they were joined at the hip, his arm slung lazily around her waist, but his palm constantly stroked her belly. Wine had nearly been her undoing.

He had her practically pinned against the wheel of the ship, working gears beside her, but how much he needed to make love was very, very apparent. She tried her best to hold still while he navigated the vessel, knowing that if she as much as flinched, her skirt might be up over her hips and it would be all over.

"Oh, look, dolphins!' she said, trying to go for any diversion possible.

"Yeah," he said, nuzzling her throat from behind. "They play in the channel between the islands all the time. Wanna stop for a little bit, find a beach, so you can see 'em?"

If they stopped on a beach to supposedly dolphin-watch, she knew she'd be picking up her boss at the Royal St. Lucien with the scent of raw sex all over her.

"Nooo . . . they look nice just where they are," she said, giggling.

"You sure?" he said, letting go of the wheel to run his hands down her arms. "Just for a little bit?"

"What time is it, Jacques?"

"I don't know," he breathed out hotly against her ear.

She glanced at his Rolex. "Near five. It'll take us an hour to get back to Rodney Bay, and my boss an hour and a half to get to his hotel. That leaves a very narrow half-hour window."

"I don't need that much time," he said, his voice low and serious as he slid his palm down her stomach and gently forced her to fit tightly against his pelvis.

"Stop," she whispered. "Steer the boat, man."

"Take off your bathing suit bottom under your skirt, and I will," he murmured, his voice growing husky. "Luv, for real, I need somethin' to tide me over until after dinner."

"Stop playing," she said, trying not to panic but swelling and getting wetter, despite her protest.

"I'm dead serious," he said. "Just leave on the skirt.

You steer, I'll work the gears. I can't make it for a few more hours."

"Uh-uh . . . Not all out here in the open where people can see."

"There's nobody out here; the closest vessel is more than a football field away." He kissed her neck, then nipped her ear. "I'll move real slow so it just looks like we're driving the boat together."

"But, but . . ."

"There's a bathroom below deck," he said quietly in her ear, "if you need to wash up, after. But I'm going below deck to put something on, and when I come back, the bottoms need to be off."

He moved away from her, leaving her to steer the boat. Her knuckles went white on the wheel, her grip was so tight. This man was out of his mind—no, correction, she was out of her mind for even considering something so wild. No. This was insane. This was over the top. But . . . then why was she inching down her tankini bottoms to mid-thigh as discretely as humanly possible beneath her sarong, one hand on the wheel, her eyes darting around like she was an international spy? This was some James Bond, off-the-wall, mad-crazy—

She stopped breathing when she saw him come back up the stairs, a mission clear on his face, and not even the slightest hint of a smile. Oh, Lord . . .

As cool as could be, he casually slipped behind her, righted the slightly errant course of the boat, and kissed her neck. He didn't say a word; his hands communicated all, as they slid down her hips, adjusted her skirt around her to hide them both, and then made her gasp.

"Don't move," he said quietly. "Let me do the work, you steer—I got da gears."

She almost closed her eyes, but couldn't; she was

the captain. Rocks and cliffs presented life-threatening realities on both sides of the channel, and she almost prayed out loud that no cruise ship or party boat would pass them or he'd have to give her instant CPR. Yet the feel of him moving ever so slightly with the natural bounce and roll of the ocean was maddening. After a few minutes, the urge to move against him for a deeper thrust was too much, and she pushed back against him hard with a gasp.

"Uh-uh," he whispered, dropping one firm hand against her hip. "Too obvious. Take it slow."

"I'm about to faint," she murmured, leaning her head back against his shoulder.

"Good."

He revved the engine and it made the catamaran hit harder water eddies, and for once she didn't caution him to slow down or be careful. *Anything* but the slow agony was all right at the moment. When he throttled back the speed, she couldn't help but question him.

"Don't stop," she whispered through her teeth.

"Had to throttle back, or we'll be in the middle of Rodney Bay waaaay too soon, luv."

"Oh, God, then park it and drop anchor and finish what you started."

"Yeah?"

He cut off the motor. "I was hoping you'd see it my way."

She nodded and waited for another thrust, but he slowly pulled out and lowered her skirt, discreetly adjusting his pants.

"Meet me below deck."

He left her and the cool breeze that bit into her back made her spin and follow him like a zombie. She only made it halfway down the stairs when he grabbed her and turned her around so that she was kneeling, then he placed one hand beside each of hers.

"It's dangerous to leave your vessel unattended in a busy channel, madame," he whispered hoarsely in her ear, entering her with a hard slide. "So this is gonna have to be fast."

"Oh, yeah . . . then make it fast."

She clung to the step before her like it was a life raft, head thrown back, gulping air, urging his thrusts with her impatient responses. Salt air, sea birds calling, the sound of surf, and his deep, melodic moans fused with hers, out in the open, him driving liquid fire between her legs, what job, what boss . . . what danger, who cared? She climaxed so hard that she bumped her chin on the steps; he collapsed against her back in a wail that resembled marine life. After a few dazed moments, she felt him withdraw, and heard him go into the bathroom. By the time he got back, she was a heap on the stairs.

He kissed her and gave her a wide, satisfied grin as he passed her. "I'm going up on deck, madame. *Somebody* has to be responsible enough to steer the ship."

Chapter 12

They pulled into Rodney Bay, her face flushed, body damp, but at least she'd been able to wash up a bit. He was back to humming. She wanted to die a thousand deaths, sure that someone had seen the madness that had just transpired.

She refused to say a word about his chipper mood, or the way he practically sang what he wanted for dinner to Mrs. Orville on the cell phone. *Just drive, collect Jonathan Broderick, remain calm, best manners, and fall on your sword in the States, Karin, if necessary,* she repeated in her head, sunglasses now shielding her eyes. This was so not right.

"Now, remember," she warned Jacques as they waited for the firm's senior partner to meet them in the hotel lobby, "no gestures of any kind that could clue this man in."

Jacques sighed but nodded and held up his hands. "I will behave, I promise."

"Please," she whispered. "You have to."

"All right, all right. I've had an appetizer and I'm good until after dinner when he leaves."

She inwardly groaned. *This is so not going to work.*

Within minutes, Jonathan Broderick was coming across the lobby. Karin gripped her purse tightly, needing something, not Jacques, to hold.

"Sir," she said, pasting on a professional smile and going toward him with her hand extended.

Broderick mopped his brow with a handkerchief, his face red, and stuffed it in his khaki suit pocket, then shook Karin's hand. "Hello," he said, and then quickly turned to Jacques. "Mr. Dubois, Jonathan Broderick. My pleasure."

Karin watched Jacques intently, but began to relax as he smiled and shook her boss's hand without incident.

"You look like you need a drink," Jacques said.

Broderick nodded. "I don't know how you do it, traveling all the time. The flight to Miami was nothing but turbulence, and the airport and security procedures down there were a fiasco. Then they lost my luggage, so I'm waiting for a call from the airport, but thank God I took my laptop as carry-on . . . and this heat—"

"How about we walk across the street and have us a couple of Pitons?"

She watched Broderick hesitate. "Beers, local."

"Oh, yes, well, that is right in order."

Jacques glanced at her, but she didn't directly return his gaze, just kept him in her peripheral vision. The muscles in her back wound around her spinal column tight enough to snap it, but she kept her expression cheerful as they made their way to the cottage-style restaurant that had been turned into a chic gourmet establishment across the street.

"After the ride from the airport," Broderick said, chuckling in the corporate tone, "I definitely need a beer."

"I know," Jacques said, issuing Karin fishy, comical

glances every chance he could. "It's long, hot, and sometimes the roads are slick."

She glared at him, but tucked it away when Broderick nodded and smiled in her direction. She smiled quickly. "Harrowing."

"I'll say," Broderick said, shaking his head as they made their way to the bar. "So, has Karin been taking good care of you?"

Jacques laughed; she blanched.

"Oh, mon . . . yeah."

"Excellent!"

She was going to slide under her barstool and hide until the next tax season.

"She's fabulous," Jacques said, needling her to no end.

"I'm glad you're turned on by one of our firm's brightest new stars."

Jacques smiled and hailed the bartender for three Pitons and let the opportunity pass. But she saw him swallow a smile.

"Mrs. Orville has prepared a great dinner," Jacques said as a diversion. "I hope you like seafood?"

"Oh, good Lord, I'm so allergic to shellfish it isn't funny."

Both Karin and Jacques paused, beers midsip.

"Uhm, then let me give her a ring now," Jacques said calmly, "and I'll ask her to make lamb."

"Oh, no, no problem, I don't have to eat while we discuss business," Broderick said, seeming embarrassed.

"No pressures, mon," Jacques said, as he slid off the barstool and went outside for better reception.

But he'd left her alone with a firm partner who was bound to pry. She braced herself, watching Broderick edge closer.

"Karin, I have to tell you," Broderick said, his voice low and calm. "Kincaid is beside himself about the hotel arrangements you left on the voice mail, and he's going crazy not being able to be in immediate direct contact with you. This is all highly irregular."

She nodded as she set down her beer, watching the overhead lights gleam against the beet-red skin that peeked between combed over strands of oily blonde hair. Even Broderick's glasses seemed smudged from the heat and humidity, and his wilted, sweaty khaki suit seemed so uncomfortable on his short, flaccid body that she felt sorry for the man. Without meaning to, she glanced at Jacques and couldn't help but note the contrast. Tall, lithe, athletic, fine, a majestic lion's mane of locks . . . designed for the environment, not an interloper to it trying to get phat-paid.

"I know, sir. It is highly irregular," she finally said on a weary sigh. "But this client is highly irregular, eccentric even. Please humor him. He's an artist."

Broderick nodded and leaned in closer. "Definitely. From his books, the man throws away money like it's water. You think he's one of those rapper drug dealer types that the firm should back away from? Kincaid is concerned. His—"

"No," she snapped and then sipped her beer.

"Karin, have you seen the poverty here?"

He was leaning closer to her than she wanted and she willed herself not to back away or show any signs of defiance in her body language.

"I have, *sir*."

"Then how did a guy like that just rise out of pigsties and outhouses to own all the crap we see on his balance sheets? His freaking books are a mess, he has idiot cousins and homeboys managing major areas of his businesses, and if you look at any one of them, they look like smugglers—you saw the vegetation around, right? They could be trafficking marijuana, or whatever, and we do *not* need to be a part of that. I mean, this whole Rastafarian getup the client is into gives me the hives."

Karin cocked her head to the side and stared at the man, considering her answer very slowly. Broderick would eat from Jacques's table, the firm would take Jacques's money, but any of the partners would slash their wrists if they thought he'd be moving next door to their bucolic, suburban lives. The stereotypes made her crazy, but not half as angry as the slanderous statement against Jacques's friends and family. No, they weren't Rhodes scholars, but she understood why he'd employed them! And screw Broderick's Anglo fashion taste. Her man was fine as hell with locks—was he blind?

"Jonathan," she said as evenly as possible, "I've had a chance to thoroughly make inquires, meet some of his people, and do a little investigating, and I assure you that while the management of his books does need more control, neither Mr. Dubois, nor any of his people, are making any profits from controlled substances.

She sat back. When she got fired, she had a chance as a press spokeswoman, because the soundbite she'd just given Broderick would have done even the White House proud.

Her boss nodded. "I guess you're right, if you're comfortable enough to stay at his home. Hard to hide nefarious activities while someone is practically living with you. I'll inform Kincaid that this travel snafu had an added benefit we hadn't expected."

She simply nodded and willed Jacques's hasty return to the bar.

This time, when Mrs. Orville came to the door, she was wearing a simple blue a-line uniform and had closed-in slippers that matched, her hair in a net, and the most dignified stiff upper lip that Karin could have imagined. She calmly offered everyone a pair of brand-new rubber slippers, spoke in low, cultured hospitality tones, gave no direct eye contact, and offered no small talk, just disappeared into the kitchen.

Broderick had hesitated, but took off his shoes and gave them to Mrs. Orville without looking at her, trying to figure out how to get his men's sandals on over dress socks.

Karin watched Jacques stiffen and the muscle in his jaw pulse. His quiet outrage was also hers, and they shared a glance. However, she also watched Jonathan Broderick's eyes as he made instantaneous financial assessments and very personal assumptions. She followed behind Jacques and Broderick as Jacques gave her boss a quick tour.

From her vantage point, she could almost see the hair bristling on the back of Broderick's neck as he spied room after room of lavish furnishings. By the same token, it was not lost on her in the least that Jacques had taken on a casually superior tone to rub salt in the wound. Great, just what they all needed: a male pissing contest by the pool.

She almost sighed aloud as they opened the studio door, half wishing that Jacques hadn't brought Broderick into his sanctuary. Oddly, as though reading her mind, he stopped short, gave a cursory view of it, and backed her boss out of it.

"I'm superstitious, mon," Jacques said without any apology in his tone. "Dat's where I work; gotta keep da vibes right. I don't let anyone in there."

"Oh, yes, I understand," Broderick said falsely. "Makes sense to me."

Karen wanted to slap him as he glanced back at her

with a smirk. She could see Jacques growing weary, but his head was held high and his back straight, and he opened the last door to the master bedroom with flourish, but almost dared Broderick to cross the threshold with his eyes.

"Last room," Jacques said flatly. "Then you can check out the garage. Like I said, everythin' in the records about the number of rooms and whatnot is accurate."

"Oh, I didn't doubt that it was," Broderick said, adjusting the glasses on the bridge of his nose. "But it is lavish, seeing it up close. The written descriptions left a lot out."

Karin stood silent, watching Broderick's mental appraisal. She wondered if he understood what having a satin-swathed rice bed like the one before him meant for a man like Jacques Bernard Dubois. Or the fact that, after having shared a bedroom all his life with siblings and wearing hand-me-downs from older cousins, why having a designer-garment-filled walk-in closet the size of a small studio apartment had been a must.

She knew that neither Broderick nor any of her firm's partners would ever understand why the man went nuts with indoor plumbing and had to have the best of the best, even a pool in his room that spilled out onto the one beside the deck—water no longer an issue, electricity at his beck and call . . . just because he no longer had to battle mosquitoes, spiders, and snakes to make a dash to the outhouse rain or shine. . . .

How could Broderick fathom why each room was infused with beauty and ivory to chase away the mud of clapboard, floral scents to kill the reminder of chicken coops and outhouses and fecal matter left by free-roaming goats? Food was the same way, always prepared to the max with plenty left over to share, give away, and savor. Before, there hadn't been enough. Now, through Jacques's music, there was.

In that brief, tense moment standing in the doorway of Jacques's bedroom, she saw what was in it for the very first time: his ultimate fears being banished . . . and he'd brought her there, shared it with her, savored her there like dessert, as though she were something added to his home to fill it up, sent to him to chase away the loneliness of being a misunderstood kid with a gift, to caress away all outside judgment . . . to really hear him . . . see him, and to tell him, "Baby, it will be all right."

Her nails dug into her palms—she so wanted to scream and tell her boss to get the hell out of her man's house with all his bad vibes. But she didn't.

"So, as you can see, Jonathan," she said in a firm tone, inserting herself into the conversation with authority and lifting her chin, "Mr. Dubois has made a good life for himself here, and as such, our firm is *honored* to have him as a client." She spun on her heels and began walking down the hall toward the dining room, unable to withstand the subtle indignities any longer.

"Oh, yes, I'll say," Broderick quipped, chortling as he slapped Jacques on the back.

She didn't need to turn to know her man had bristled from Broderick's touch. But she also knew him well enough to know by now that he would take it in good form as a best performance.

"Well, with this layout, I understand why you built in St. Lucia. You couldn't do this in the States at the same cost, given how weak E.C. dollars are compared to U.S.," Broderick prattled on. "Wise move, and some of the other musicians who've stretched themselves thin in Beverly Hills and such might need to take a page out of your book."

She said a quiet prayer, because she saw Jacques' eyes flash with a lethal glare. The snide, backhanded compliment had the potential to derail everything.

"Mr. Dubois made a personal choice to build here because of commitment to his family and community, Jonathan, not for financial reasons. When he began building some years ago, he was definitely in a position to set up an estate in Beverly Hills, had he wanted to, but *chose* to locate here to help the local economy."

"Of course," Broderick said, smiling tensely. "Er, yes."

Jacques glanced at her, a thank-you in his eyes. Her comment seemed to mellow his mood, and he walked through the house more casually with her boss toward the garage.

"Wow . . ." Broderick said, and then whistled. He laughed nervously and let his gaze take in the array of vehicles that included the Jeep Grand Cherokee, a Jaguar, a Mercedes, a Lincoln Navigator, a Ford F150, an H3, and a candy-red Porsche. "You need all these?"

"Yeah. I do," Jacques said, and then went back into the house.

"Touchy," Broderick whispered to Karin as they followed behind Jacques, twenty-five paces back.

"Yeah. He is," she said without even turning to look at the man.

"Dinner was fabulous, J.B.," Broderick said, wiping his mouth and casually dropping his cloth napkin by his plate. "Do you eat like this all the time?"

Jacques stared over the rim of his tea cup. Karin raised an eyebrow. In a very short time, Broderick had gotten very familiar, and was calling Jacques by his stage handle. Why did corporate jerks do that, just pick up and give someone a nickname like they could, without permission, she wondered?

Oblivious, Broderick pressed on, leaving half of his

key lime pie for Mrs. Orville to take away. "How do you stay in such good shape with her feeding you like that?"

Karin almost closed her eyes. If Broderick didn't call Mrs. Orville by her surname and give her proper respect, she wasn't sure whether or not her man would go across the table and kick her boss's ass. It was brewing.

"I work out, Jonnie," Jacques said in a near rumble, shortening Broderick's name to an awful nickname of his choosing.

"*Mrs. Orville* is a *wonderful* cook," Karin said, trying her best to keep an atmosphere of détente.

"You are so right, Karin," Broderick said, running his palm over his balding scalp. "It is so hard to find good help back in the States. Bet you were able to hire her at a—"

"Jonathan," Karin said quickly as she watched Jacques set his tea down too slowly for comfort, "did I mention that, uhm, I was able to get that first report off to Mr. Kincaid before I left, but that you have to go to Cable and Wireless to be sure your Internet connections work?" She fidgeted with her napkin and spied Mrs. Orville in the kitchen doorway. Karin prayed to Jesus she hadn't heard Broderick's social faux pas. "Thinking of all the fine people Jacques has hired when you mentioned Mrs. Orville's efficiency just reminded me of that."

"Karin, you're right!" he exclaimed. "I'll have to get that established first thing in the morning. Is your service available yet?"

"No, sir," she said quickly. "I'm going back tomorrow myself to be sure that it is."

"Good, then maybe you can get a taxi over in the morning; we can have breakfast and ride over there together to do some of the boring work of file setup that J.B. needn't be bothered with."

"That sounds like a plan, sir," she said as calmly as she could, and watched Mrs. Orville melt away from the door like a ghost.

Jacques glanced at his watch and stood up. "Well, it's getting late, and you've had a long day—so have I. So I'll have my driver come and collect you to take you back to the hotel."

"Thank you so much," Broderick said, beaming. He waited until Jacques left the room and then leaned in to Karin to whisper. "Would you get a load of how this guy is living? Maids, cooks, drivers, and shit. Fancy cars, *bedroom pools* for cryin' out loud. This is one of the most outrageous displays of conspicuous and unnecessary consumption I've seen in all my life. All that's missing is the gold teeth and a bling-bling medallion hanging around his neck. No wonder he's going broke."

She did not move. She was stone. She would not speak. She was invisible. She would not breathe, for it would be fire. Rockko's hulking form in the doorway was the only thing that made her avert her eyes.

She watched Broderick shake Jacques's hand. She watched her boss walk away looking nervous, being led to a big black sedan by a big black bouncer. She waited until the car pulled off, watched Jacques shoulders like a hawk. The muscles under his skin twitched as he gently shut the door, brushed past her and went into the kitchen to find Mrs. Orville.

Right on his heels, Karin was three paces behind him. The moment he hit the kitchen, he whirled around, slapped the butcher block island and exploded.

"I do not want that sonofabitch to ever cross me threshold again! That arrogant, no good piece of—"

"Jacques, son," Mrs. Orville said, going to him, "you know how—"

"No, Ma! I work too damned hard!"

"He does," Karin said quietly, making Jacques and Mrs. Orville grow still.

"Broderick was out of order," Karin said, seething. "Arrogant."

She rubbed her cheeks with both palms and began to pace, then stopped and screamed. It was totally primal sound, like that of a crazed Zulu warrior ready to fight with bow and arrow raised. "He has no right and everything you've got is, to my mind, freakin' reparations! I don't care how we have to hide it, how we have to show it on the damned books, you are not, Jacques, NOT, paying the IRS in the U.S. any more than you have to! Day and night I will stay up. I don't care what I have to do. If I have to call in every professor, every coworker, every person I know in this profession for assistance, I will do it, dammit, you hear me—and you are NOT going to pay that arrogant jackass one penny more than you absolutely have to. I'll go into your offices on my own time, I'll go over the books and bill one hour—even if it takes me three weeks to do the work. NO! Oh, Lord have mercy Jesus help my soul, I'll do it on my own time, do it on weekends, will underbill the firm for my time, will make this account so freakin' unprofitable to them that the partners will have an aneurysm!"

Her voice had exploded with sudden fury. Mrs. Orville stood by the sink wringing a dish towel. Jacques stared at her, slack-jawed. Hot tears of frustration formed in Karin's eyes.

She pointed at him. "They do not know who you are, what your real value on this planet is, what your gift is, and what you deserve! Who the hell are they to judge, huh? I'm looking at pure genius with a heart of gold. They see some thug rapper. I'd stand my own momma down for you, after what you showed me today, Jacques. So you play the game, be cool, chill in front of *the Man*. Keep doing your music. I'll work behind the scenes to hook a brother up. And when it's all over, you walk—clean, you hearing me!?" By the time she'd finished shouting, she was breathing hard.

"I hear you," he said quietly, his eyes never leaving hers.

"I'm gwan leave these dishes, and let you all put away the food. I'm tired," Mrs. Orville said with a sly smile. "Tomorrow, call me when you're ready for me to come over and begin my day. I'll let Rockko know to jus', 'um, drive the car home, and you'll call when Karin needs a ride into town."

"I'll walk you across the street, Ma," Jacques said, still staring at Karin.

"Oooohhhh . . . nooooo. Not tonight, son. I'll be jus' fine on me own."

He didn't argue. Karin didn't move. He stood rooted to the floor as Mrs. Orville passed him, gently pecked his cheek, and left. The door slammed decidedly behind her after a moment. The kitchen suddenly became very quiet, almost still. Not even the faucet seemed to drip.

"I ain't never had no woman, 'cept the one that just left, have my back like that," he said in a quiet rush.

"I've never been so personally outraged in all my life," she said, her voice thick with emotion. "*Ever*." She wrapped her arms around herself.

"I could tell," he murmured, pushing off the wall to come to her. "It was the most profound gift I've received."

She looked up at him. "I meant what I said," she whispered, still furious as his arms enfolded her.

"I know. I heard you," he whispered, stroking her back. "That's what makes it so special."

His touch made her unbundle her arms and return his hug. His mouth found hers and, gently probing, began to extract all the fury, all the tension, and every bit of the stress that had been levied against her since Broderick's arrival. What began as tender slowly turned more aggressive, and then feral.

Time and distance collapsed in on itself. She wasn't sure how they'd arrived at his room, just knew that there was motion as they blindly kissed, moved as one, and he kicked the door open with his foot. Clothing had gotten abandoned piece by piece along the way, leaving an exotic trail of fabric that began at the kitchen threshold and terminated at the bedroom.

He fell first, taking the brunt of the backward fall with her weight on him. Pillows slid away at the intrusion of brown bodies against an ivory-satin duvet. Her kisses washed his face, making tears slide from the corners of his eyes and run down his cheeks. Her hands splayed against his chest as though trying to wipe away every hurt and in-dignity, her mouth a soft, quick, wet brush of tender trib-ute to the rapidly beating heart encased within it.

She paid attention to his stomach that had had to digest too little respect for too long. Her hands rubbed that foul meal of injustice away, then her cheek nuzzled against him there, and her kiss tried to fill him up with anticipation till he arched. She found his belly button, the place where he'd been once nourished in the womb, and blew life into it with a hot stream of air to make him know she knew from whence he came, and respected that connection to who bore him. And as her hands traced over his hips, her mouth revered the man that he was with every flick of her tongue, palms encir-cling his engorged base, steadying his frenzied move-ments, her tongue being sure that he knew how much she understood all that he needed from her . . . she let him hear it, the sound, wet suction a steady rhythm . . . intermittently sending a cool waft of air over burning skin, whispering, "I know," against the place that had been most damaged, his manhood.

Half sitting up, half jerking with her every pull, his hands were in her hair, his eyes crossing beneath his lids. She'd taken him to a place in his soul so deep that his body was not his own. His mind was gone. She'd heard him in her office, in his kitchen, in his pool eating ice cream . . . in his studio, in his bed, the shower, on the drive, even in Martinique . . . and on the catamaran . . . in the bar, at his dining-room table; she'd heard him without words. She was the only one that ever understood, but she could never comprehend where she'd taken him now.

"Oh, God, Karin . . . *take me there*," he said between his teeth, and arched so hard that the top of his skull dug into the duvet.

Then she heard him for real, understood exactly what he was trying to say. Her body replaced her mouth, and he almost sobbed, she felt so good. He couldn't even kiss her as she ground against him in a hard, torturous circle. His body was jerking, his rhythm unsteady, his breathing irregular, her hips his only anchor. Her hands suddenly held his locks tight, her kiss crushing air from his lungs, her thrusts determined, making him grab her waist tighter.

She broke away, throwing her head back just to breathe. Words spilled up and out of him from nowhere, as though the broken kiss had drained him.

"Jesus, woman, I love you so much I can't stand it!"

His name, embedded in her wail, spent him. The sound of her voice cut his reason like a razor, a swift slash through it, halving it, spilling spasm-ejected seed deep within her. Her body was still moving, running hot lava over his groin, erupting more emotion from him as she quaked and hugged him tightly to her breasts, trembling, her voice softly whispering, "Baby . . . oh, baby, it'll be all right."

When the tremors had passed, he buried his face in the crook of her shoulder, bewildered. She was still holding him tightly, petting his hair, rocking him in her arms, and cooing softly to him. She knew. She'd heard him. His voice was unreliable. His chest was too filled up. She was patient. She was kind. She wouldn't ask questions. But she knew. She heard the storm coming in the distance. Lightning was opening up his chest. His thick breathing against her shoulder was a low, rumbling thunder of pain that needed release.

He fought against it, sucking in huge inhales. But her soft strokes against the crown of his head and her tender whispers released the sob. And he let it rain down on her shoulder real hard, for all the years of faking the game, acting like he didn't care or didn't need a soul. It rained, torrential downpours for all those who disbelieved . . . for all the lies he'd told and had been told, for all the necessary drama to get to this place of peace.

She rubbed his back and silently wept with him, for him, for herself. Never in her life had she taken such a risk, which oddly didn't seem like a risk at all. What had happened was necessary, natural. The man she held in her arms so needed to be unconditionally loved, as did she . . . and that was all she had to give, a small gift that she inherently knew he'd cherish. And he'd blessed her by opening up and letting her know without words that he had.

They lay together for a long time, just breathing, just touching tender strokes against sensitive skin. There was no need to say anything. They both knew the deal. There were possible consequences to unplanned freedom. Truth was, freedom wasn't really free.

He rolled her over on her back and stared down into

her eyes, wiping her tears, his tears, his gaze both sure and uncertain. Her palm cradled his cheek, understanding some, if not all that was on his mind.

"I know," she whispered. "I'm sorry."

He shook his head no, his majestic locks falling over his shoulder as he took her mouth. "Don't be," he whispered. "No apology necessary."

She looked deeply into his eyes, trying to understand.

He saw uncertainty flicker within her big brown eyes, and he tried to kiss it away as he made her close her eyes. "Marry me," he whispered. "I'm old-school and Catholic. We need to do this right."

She opened her eyes. "We just met," she whispered.

He smiled a half smile and closed his eyes and sighed like a big, contented lion. "I know. But I can't go back to latex after this." He gave her a sheepish look. "Ain't supposed to be using them nohow, me being a Catholic."

"That's not a reason," she said, chuckling and making him open his eyes.

"That's not the reason," he said, growing serious.

She touched his mouth with a trembling finger. "Jacques, talk to me."

"I had almost made up my mind in Martinique, but you still seemed unsure. But I made my mind up in the kitchen, when you went to war for me."

She closed her eyes and cupped his cheek. The kiss he delivered was so gentle that it almost hurt.

"Karin . . . don't you think that after all I've seen out here in the world, and all that I have at risk, that I would never do this with anyone I wasn't sure about?"

She couldn't open her eyes.

"Sweet, sweet, Karin . . . don't you think that I know what it means for a woman like you to throw caution to the wind for a man like me? I'm a variable, a risk, a rogue, a career hazard, and probably your mother's worse nightmare. But you didn't care, asked for no guarantees in return, and did it simply because you heard me."

He delivered a soft kiss to the bridge of her nose as two huge tears slipped from beneath her shut lids. His voice was the barest of whispers in her ear. "I even heard your heart quietly say, 'Jacques, please wait until your tax troubles are solved, so that my job doesn't think a certain way about me.' I couldn't hold off on touching you, but I will never humiliate you on your job. So I can wait until they straighten out my books, even though in my mind, that doesn't change a thing. But the offer stands. Marry me."

She hugged him hard and hid her face against him. She fought hard against the tears, but they came anyway, hot and sudden. The man had heard her all the way down to the core of her soul. His embrace was gentle, just like his slow, comfort-rocking of her body. He heard her. This wasn't a dream.

"I love you," she said thickly into his shoulder.

He nodded. "I know. I heard that, too, even though you didn't say it." He stroked her hair as she cried harder. "But there is one thing you never told me."

"What?" she wailed, almost dissolving into hiccupping sobs.

He chuckled softly, cradling her head with his broad palm. "What cut emerald you like best."

Chapter 13

In the deep recesses of his mind, he heard his phone ringing, his front door open, hard footsteps bearing outside shoes running down his hallway, and his name being called. But Karin had rocked his world so hard time after time all night long, he had to be hallucinating. Then the shrill pitch of an older woman's voice that he knew by heart pierced his coma.

"Jacques! Oh, Jesus Lord, son, don't make me open your bedroom door. EMERGENCY!"

He was up like a shot, disoriented, grabbing a fistful of sheets. Karin had snatched the duvet up around her. His heart was pounding, 'cause someone had surely died.

"Coming, Ma!" he hollered, stumbling forward to open the door.

Mrs. Orville's face was streaked with perspiration and tears, and she yanked him by the arm and walked him in a mad flurry of patois down the hall clutching papers.

He grabbed her by both arms the moment they entered the kitchen, his rumpled toga of sheets precariously sliding down. "What's happened?"

"Oh, good Father Jesus," she said, thrusting papers

toward him. "Her office faxed this to us this morning. That po' chile gwan die!"

"What?" he said, trying to unfurl the sweat dampened papers and make sense of what he saw in the gray-speckled images.

"*National Star,* son! Dey seen you two out on the catamaran and got photos no modder should see! Da girl's momma called the office in a shriek, her office called Mr. Broderick, he called me and got me fax, awww Lordy, Miss Claudy," the older woman wailed, beating her chest. "Rockko is on his way to get dat chile somewhere before you have media at de door—got photos of you buying her a ring in Martinique, son, are my eyes deceiving me? Your modder called, her girlfriend in New York sent her a fax, and now Annette, Ginette, and Jean are on the drive over here—"

"Oh shit!"

"Yes, son, dat's what I been sayin' but you gwan def dis mornin'! Get her cleaned up, showered, to preserve what little is lef' of her dignity and job." Mrs. Orville walked back and forth wringing her hands, her eyes a hot glare, and then she spun on Jacques. "She's a nice girl! A good one! Boy you know I don' brook da' bachelor playboy mess wit da nice ones!"

"Ma, hol' up—"

"No! *You* hol' up and put your dick back in your pants and do right by her. Now, lissen! She was ready to fight tooth and nail for you, was ready to—"

The front door opening and slamming made them both stop talking with their hands. Heavy male combat boots thudded down the hallway like a SWAT raid.

"Yo, boss—I'm on this thing stat! Media vans at the bottom of the hill. Where's Ms. K? We gotta break camp now or never."

"Karin!" Jacques hollered, brushing past Rockko

and Mrs. Orville, intermittently picking up her clothes as he raced down the hall.

She peeked out the door, never expecting him to grab her out of the room in a bedspread. When Mrs. Orville and Rockko entered the hall from the kitchen, her eyes went wide enough to split at the sides.

"Ohmigod!" Karin turned around and bumped into Jacques's chest.

"Cat's out the bag, luv," Jacques said, rushing her past Rockko and Mrs. Orville so fast that he and Karin both almost lost their bed linens. "*National Star* saw the boat. Your mom called the firm—"

Karin's scream cut off his words and ricocheted through the house.

"I didn't want you to meet my mom and family this way, via a fax from New York—"

Another shriek pierced that hallway as she ran ahead of him.

"Get dressed; news vans are on the lawn!"

He dashed down the hall in the opposite direction of the main guest bedroom and skidded to a halt in the kitchen doorway. "Mrs. O, she didn't take it very well— you got some aspirin or something you can give her?"

"From the sound of her voice, girlfriend is definitely gonna need a Valium this time, if you ask me," Rockko said flatly.

"I ain't ask you, mon!" Jacques snapped.

"Cool. But want me to call Danny and get his legal take on if you got any legal issues? Like, I'll know if they consider screwing on the high seas a public exposure crime, boss, seein' as how you was on your own boat and shit, and it might have even been in international waters, anyway, feel me—but a brother should be advised—"

"Don't say nothin' to me right now, Rockko," Jacques said, wiping his palms down his face.

"I'm just sayin'."

Jacques forced himself to ignore his buddy. "Mrs. O, Jesus wept . . . Tell me why news vans are on my front lawn?"

"St. Lucia's most eligible bachelor chooses a girl from the States." She placed one finger to her lips, her glare breathtaking. "Oh, wait, how about, this: Tax firm selected to fix superstar's U.S.-based IRS problems, sends call girl?" Her voice dropped to a lethal hiss. "Broderick was stuttering into the phone like he had rabies, Jacques! The girl's modder is on a flight as we speak and some young man over dere called her job—"

"I will kick his punk ass—"

"I will kick your behind so help me if you don't get dressed, Jacques Bernard Dubois, before your modder and family gets here!"

He and Rockko went still. He'd forgotten about his mother. This couldn't get any worse. He was down the hall in a shot. His doorbell was ringing. He heard Jonathan Broderick's name fall out of Mrs. Orville's mouth at such a high pitch, he squinted.

In and out of the shower, slacks on, shades, leather slip-ons, T-shirt, Rockko body blocking Broderick, and Karin holed up in her room, probably having a nervous breakdown. How did his life get so out of control overnight? It wasn't supposed to go like this.

"Mr. Dubois, I demand an explanation!" Broderick hollered while being shoved back out of the door by Rockko.

Jacques didn't even look as media sharks covered Broderick and his taxi driver hung around to see the show, no longer seeming interested in the fare. Jacques kept moving through the house. He found

Karin sitting on the edge of the bed in what could only be described as shell shock, wearing a black linen suit, dark shades, her bags packed, no make up, and her hair standing on top her head.

"My life is over," she said way too calmly, her voice building in volume and momentum as she spoke. "Please give me a phone, Jacques, baby, so I can find out what flight my mother is on and inform them to put a spoon on her tongue when she has an epileptic seizure!"

"Baby—"

"Ohmigod!" Karin jumped up off the bed like a bee had stung her. "I told you—but you didn't hear me!"

"Baby, I'm sorry about da boat ting, luv—"

"Ohmigod—in the *National STAR!*"

"The jewelers must have tipped them off, because they get VIP clients in dere, luv, then they must have followed us, and under normal circumstances, over here dey don' mess wit me, but when dey saw de ice, and de kiss, and the way we was whispering and the solitaires was glitterin' on de counter—it brings the stores business if they can say dat so and so star bought his woman's trinket from dere establishment, understand, and den they see if dey can get a photo glimpse of your honeylove, and—"

"Ohmigod—the name of your boat is *Wild Thing*!"

"Baby, I was so caught up, I forgot about paparazzi. So, what we gwan do is get you into a vehicle with blacked-out windows, all right? Den Rockko gwan drive you past your boss, but act like—"

"Broderick is on your lawn?" she whispered. "Right here, right now?"

He closed his eyes and nodded. "I ain't worried 'bout him. You don' need ta be meeting me modder and sisters and brother under dese circumstances or conditions—let everybody cool off and—"

"Your *mother* is actually on her way over here as we speak?" she said in a quiet tone, sitting down slowly.

He nodded and leaned against the door with a thud. The doorbell rang. Their heads jerked toward the door.

"This is built like an old French castle. Tell me there's a tunnel, a secret passageway behind the fireplace, and I will see my way out," she said between her teeth as she shot up off the bed.

He shook his head no. "Modern architects. New development."

Angry female voices were coming down the hall. Karin just sat down again on the edge of the bed and folded her arms and closed her eyes. The most bizarre thought crossed her mind as she waited for the inevitable; she wished her hair was in better shape for this media travesty. If this had been day one, she would have represented Philly much better. Sharon would have been proud. Her girlz in the office and her homegirls from long ago would have given her a high five, but *not* today. She looked like a chickenhead.

Karin let out a plaintive sigh. Rockko's voice sounded like he was getting beat down by a group of angry women. Mrs. Orville sounded like she was serving fisticuffs, too. A lone male was verbally siding with Rockko in the hallway, clearly trying to back the females away from the door. Had to be Jacques' brother—she'd thank him later. St. Lucia was a pretty island for a wedding. In five hours, her mother would be there any ole way. His whole family had turned out, and would get over it. The jeweler in Martinique was picked already. The photogs were there. There was no job conflict of interest, given that she was obviously now unemployed. All she had to do was comb her hair and put on her white suit and a little make up. Good thing Aya had advised her to pack some comfortable low heels. The backyard could work. Maybe even onboard the catamaran. Karin chuckled, as the last of her sanity slid away. She began unzipping her suitcase.

"Luv, you aren't falling apart on me are you?" Jacques calmly turned the door lock when his mother called his name. His cell phone was vibrating.

"Philly area code," he said quietly. "Wanna let it roll over to voicemail?"

"Nope," Karin said, accepting the phone as fists pounded on the door. She clicked the call on. "Hi, Mr. Kincaid. How are you today?" She pulled the phone away from her ear and started laughing.

Perhaps the nervous breakdown took a while to kick in. Maybe it was just that there was nothing left to do but laugh. She hung up and counted to ten. Jacques stared at her. The phone rang again, and Betty's nervous voice filled the receiver.

"Uhmm, hmm . . ." Karin said, unruffled. "I know. I called from his phone yesterday like a nut. Uhmm-hmm . . . that was me." She pulled the phone away from her ear as a sonic-boom scream filled it. "Please tell Lloyd to leave your office, and would you politely ask him to kiss my ass, Miss Betty? Yes, yes, I know you don't use such language—substitute "butt," then, and call security. Yes, yes, I know I have to turn in my laptop, badge, and keys, and no, hon, it's not your fault. I enjoyed working with you, too. Oh, what flight is my mother on? Uh. Okay. I love you, too. Bye."

She handed Jacques back his phone. He just stared at it for a moment and hooked it onto his belt. Her face was so serene, yet her hair looked so wild, that he wasn't sure what to do. Against his better judgment, he opened the door to try to back his family down the hall, but like lemmings they slid over, under, and around him and came barreling into the room. Four angry female bodies knocked him aside and stood like gunslingers with their arms folded. Only Mrs. Orville stood at Karin's side. His brother and Rockko shrugged an apology and had his back.

"Who is dis *shameful* floozy dat you takin' up wit, Jacques?"

"Yo, Mom, she ain't—"

"Hello," Karin said calmly standing, her voice dignified and quiet, her outfit looking like she belonged at a funeral, sunglasses still in place. She extended her hand. "My name is Karin Michaels. Pleased to meet you, Mrs. Dubois."

Chapter 14

She finger-combed her hair into place, added some lipstick, and held her head up. Jacques opened the front door to a hail of flashbulbs, but didn't stop to answer questions. She didn't say a word as Rockko helped her into the back of the Lincoln Navigator, and she noticed that Mr. Broderick seemed to be less angry and very solicitous of her as she passed him, given Mrs. Orville's press statement—backed up by Jacques' mother's pleasant media smile. Yes . . . Broderick would have to deal with her ghetto-fabulous reality now, so would Kincaid, as she would be a knowing, very astute spouse in a matter of hours.

She boarded the *Wild Thing* catamaran that had sealed their fate, and calmly ignored the helicopter that circled the bay with a telephoto lens. Her new attitude: There was no bad press. Controversy sold CDs.

Jacques sipped a rum and coke slowly to steady his nerves, poor man. He was still salty about the fact that one of the DJs in Philly had given the tabloid a quote about him singing to a Miss Karin at the Philly concert, and how he knew there was something going on before anyone else did. Jacques had thought they were tight. Karin simply told her fiancé to leak that there would be a new ballad coming out about this torrid affair so his stock would go up. He did.

The ride over to Martinique was uneventful, calm. Jacques stood at the helm with his eyes set on Forte de France. When they got there, more media swamped them, much to the jewelry shop's delight.

She entered the store in all black linen, like a mysterious widow. The same salesman that had formerly waited on them hung back, seeming ashamed. His loss. The commission on the sale was ridiculous.

Jacques asked her brief questions.

"Emerald, luv?"

"Yes, baby."

"Diamonds on the side?"

"Absolutely."

"Cut?"

"Same as the center stone—square."

"Size?"

"Very, very large."

The manager asked only two questions. "Cash or credit?"

Jacques's answer was basic. "Platinum."

"Should we wrap it?"

"No, she'll wear it."

Karin stood still for a moment outside the shop for the photo op. Hair was a non-issue at this point. She held up the ring; camera angles seized on that. And she didn't care as they got back on the boat that Jacques kissed her long and deep and hard in a full public display of affection. It really didn't matter, not one bit.

Mrs. Orville had put flowers on every table that the caterers brought. Paperwork would be well behind the ceremony, but it was a matter of principle. A local judge obliged. Being a VIP had certain privileges, although Jacques's mother wept herself sick in the kitchen. Her own mother was prostrate on the bed while she blow-dried her hair. The plug adapter finally came in handy. Broderick was even staying to make a good show for the firm, and had reminded her that now Jacques got an extra deduction with a spouse for the coming tax year.

The guest list was small; immediate relatives and associates who had visited, or rather, crashed the house that morning. But the media was large.

Karin turned off the blow-dryer and tested the curling iron. It was hot enough. The moment the hair-dryer stopped, her mother began wailing again. She flipped it on, and just gave her mom the eye. Mrs. Michaels sat up and blotted her face.

"You done?" Karin asked her mother.

She nodded. "I'm just sooo happy," she wailed, and began crying all over again.

"Huh?" Karin almost dropped the curling iron.

"My baby's getting married to a man who has all this, and he went to Julliard!" Her mother covered her face with her hands and wept.

Karin sighed, stood, and went to her mother and kissed the top of her crazy head. "Mom, I thought he was a thug and his family was a bunch of dysfunctional hicks—per your first words when you got past customs?"

"He's an artist," he mother sniffed, turning her under the light. "And who's to throw stones about dysfunctional families?"

"What changed your mind?" Karin asked flatly.

"I had a chance to come to the house, sit in the kitchen and have tea with Mrs. Orville—lovely woman."

"You came to the house . . ."

"And *had tea*," her mother said, lifting her chin. "Don't be silly, Karin. You know I'm not like that." She pushed a stray bit of half-straightened hair behind Karin's ear. "You should have at least gotten a gown while in Martinique. I'm sure in the French designer boutiques there would have been superb finds, rather than a plain white linen pants suit."

"This is a media shotgun wedding, Mom," she said, her tone so flat that she could walk on it. "He likes me the way I am."

"Of course he does. And poor Lloyd just couldn't get himself together. Imagine a doctor carrying on like such a hoodlum. Good riddance. He wasn't a surgeon yet, anyway."

"Mom, you are . . ." Karin counted to ten and sighed, then kissed her forehead. "I love you. Always will." She glanced around the room, needing a moment alone. "Now that you're feeling better, how about if you go try to cheer Mrs. Dubois up? Since we'll be family and all. . . . Or you could talk to Mr. Broderick, seeing as how he's still pretty shaken about the firm's image after the fax they received from you."

At this juncture, she'd propose *anything* to get the woman from underfoot. Her mom was at her best when she had something constructive to do, like détente. Besides, it only seemed fair that the most annoying person in her life would be set upon the most outrageous one in Jacques's.

To her amazement, her mother stood and agreed. "Yes, that makes all the sense in the world, to mend fences."

Mrs. Michaels gave a very gracious sigh and went to the bathroom to dab her face with water. But before Karin could lift the curling iron again, her mother was back in the middle of the bedroom clutching her pearls.

"Did you see the bathroom, Karin?" she gasped.

"Yes, Mom."

"They have *a bidet*," her mother whispered.

Karin chuckled, and whispered back, "I know."

Her mother fanned her face, kissed her in passing, and went toward the door. "Mrs. Dubois and I should really mend the fence, and I'll make professional amends with Mr. Broderick and Mr. Kincaid on your behalf. That's the least a mother can do."

"Yep," Karin said, turning toward the mirror and pushing a wad of hair onto the iron rod. She briefly closed her eyes once her mother left and pulled her hair off the hot surface before it burned.

She thought of her father and tried to hear his laughter all the way up in heaven. In her heart she knew that only he could have orchestrated such a crazy turn of events that humbled even Eloise Michaels. Then it dawned on her that she didn't even have anyone to walk her down the aisle, much less help her make herself pretty for the biggest day of her life. She was plain. Jacques seemed to like that, but at the moment, she didn't. She opened her eyes and just sat there, the ring weighing heavily on her hand.

A knock at the door didn't even make her turn. She wouldn't be surprised if it was her mother who'd found some new facet of the house to ogle, or Jacques to say that they'd taken his mother by ambulance to the hospital, and therefore the wedding was off.

But a soft voice called through the door in a familiar female island lilt that she'd grown to love. It was Ma, calling for Miss Karin. She would not cry, she would not cry, no, Lord, no she would not cry.

"Be right out, Mrs. Orville," Karin said, sniffing.

"Oh, no, no, no," the older woman said, slipping into the room with a big shopping bag. "It is bad luck for de bride to be seen so close to the wedding, and I've tol' Jacques that he needs to observe *some* traditions."

Karin chuckled and dabbed her eyes. "You are the one person in the world who I am so glad to see right now," she said quietly and stood.

"Sit," Mrs. Orville ordered. "Every natural mother in here has lost her natural mind. But, me, well, I've done this many times and I'm over de shock of impromptu weddings." She hoisted her heavy parcel onto the bed and began to pull items out of it, occasionally glancing at Karin with a sheepish smile.

"My middle daughter is about your size," she said, and unfurled a handmade, strapless, white satin gown with petticoats and small handsewn seed pearls. "Somethin' old."

Karin stood.

"Jacques gave you somethin' new. Probably a baby, too—so you're good to go." She smiled when Karin laughed, and pulled out a long white veil that had an open halo top. Then she whipped a spool of blue ribbon out of her shopping bag. "I'll be tying white flowers to this from de yard, ta give you something blue. You have white shoes?"

"Yes," Karin whispered, allowing the tears to stream down her face.

"You may borrow my lace gloves from when I was a girl your age and married," Mrs. Orville said, misting up, and gingerly presenting the gloves to Karin with a kiss on her cheek. "There. All set. Something old, something new, something borrowed, and in a moment once I work me magic, something blue. Okay. But no more crying, because it don' say nothin' about something red and puffy, like your nose and eyes will get."

"Okay," Karin said, hugging Mrs. Orville. "I know my dad sent you."

"Got him right here in me pocket," Mrs. Orville said, extracting a small color photo from her uniform and giving it to Karin.

Karin clutched it and looked at her father's photo that she'd only ever seen on the dining-room mantle. "Where did you get this?" Her voice was a reverent whisper.

Mrs. Orville cupped her face with both hands. "Chile, me and that nice lady, Miss Betty, we talked for a loooong time on the telephone, she and I. I knew you would be the type of young lady to miss her daddy on a day like this, and she agreed. So, since we knew your mom was heading to the airport—Miss Betty called and sent another woman over to meet her before she left, uhmm . . . a Brenda somebody or other, to beg your mom for the photo. We said we were doing a collage of employee's families—sorta stretched the truth so your mom thought you might still have a job. Brenda brought the photo to Miss Betty, who scanned it and e-mailed it to me, and I printed it off. Now, when Rockko walks you down the aisle, he can wear it under his boutonnière. This way, your da can be there in spirit, and you can glance back to him when Rockko steps away. Plus all de girls in the office said . . . wait, lemme get dis right. 'You go, gurl,' I tink."

She barreled into Mrs. Orville's arms so hard that they both almost fell and the photo was in jeopardy of getting crushed. Boo-hoo wails echoed in the room, and there was nothing Mrs. Orville could say to stop them. They just had to come out.

"You sure about this, boss?" Rockko asked, fidgeting with a pin and a white hibiscus flower at Jacques's lapel.

"Don' ask me again, mon. I'm sure."

"But it happened kinda fast, yo—didn't it?" his brother asked, shrugging as he straightened his tie.

The guys in the band that had spread out throughout Jacques bedroom looked up.

"Happens fast like dat sometimes, dude," Blind said.

"My wife's pop put a nine to my skull. It can happen real fast. J.B. went out easy," Puff said, scratching, his chin.

"She good wit dat numbers, and is cool peeps," Sweet shrugged. "Makes sense to me. Sista gonna get his business straight, so hey."

"She's fine, too, man," Chewy said.

"Word," Frank agreed. "If from Mrs. O's mouth to God's ear, Miss Karin is a'ight, it works for me."

"See," Jacques said, dabbing his brow. "It's all good, mon."

"Den why you sweatin' like a pig?" Rockko smiled, and straightened Jacques' tie.

"It's just warm in here, mon. I been runnin' all day."

"Uh-huh," Jean said. "You shoulda kept runnin', if you ask me—or at least gave us a heads-up so we coulda had you a bachelor party, mon."

Jacques dabbed his brow again. "My *life* has been a bachelor party, brother. I don't think there's too much you could show me at this point. It would have to be so good, it would kill me."

"Word," Frank said, looking over the tops of his shades at Jacques' brother. "Just shut up and let da man take the long walk."

Jacques knew he had to pass by the kitchen to get out to the deck, and that was the last place he'd left his mother and sisters. One more crying jag from them and he was permanently moving to another country. But to his amazement, they were all sitting in the kitchen with Mrs. Michaels, having tea, the two mothers seeming enthralled with each other. He had no idea what they were saying, and didn't wanna know. If he could have made himself invisible to slip past them, he would have.

"Did you know dat Karin's modder was a principal of a school dere, Jacques?" his mother asked as he entered the now too-small kitchen.

He shook his head no.

"She is very educated, and her daughter is, too," his mother announced.

"That's nice, Mom."

"That means that the potential modder of your children will know to educate them well—which was always my main concern." His mother stood and folded her arms over her chest. "You really owe dis nice, educated lady a form of apology for the situation dat embarrassed her child so publicly, son. I raised you better."

He just stared at his mother for a moment. What *the hell* had transpired in his kitchen?

"Dat's right," his sister Ginette said.

"Dat's de only reason Mom was upset," Annette fussed. "Because she didn't know what kind of lady Karin was—but we're *all* glad you're finally getting married and have stopped running the streets. Dat was all we been saying for years."

He blinked twice, stunned.

"He looks so handsome," his mother said tearing up. "Would make his father proud."

Mrs. Michaels nodded and dabbed her eyes. "I wish my late husband were here to see this, too."

Frozen, Jacques stood by the door. Both mothers

looked at each other and burst out crying. His sisters were up out of kitchen chairs in a flash grabbing more paper towels. He backed out of the door, trying to find a way out of the house, away from any and everyone.

But media was at the front and sides of the house, waiting like buzzards. His boyz had taken over his bedroom. Mrs. Orville was in with Karin. Eager caterers earning premium dollar for the rushed event were out back, in the living room, and in the dining room, making a way out of seemingly no way. Nieces and nephews were running around in the rec room, and the guest rooms were loaded with folks who just needed a moment to crash and burn. The man who would perform the quick civil ceremony was out back, too, glad-handing with Karin's boss. The hallway was the only place he could quietly stand for a second, albeit also a high-traffic zone. Everybody was crossing his threshold with shoes from outside. What *the hell* had just happened to his life? The studio was calling his name.

"I think our boy got cold feet and rolled," Rockko said quietly to the band.

"Happens," Blind said with a shrug. "Cool sister, though. Shame."

"You should go tell Mrs. O," Jean murmured. "She gwan be fit to be tied."

Rockko nodded and glanced around the deck one more time. "But you know that's really your job as the best man."

"You security," Jean argued in a whisper, looking at all the family sitting on white rental chairs.

Roccko didn't answer as he left the deck rail and walked back into the house.

* * *

Mrs. Orville stood behind Karin as they both stared at her in the mirror. Long baby-blue ribbons flowed over her Karin's shoulders with the veil, and the freshly picked yellow and white flowers had also been tied with blue ribbon streamers, courtesy of Ma. The pearl, ivory, and crystal necklace and earrings from her first day on the plane worked perfectly. And her hair did just what Sharon and Mrs. Orville commanded that it do.

"You look soooo pretty," Mrs. Orville breathed out. "For an instant bride, you made this looked like we've been working for six months."

"You did this, Ma," she said quietly. "Bless you."

"Good stock, good foundation. I just added some ribbon and flowers," the older woman scoffed, and then kissed her softly, careful of her makeup.

Rockko's power knock made the both start and then giggle.

"You ready?" Mrs. Orville asked, squeezing Karin's arm.

"As I'll ever be," she whispered. "Thank you."

"Okay, Rockko. You can come in," Mrs. Orville shouted.

He peeked his head in the door. "Ma, we got us a little problem. The band is gonna play to keep people chilled out, and uh, the caterer is going around with trays of food and drinks, but um, can I speak to you for a minute?"

"He changed his mind," Karin whispered.

"Well, we'll just see about dat," Mrs. Orville said, hands on hips.

"No, it's all right," Karin said quietly. "This was crazy any ole way."

"I can't profess to say what he did, K . . . 'cause, all I know is, I can't find a brother, feel me? So he mighta took one of them long, gotta-think-it-out walks, or, you know, needed to clear his head, 'cause there's been a lot of chaos 'round the joint today."

Karin nodded calmly. "I know where he probably is," she said, slipping past Rockko.

"No, no, no, chile," Mrs. Orville fussed. "Dat's bad luck!"

"I know, generally speaking it is. But under these circumstances . . ." Karin shrugged.

Mrs. Orville sighed and nodded. "I'll keep people fed and occupied."

Her dress floated down the hall behind her as she passed nervous caterers. She kept walking till she found the room that no one entered but him. She knocked lightly, and then remembered it was sound-proofed, and pushed the door open. The saddest melody had filled the room. It was also so beautiful that it made her chest tight.

Karin took her time going up to him at the piano bench, and she waited for him to stop playing. She stood behind him, voice soft, and no acrimony in her tone; she understood where he was at. She allowed her mind to take a mental snapshot of him, where he naturally belonged: here, in deep concentration, locks pulled back over broad shoulders, composing his heart out, handsome all in ivory . . . talented beyond all imagination, and free.

"Hey," she murmured.

He turned and hesitated.

"I understand, Jacques. You can't do this. But like I

told you, I'll help you, and will *always* think well of you."

He simply stared at her. His mind couldn't comprehend what she was saying while white satin bathed her gorgeous brown skin. He didn't hear her at all, as a lace veil pelted with seed pearls glisten in the lights and long blue streams of satin ribbons ran over her shoulders like waterfall runnels. She had white flowers in her hair and in her hands, with splashes of yellow. More blue ribbons seemed to spill down her dress from her bouquet. Her throat was encircled by that necklace of crystals and pearls and ivory he adored on her. He was deaf, he was mute; what was she trying to say?

"Huh?"

"It's all right." She looked down at the floor.

"Is it time?"

She looked at him and stared long. "Are you ready? Do you want to do this, still?"

"Are you crazy? You changin' your mind on me—now? What did I do wrong, K?"

"Nothing," she said, smiling. "I thought you'd walked out."

"I got out of the path of mayhem and destruction in my house to the only place of peace to be found, but walk? No. Why would I do that?"

"I don't know . . ."

"Did you hear the words?"

"Just the melody. It was so sad."

"It was saying, 'Run away with me, girl—away from the madness. Run away with me, girl, where you and I can be free.'" He raked his hair. "Karin, you are exasperatin', woman. . . . Don't you remember when I tol' you don't move, I was still composing?"

She covered her mouth with a slow hand.

"Yes!" He said, shaking his head. "My pilot is on

standby, sitting in da front row under orders to take all drinks virgin, so as soon as we do dis ting, my boy, Rockko, can get us da hell out of here. Da house is overrun. Infested with family. My new wife can't be bothered with all dat. I'm not honeymooning with your mother, my mother, my second mother, my family, the band, your boss, and half of St. Lucia and the media in my personal space!"

"Where are we flying—"

"I don't know and I don't care—dis is hell, not paradise, under these conditions, K!"

She laughed so hard that he had to stop pacing and laugh with her. They laughed, a good, crazy, down-to-the-soul laugh. They laughed, because she finally heard him and he had definitely heard her. They laughed, because they both knew and understood.

She laughed even harder because her period was due that morning, but had never . . . ever . . . come on.